Gruesome Gary's
Home for the Dead:
A Funeral Alternative

by Gary Freeman

gfreemanbooks@gmail.com

Manufactured in the United States of America

~

Special thank you to the Crocker House Museum of Mt. Clemens, Michigan, for use of the Crocker House on the front cover. www.crockerhousemuseum.com.

Also a special thank you to Maurice Greenia Jr. for use of his well-traveled red wizard's cape on the back cover. http://research.udmercy.edu/find/special_collections /digital/greenia/

Gruesome Gary's
Home for the Dead:
A Funeral Alternative

by
Gary Freeman

CHAPTER 1

The fully-loaded 747 bounced hard once, twice, then skipped and shuddered as all wheels caught firmly on the cracked and uneven surface of the runway to the loud strains of jet engines pumping out reverse thrust. The plane rolled hard and fast, bumping and swerving before slowing and making two turns, coming to a stop near the terminal. The pilot gave a thumbs-up to the rookie copilot. Together they had conquered Nandi International Airport.

As tourists rose to disembark, either for a stay in Fiji or to transfer to a flight to New Zealand, Gary, Dinah and Gilbert, seated three abreast, paused. Gary finally spoke, "I don't believe it. We're here. We're actually here, half a million miles away in Fiji."

Gilbert said, "What kind of business were we in, anyway. I forgot already. Hey, hand me Kevin's letter. I want to read it one more time."

Gary reached into his shirt pocket and produced the letter, written on frail airmail paper. "It'll be good to see Kevin again after all this time," he said, passing the letter across Dinah to Gilbert.

Dinah intercepted it, saying, "I want to read it again, too." She steadied her hand on the armrest between her and Gilbert. Gilbert leaned over, and together they silently read:

Dear Gary and Dinah,

Much belated congratulations on your marriage. What a surprise to hear from you! I thought everyone over there had given me up for dead. Too bad about Aunt Winifred. I don't remember much about her except that house full of creepy old furniture. Do you remember that crappy rattan stuff she had?

So, when are you coming to Fiji? Hurry up, we're developing. You got to see this place before it disappears. You're going to love it. Everyone is real friendly and there's lots of weird things to see. Be careful, though, that the tropics don't mess up your mind. They've messed up mine, plenty—lately, for example, I've been having flashbacks of when I was a drunken beachcomber who jumped ship here after being shanghaied from a filthy whorehouse in Sydney ONE HUNDRED FIFTY YEARS AGO! It seems like I've lived here forever!

Give me a call and tell me when you will arrive. I'll meet you at the airport. The best time to reach me is around noon. I don't know what time that is in your zone. And every time I try to figure out time zones I get screwed up because of the International Date Line. I'm practically sitting right on top of it, you know. It's just one of the many things that'll blow your mind.

Your long
 lost cousin,
 Kevin

Dinah looked up. "Come on, you guys," she said, "The aisle's clear now. Let's go!"

As they climbed down the stairway to the tarmac, the tropical heat seared their bodies, and steam rose from the puddles of an early morning rain. The sun shone brightly. "I brought these sunglasses with the fake nose and mustache as a joke on Kevin," Gilbert said, reaching into his carry-on bag, "but I'm going to wear them for real. That sun is something else. How do I look?"

The sunglasses hid Gilbert's bushy eyebrows and slightly protruding eyeballs, but the fake nose and mustache barely covered his own bulbous nose and thick, unkempt mustache. "I'm embarrassed to be seen with you," Gary answered, wishing he had remembered sunglasses, any kind of sunglasses. "Kevin won't have any trouble spotting us, at least."

Gilbert joked, "You should have worn sunglasses to cover your shifty eyes. These Fijians are going to think you're a con man."

"My eyes aren't shifty," Gary said, knowing Gilbert was right.

"You know," Dinah observed, "you do have shifty eyes. All the years we've been married, and it's just now that I realize why my parents didn't trust you— you have shifty eyes!" She studied Gary's face a moment then added with a warm laugh, "Well, with all the bags under them, how was I to notice?"

Gary sighed and scratched the stubble on his chin, and made a pretense of rubbing a speck of dust from under one eye, using his thick, clumsy fingers to hide what he feared might be a shifty look.

Gilbert chuckled, and Dinah giggled at his effort. "Don't worry," Dinah said, putting her arm in Gary's, "we still love you."

"Sure, we don't care what you look like," Gilbert added, as he put his hand in his pants pocket, surreptitiously slipping on a joy buzzer.

They collected their baggage, passed through customs, and entered a waiting area filled with taxi drivers and touts. All along the way people smiled and pointed at Gilbert. "These people sure are friendly," he said.

Dinah shook her head and smiled, saying, "They must think you're a movie star, Gilbert."

A tall, bony man with long, thinning hair, wearing white pants and a bright floral pattern shirt approached hesitantly, holding a cardboard sign with their names on it. "I'm looking for some cousins of mine who were supposed to be on this flight. Have you seen them?" he asked Gary, giving Gilbert odd sidelong glances.

"Kevin? Is that you?" Gary asked. "What happened to you?"

"The same thing that's happened to you," Kevin replied. "Time." Turning to Dinah, he said, "You must be Dinah. You look good. Cute bobbed auburn hair — my favorite! How did you get mixed up with these guys?"

Before Dinah could respond, Gary took Kevin's hand. "How've 'ya been, Kevin? Really, you look great. Fiji's been good to you."

"I'm glad I stayed." Turning to Gilbert, he said, "Gilbert. What can I say? Still up to your tricks, I see."

"No," Gilbert answered earnestly. "I'm above all that now. I haven't played a trick in years."

They shook hands. Kevin jumped. "What the...I should have known better." Kevin shook the sting out of his hand, turning to Dinah. "You poor thing. You were actually in business with these two? You must be a saint."

"I can't believe it either. Nice to finally meet you, Kevin. You're something of a mystery figure in the family. Your name comes up at family get-togethers, but nobody seems to know what you do."

Kevin answered quickly, "I guess I'm not the best letter writer in the world. But never mind that. Come on, I got a car. I'll drive you into Suva and show you around a bit."

He picked up Dinah's suitcase and led the way to the parking lot, Gary and Gilbert bringing the remaining bags. Outside, Kevin nodded toward the middle of the parking lot. "Wait here with the bags, I'll get the car," he said, adding, "Gary, come on, I want you to check out the turbocharger in my car. Tell me if it's making a noise."

Gary and Kevin crossed the road outside the airport terminal. Kevin confessed, "I don't have a problem with my car. I just wanted to ask you: Last time I saw you, you were living in some rat hole apartment, on your way to jail. I never did find out what happened."

Gary shivered. "I never did any time. Except for the one night when they let me sleep it off. The concessionaire didn't want to press any charges, and the owner of the speedway was satisfied with barring me from his track for a year." Gary paused and gave Kevin a quizzical look. "You were talking about that time I got mad about being knocked out early in the demolition derby, weren't you?"

"I guess so."

Gary shrugged and threw his hands in the air. "I don't know. I was just a jerk kid back then." Gary looked over his shoulder. Seeing Gilbert and Dinah busy pointing out new sights to each other, he continued, "Then I met Dinah. She wasn't as chunky back then, really kind of cute, actually."

"She's still cute. Seems like a great person. Congratulations on your good luck."

"Thanks. She's all right. Kind of sexy in her own way. So anyway, I finished school, married her, and got a decent job working for the state interviewing welfare applicants. The job paid the rent, but I got to tell you, after eight years of that crap, it damn near drove me nuts."

"That's when you, Gilbert and Dinah started your own business?"

"I suppose it made me want to get into business for myself, yes. Dinah was sick of her job. She was an illustrator for some stupid little trade magazine, *Concrete Production Stats Quarterly*," he said, looking at Kevin with a wry grin.

"Sounds exciting."

"And Gilbert was doing pretty well," Gary continued. "Part owner in an old movie theater that showed mostly cult classics. Sold his interest to join G&G's."

"Gutsy move," Kevin said.

"Anyway," Gary continued, "he was as pissed off as I was over Aunt Winifred's funeral."

"Ah-ha," Kevin said. "Aunt Winifred's funeral. That's how it all started. My dad wrote me about how you and Gilbert botched the arrangements. What happened?"

Gary grimaced at the thought of Uncle Thomas,

reminding himself not to speak too harshly of him in front of Kevin.

Kevin said, "It's all right, I know the old guy is the world's biggest ass. That's why I came here and never went back. But Dad couldn't have been the reason you started your own funeral home. And where did you get the idea to open the kind of home you did? Sounds like the damnedest thing. I've seen the stories about it on the wire services down at the newspaper."

Gary relaxed knowing Kevin shared his opinion of Uncle Thomas. "No, your dad isn't the reason we started G&G's Funeral Home, but he did seem to enjoy telling everyone how he thought me and Gilbert botched Aunt Winifred's funeral."

"So you really did botch it?"

"We might have done a few things differently," Gary answered, rubbing his eye, turning from Kevin to conceal the broad smile he couldn't repress.

They reached Kevin's car, a large white Holden from Australia. Kevin circled around to the driver's side and opened the unlocked door. Gary looked over the roof of the car at him, knowing he had a long story to tell his cousin, whom he hadn't seen in over a decade. Gary climbed in the front seat. "It all started when Aunt Winifred died," Gary explained. "Sorry you couldn't make the funeral."

"Well, I didn't really know her that well. Spooky old lady, I always thought. Rich, spooky, old lady. That house of hers always gave me the creeps when I was a kid," Kevin said, putting the car in gear and backing out of the parking space.

"Yeah, I know. That house gave everyone the creeps. She hadn't changed a thing since her husband, Uncle...what was his name?...died back in the Fifties."

"William. Uncle William. My folks told me I once met him. He bounced me on his knee when I was a baby, and I puked all over his silk smoking jacket."

Gary chuckled. "You puked on him? How could you? Aunt Winifred used to say he was the most patriotic man in the country, supplying K-rations to the military."

"Yeah, I know. Korea made him a millionaire. If he had lived a little longer, he could have been a billionaire off Vietnam."

Kevin pulled the car over to the curb in front of Gilbert and Dinah, got out and opened the trunk. "I think it'll all fit," he said, helping Gilbert hoist his suitcase into the trunk.

"Never mind this, Kevin," Gilbert said. "We can handle it," he added, motioning toward Gary.

Gary got out of the car and dragged one of Dinah's suitcases to the trunk, sweat beading on his reddened, slightly pockmarked face. Seeing Gary struggle, Gilbert offered, "Here, let me help you with that one. You got to get in better shape, cousin."

"Thanks cousin," Gary answered, poking the tight roll of flab above Gilbert's waistband. "You should talk."

Together, they threw Dinah's suitcase in the trunk. It bounced off the spare tire and tumbled on its side, landing handle side down. Both Gary and Gilbert reached for a smaller bag. Each thinking the other would take it, they grabbed hold of other bags, leaving the small bag where it lay. When all the remaining bags were strewn in Kevin's trunk, both Gary and Gilbert picked up the small bag. "Got it?" they asked each other, letting go, sending the bag plummeting to the ground.

Gary turned to Kevin and Dinah, saying, "It's OK, this is one of those bags they have gorillas stomp on in their TV commercials."

"Yeah," Gilbert added, "me and Gary can handle it."

"After you," Gary said, offering a clear path.

"No, after you," Gilbert answered politely.

Again, they both reached for it. Again they both backed off. They slowly reached again, then slowly backed off, like two mimes in a mirror image routine.

Kevin motioned them aside. "Allow me," he said.

As Kevin lifted the bag, he read the name on the baggage label. "Millie Foster? Are you sure this is your bag?"

Gary said to Gilbert, "It's not mine, I thought it was yours."

"It's not mine, I thought it was Dinah's."

"No, it's not mine," Dinah said.

A porter and a hysterical woman ran over, the porter blowing a whistle and waving his arms, shouting, "Sir. Sir. Pardon me, sir."

"That's my bag!" the woman screamed.

Kevin offered her the bag, apologizing, "We're sorry. It was our mistake."

Gilbert offered his hand, "You must be the real Millie Foster. Hi, Gilbert Jackson."

The bag fell to the ground as Kevin released it and Millie Foster instinctively moved to shake Gilbert's hand, a suspicious and wary expression on her face. The porter picked up the bag, squinted at Gilbert and followed Millie back to the terminal, looking back once at Gilbert's sunglasses and fake nose.

"Well, that takes care of that," Gary said, slamming the trunk. "Let's go." The trunk's latch caught with an audible click. Kevin winced at the bow in the trunk's sheet metal, but said nothing. They piled into the car, Gilbert up front with Kevin, Gary and Dinah in back. The car's suspension sagged nearly to the ground under the weight of passengers and luggage. Kevin turned the ignition, shifted gears and floored the gas pedal. The car inched away from the curb, picked up momentum through the parking lot, and sputtered and strained onto the highway heading east, along the southern coast of Fiji's biggest island. Gary leaned forward and whispered in Kevin's ear, "Great turbocharger, Kevin."

Dinah leaned forward, resting her arms on the seat backs. "Kevin, it's so nice of you to come get us like this."

"I'm glad to do it. I haven't seen Gary and Gilbert since we were kids, practically. And I heard Gary got married, and I was always curious to see who would marry Gary." Kevin added quickly, "He's one of a kind, and I knew his bride would have to be something extra special."

Gary bowed his head and scratched his forehead to hide the smile on his face. Kevin was good. He would have been a good business partner. He could have been president of G&G's overseas operations. Gary put the thought out of his head; it was useless to daydream of G&G's anymore.

Kevin continued his conversation with Dinah. "You're going to enjoy Fiji. Have you been abroad before?"

"No. But we did have a Mexican family living down the street from us when I was growing up. And the printer where I once worked did a lot of jobs for a travel agency, so I got to see a lot of pictures of places. That's about it, though."

Gilbert joined the conversation. "Dinah, didn't your father used to travel quite a bit?"

"Oh yes, he did. But never abroad. He was a buyer for the housewares section of a big department store. He always brought home samples—shower curtains, hand towels, that sort of thing. And fudge. He had a thing for fudge. It was his hobby, finding the city with the best fudge. I guess that's where I got my sweet tooth."

"Well your sweet tooth must be what made you so sweet," Kevin said. "They're going to love you here in Fiji."

Gary bit his lip. Kevin was good. Damn good. What would have happened if he had handled Aunt Winifred's funeral arrangements? Would he have trusted Mr. Wiggins to find an answer to the "green problem"? Being in the newspaper business, could he have foreseen that Mr. Westlaw was such a rat? With his savvy, could he have handled Mr. Devine better? Or Gilbert and Dinah, for that matter?

Gary looked out the car window into the distance, thoughts of the long flight and the events leading up to it forming a whirlwind in his mind. Nonetheless, he felt safe nestled in the back seat of Kevin's car, next to Dinah, oblivious to the words, but clearly hearing her cheerful, feminine voice engage in small talk with Kevin and Gilbert. The gentle rolling of the car over highway pavement lulled him into a trance. He recalled everything, even the leg cramp he got as he and Gilbert squatted on his patio cleaning the winter's rust off his hibachi. He could hear the gravity in Dinah's voice when she called him to the phone, the gravity that told him someone had died, leaving the moments until he reached the phone suspended in time and emotion until he found out who. By evening, everyone had heard the news, and the next day all the family members who could make it gathered in Aunt Winifred's living room.

Gary closed his eyes. He heard snippets of conversation from the front seat, Gilbert mentioning "G&G's" and "funeral homes," beginning to recount the whole story to Kevin. He could see Gilbert's mother, Eunice, standing in Aunt Winifred's spacious living room, as Gilbert told Kevin how she had asked him to help make the funeral arrangements.

"Just call the funeral home and tell them what hospital she's in," Gary imagined Gilbert's mother saying, "and they'll take care of everything. There's a nice funeral home we used on your Uncle Barney...oh...I forget the name of it. Go ask Gary; maybe he'd know."

CHAPTER 2

Gilbert elbowed his way through the crowd to the kitchen to find Gary, and pour himself another whiskey sour. He asked, "Hey Gary, what funeral home did they use on Uncle Barney?

"Devine Funeral Home. Is that where they're sending Aunt Winifred?"

"I don't know. I'm the one who's going to do the sending."

"How'd you get stuck with that job? Don't you know enough to duck out when they start talking about arrangements?"

"Guess who's going to help me?" Gilbert asked with a wink at Dinah and a nod toward Gary.

"No way. I don't know anything about arranging for a funeral. What help can I be?"

"You can help share the blame if anything goes wrong. Anyway, it's real easy. All we have to do is call Devine's and tell them Aunt Winifred is at Holy Shrine of the Epiphany Hospital. They'll take it from there."

"It can't be that easy," Gary said. "Did you call?"

"Not yet. Let's go down the basement where it's quieter."

Gary asked Dinah, "Do you know anything about arranging for a funeral?"

"Not a thing," she answered, "but let's give it a try, maybe we'll learn something."

Down the basement they marched, Gilbert with his phone, Gary with the blender, and Dinah with the enthusiasm. They made themselves comfortable in the rickety old rattan furniture Aunt Winifred bought when she was first married. Gary poured a round of drinks then settled back in the couch, putting his arm around Dinah's shoulder, pretending to comfort her, keeping too busy to make the call himself. He found it hard to suppress a wide grin as he thought, 'Wives come in handy at the strangest times.'

Gilbert frowned as he downed his drink and picked up the phone. "Hello. … Yeah. My aunt died at Holy Shrine of the Epiphany Hospital. Can you go pick her up? … Aunt Winifred. Winifred Gladstone. She's about five foot three, gray hair, eighty-two years old. You'll know her when you see her, she'll be in Epiphany's morgue. What time can you get her? … This is Gilbert Jackson. I'm handling the arrangements. … Ten o'clock? OK."

Gilbert put the phone down. He looked at Gary and Dinah and shrugged, "That was easy. We'll go over there at ten tomorrow to sign all the papers or whatever. You two will come with me, won't you?"

Gary tried to think of an excuse, but could only think of how he and Gilbert used to hang around together as kids getting into all kinds of mischief. He remembered the time Gilbert lied for him when he set the porch on fire playing with firecrackers. He couldn't let Gilbert down now. "Sure I'll come. Dinah?"

"Ten o'clock? Sorry guys, I got to be at work tomorrow morning. I have to paste in the load-bearing specifications on my illustration of the concrete footbridge they developed for spanning floodwaters in the Serengeti."

Gary and Gilbert stared at her with blank expressions. Dinah added defensively, "Well you never know, someone might have to build one someday. Anyhow, the magazine is supposed to go into production by the end of this week, and we have to stay on schedule."

Back upstairs Gilbert told his mother that everything was taken care of. She looked relieved, and several people standing nearby acted surprised that arrangements had been made so quickly without their help. Uncle Thomas shook Gilbert's hand with approval, saying, "I had forgotten all about funeral arrangements. It's so good of you to help us out like that, Gilbert."

The next morning, Gary and Gilbert paused in the deserted vestibule at Devine Funeral Home. They peeked inside the first room on their right. A thin, white-haired man lay in a mahogany casket. The room was dark except for a fluorescent light that shone from behind the casket upwards onto a red velvet curtain. Gary was admiring the aesthetics until he remembered there was a dead man in the room. He silently apologized to the man and exited.

They peeked inside the next room, where a woman was placing prayer cards on a podium near the door. She looked up, startled, "Mrs. Greene won't be displayed until this evening."

Gilbert said, "No, we're not here for Mrs. Greene. We're here for Aunt Winifred... Mrs. Gladstone."

The woman looked puzzled. Gilbert continued, "She's new here...she just came in...she hasn't been set up yet. We're here to talk to an arrangements counselor. I called yesterday."

"Oh yes. You're Mr. Jackson. Right this way."

She led them to the office and buzzed the intercom. "Mr. Jackson is here to see you, Mr. Devine. Along with a Mr.," she looked at Gary.

"Colbert. Gary Colbert."

"Along with Mr. Colbert. Shall I send them in?"

"Yes please," crackled the answer.

Gary straightened his back and checked his fly. He would have worn a more conservative tie had he known they were going to talk to Mr. Devine himself. The man whose name is plastered all over the building's ornate facade, in gold letters two feet high!

Certificates, shining plaques, and leather-bound books strategically focused attention toward Mr. Devine's big oak desk, which dominated the office. An overstuffed sofa and two matching chairs lay across the thick carpet, at the opposite end of the office. Two wooden chairs with leather seats and hard, straight backs stood in front of the oak desk.

Mr. Devine rose from behind his desk. His tailored three-piece dark blue suit and starched white shirt radiated power, strength and position like a coat of mail. A gold pin from a local community service organization adorned his lapel. Properly coifed snow white hair framed to perfect proportion the face, not of a man, but of, perhaps, an adult cherub, or at least a trustworthy eunuch, whose crystalline, angelic blue eyes were to be used as much to see as be seen. Mr. Devine paused, as he always did, to let his visitors gaze upon his visage and wonder at the total effect of his persona, a persona that, while clearly placing him above ordinary mortals, stopped just short of presuming divinity, a conclusion he tactfully left to his beholders.

Gary and Gilbert, dressed in department store suits, Gilbert with brown wingtips and wide, green and blue striped tie, sheepishly accepted Mr. Devine's commanding gesture to sit in the two wooden chairs next to his desk.

He spoke. "I was so sorry to hear of your aunt's passing. It's always such a tragedy. But these things happen and we're here to help you make the transition in your lives as smooth as possible. If at any time there's anything I can do to help you and your family through this difficult period, please don't hesitate to ask."

Mr. Devine smiled and continued, "I'm sure you'll want only the best for your dear aunt, so I've made up a little list of what I think will make a very nice service. These items are inclusive in our package deal, and I'm sure you'll find the cost reasonable, not that cost is anything you'd think of at a time like this."

As Mr. Devine explained each item on the list…filing death certificate, submitting death notice to local paper, hearse rental, attendant fees...Gary's mind spun into catatonia. The list, spoken in the funeral director's most sonorous tone, was meant to be heard and experienced, not understood. He nodded on cue as Mr. Devine occasionally looked up.

When Mr. Devine got to the bottom line, he paused for a reflection on the ancient Egyptians and how they spent the equivalent of millions of dollars providing for the burial of their beloved rulers. "But with the package deal," he said, "you'll not have to spend anywhere near that much.

"Of course," he went on, "this list just represents the essentials. We'll help you arrange a marker, and I'm sure you'll want a good, sturdy vault," he said, looking up to solicit an affirmative nod. "It isn't included in the package because we've found that people's tastes in vaults vary. Some want basic concrete, some prefer steel-reinforced concrete. In these days of nuclear accidents just waiting to happen, some even choose to protect their loved ones with our special lead-lined vaults. And of course, all our vaults are guaranteed not to crack or leak for twenty years. That's an important consideration when you stop to think about the water table in this area, and of course, earthquakes. We wouldn't want Aunt Winifred disturbed, would we?" he asked in a tone that forced his clients to agree, or be damned.

"Personally," he continued, "for my own aunt who passed earlier this year, I chose the steel-reinforced, copper-lined vault. It affords the best protection and I can enjoy peace of mind knowing she's taken care of. Although the caskets we offer are the most durable known to man, if left to the open environment they'll eventually decompose. And we all know that raw soil, anywhere but the driest desert, is rife with bioinvaders. I couldn't bear the thought of that happening to my own aunt."

Gary glanced over at Gilbert and shivered, succumbing to Mr. Devine's suggestion. Images of bioinvaders with groping, slithering tentacles and acidic saliva filled his mind. Mr. Devine paused just long enough for the image to form.

"So, just for now," he said firmly, "I'll put you down for the steel-reinforced, copper-lined. And that leaves gravesite. Had your aunt purchased one already?"

Gary and Gilbert looked at each other and shrugged.

Mr. Devine continued, "Well I'm sure she would have told you if she had. But don't worry, there are several fine sites in the immediate area. They're going fast, though. In another few years I'm afraid all the sites within fifty miles will be taken. Perhaps it's not too early to think of reserving a couple of these sites for yourselves. You look like a couple of fine, conscientious young men who wouldn't want to burden those you leave behind when it's your time to pass. And let's be realistic, I think we all know it's going to happen."

Gary instinctively thought of Dinah, and how he

could spare her this ordeal. His eyes started glassing over, and he nervously played with the wedding ring on his finger. Mr. Devine continued with enthusiasm, speaking directly to Gary. "When a husband dies unexpectedly, there's enough for a poor, bereaved widow to worry about…grieving over the unfairness of life, dealing with insurance people, wondering how to go on. I know of four very nice sites in Elmwood Lawns overlooking a delightful little valley just filled with crocus and mums. If you'd like, I could reserve them for you and we could find something else for your aunt."

Gilbert crossed his legs, using the motion to kick Gary in the shin. The pain snapped Gary back to attention, serving as penance for burdening Dinah. Gilbert said to Mr. Devine, "That's certainly something to think about. But for right now, we would like to concentrate on Aunt Winifred."

Gary's eyes cleared. The spell had been broken.

"We'll keep those four spots open for now," Mr. Devine said. "They really are intended as a family unit."

Mr. Devine shuffled through a long computer printout, running his finger down its many columns and ponderous codes. "There is a single space left on Lot B at Elmwood," he noted. "I think your aunt will be very happy there. Elmwood is so nice this time of year. The grounds are kept immaculate, and you can be assured that all gravesites are trimmed and all flowers removed before they wither and become unsightly. Now then, for your choice of casket; we've got several to choose from."

Mr. Devine led Gary and Gilbert with brisk, confident strides to the showroom, next to his office. "Any of those marked with a yellow tag are included in your package," he advised. "And, of course, if you prefer something a little more expensive...I don't know how close you and your aunt were...but if you'd like something a little nicer, any of those to the right can be substituted and we'll just make an adjustment to the package price. Normally I'm not supposed to allow adjustments, but I feel that just because someone takes advantage of the package deal, it doesn't mean they want to scrimp when it comes to the casket, something the whole family will see at the service. I'm sure you'll want to do the right thing. Well, I'll leave you, and when you've made your decision, I'll be in my office and we'll just do a quick signing on the dotted line. Then we can begin restoration on your aunt so we can present her tomorrow."

When Mr. Devine was gone, Gilbert whispered, "Hey Gary, we got to get one of the caskets with the yellow tags. Look at the prices on those others."

"No way! We want the best for Aunt Winifred," Gary teased. "Remember, the whole family will see it. How about this one over here? Titanium alloy with proof-minted nickel ornamentation and hand-tooled leather end pieces. It's only $22,000."

"I could buy a whole house for $22,000! A decent used mobile home, anyway. These ones over here are already included in the package, let's pick one of them," Gilbert said, taking Gary by the elbow, steering him away from the more expensive caskets.

The two caskets included in the package were made of particle board covered with what looked like second-hand drapes from the thrift shop. One was an olive shade of green, the other a dirty pink. Either would be an embarrassment, but the cheapest upgrade would add $750. And even it looked tacky.

Examining the yellow-tagged caskets closer, Gilbert fretted, "These caskets look like hell. How are we going to face everyone when Aunt Winifred is wheeled out in one of these?"

Gary stroked his chin and rubbed his eye. "It's OK," he said at last. "Here's what we'll do: I'll ask Dinah to go around saying how nice it looks. Everyone trusts her judgment, and we won't get ripped off."

"I don't know," Gilbert said. "It's so obvious how ugly it is. I don't think it'll work."

Gary thought a moment, his eyes moving across the showroom, from casket to casket, price tag to price tag. He observed, "Some of these caskets are really beautiful. Real works of art. I wonder how the craftsmen who made them feel about them being buried, never to be seen again?"

"Maybe they don't know," Gilbert began. "Maybe the craftsmen are kept isolated in little workshops underground and told that they're making stereo cabinets or port-a-beds. Maybe they're a whole unseen class of humans, like a lost tribe of troglodytes who labor day and night, happy if their masters allow them a few crumbs of bread every now and then. Maybe..."

"OK, Gilbert. Enough!" Gary said, sorry he had brought up the subject. "Anyway," he continued, "I think I have the answer. We'll tell Devine to drape an American flag over the coffin. That way, no one will see it until we get to the cemetery. And by that time, everyone will be thinking about getting some lunch, and they won't care."

"It might work. It's worth a try, anyway. OK, should we get the pink or the green?"

"Pink for Aunt Winifred."

"No," Gilbert said, rubbing his fingernails at a stain on the pink casket. "Green. It doesn't show the dirt as much."

Gary and Gilbert re-entered Mr. Devine's office without knocking. Mr. Devine closed the latest issue of *Mortuary Market* magazine and stuffed it into his desk drawer. "Well, you've made your choice, I see. I have all the paperwork right here so we can make that adjustment."

"No, we don't need an adjustment," Gilbert said. "That green casket in the package deal looks really great. Aunt Winifred had a pair of drapes that color in her living room. I think she'd like it."

"Also," Gary added, "if you could drape an American flag over the casket, we'd appreciate it. Aunt Winifred, and her late husband, were quite the patriots, you know."

Mr. Devine's nose twitched, like a cat smelling a

rat. He stared blankly at Gary for a moment, then smiled slightly. "All right," he said, "I'll assign one of my people to take care of it."

While Mr. Devine stuffed their bill into an envelope, Gary and Gilbert nodded and smirked at one another.

As they walked out of the funeral home and crossed the parking lot, Gilbert opened the envelope, and read each item on the bill. "Hey Gary, what's this? $180 consultation fee?"

"What! Let me see that," Gary said, grabbing the bill. "You mean we had to pay that scoundrel $180 for selling us a bunch of crap? We've been had. No wonder nobody wanted to make the arrangements."

"Oh well, it's over," Gilbert said. "The money'll come from the estate, so we're really not out anything. Come on, let's get out of here."

After Gary and Gilbert left his office, Mr. Devine paused, allowed himself a brief chuckle, then stepped into his secretary's office. "Miss Krofchak, do you have a postage stamp with the American flag on it?"

"Yes, sir. Right here," she answered, reaching into her desk drawer. "Just one?"

"One will do nicely, thank you. Oh, and do you have any strong glue?"

"I think so," she answered, walking to a supply cabinet in the corner, fishing through its shelves. "Oh, yes. Here we go."

"Thank you very much, Miss Krofchak."

Mr. Devine returned to his office, allowing the smile to return to his face. He stepped into the adjoining showroom and glued the postage stamp to the top of the green casket.

At the service the next evening, Uncle Thomas waited until Gilbert and Gary were within earshot. "God that casket looks cheap. You'd think they would've chosen something more presentable. And what's the big idea putting a postage stamp on it?"

Gary pulled Dinah aside. "Dinah, weren't you able to get that postage stamp off?"

"I tried, but it's really stuck on there. I did get a little corner off, but it looked worse torn, so I put it back. Gary, is this some kind of joke?"

"I don't know. I asked the funeral director to drape a flag over that God-awful casket so people wouldn't see it. I'm going to go have a talk with him. Meanwhile, you better get circulating about how nice the casket looks. People are starting to talk."

"I don't blame them. Gary, promise me that when I die you won't put me in something that crappy looking."

"If you circulate and talk up the casket, I'll promise you anything."

Gary found Mr. Devine standing in the hallway giving instructions to the attendants. As Gary approached, Mr. Devine gave the attendants their leave and turned toward Gary, smiling. "Ahh, Mr. Colbert. I trust everything is satisfactory."

"Satisfactory?" Gary asked indignantly. "No, it's not satisfactory. I asked for a flag over Aunt Winifred's casket, instead I get a postage stamp."

"Oh, yes, that," Mr. Devine said, taking Gary by the elbow, leaning toward him, whispering, "I'm so sorry about the misunderstanding, but you see, I gave explicit instructions to one of my people. It turns out, however, he couldn't find a full-size flag. So, thinking any representation of a flag would suffice, he affixed a postage stamp. I'm very sorry. He will be severely reprimanded, I assure you."

Gary frowned and hesitantly turned to rejoin the service. Out of the corner of his eye, and too briefly to be certain he even saw it in the large gold-framed mirror in the hallway, he thought he saw Mr. Devine smile and slap himself on the wrist.

It rained the day of the funeral. Nothing heavy, just the right amount for a funeral. When the service was over, most everyone went to Aunt Winifred's big house for an array of hot food, cold cuts and mixed drinks. Uncle Thomas and the other beneficiaries of Aunt Winifred's ambiguous will took the opportunity to argue over her remaining possessions, hoping to preempt any later decisions by the executor. Uncle Thomas, with second drink in hand, argued with Gilbert's mother, Eunice. "I don't care how much you like the painting, I helped Winifred hang the damn thing twenty years ago when she bought it. Do you hear me? Twenty God Damn years ago! I think that gives me some rights in the matter."

"Now Thomas," Eunice began, "You don't appreciate art and you know it."

"That's not the point," Uncle Thomas bellowed, "it's the principle of the thing. Twenty years ago I put labor, my labor, into hanging that painting. What have you done to earn it? I'll tell you what you've done: NOTHING!"

Edgar, a wily relative of Aunt Winifred's late husband, had been sent to the funeral to look out for his side of the family's interests. He pulled Uncle Thomas aside, whispering, "You know, Tom, old buddy, that painting isn't worth doodle. Let Eunice have it. That way you'll be in a better bargaining position to snatch Winifred's collection of paste jewelry...some of that stuff's antique and quite nice, not worth much, but still quite nice. I know Eunice wants it and you can trade her for the painting and the big-screen TV I hear she snuck out of here last week when Winifred was in the hospital. Then later you and me will get together and I'll be satisfied taking the painting, it does have sentimental value for me, being from my favorite aunt's house, in exchange for some bona fide stock certificates my family's been holding for Winifred all these years. Who knows what they could be worth today? And you keep the TV set on top of all that. Wouldn't it be great to watch the Superbowl on your own big-screen TV?"

Uncle Thomas' eyes shifted from Edgar to Eunice, to the painting, to the crowd of other relatives mingling in the next room. Edgar pushed, "Hurry, before someone else gets in on this."

Uncle Thomas nodded secretively at Edgar. He approached Eunice, and in his gruffest voice, said, "There is a principle involved here, Eunice, but I'll be reasonable if you will. I'd like you to have the painting if you appreciate it that much. And I appreciate Winifred's jewelry. And, I'll have you know, she promised on her deathbed, ON HER DEATHBED, FOR GOD'S SAKE," he yelled, "that Silvia would get every piece of it. Do you hear me? EVERY GOD DAMN PIECE OF IT!"

"That's insane," Eunice shrieked. "Winnie didn't even like you or your wife. She wouldn't give her jewelry to anyone but me." She quickly added, "And maybe a few pieces to Livia."

Taking the mention of her name as an invitation, Livia stepped over and offered, "It's too bad Winifred sold all her real diamonds and pearls when William died. But what she has left is still nice. I wouldn't mind having a piece or two."

Uncle Thomas turned red and stamped his foot and shook his fist in the air, spilling ice cubes and the last ounce of liquor in his glass. "Great!" he bellowed, "Now we got you involved in this."

"Well she should be involved," Eunice countered, "after all, Winnie was her sister too."

"I don't care if she's God Almighty's sister! She's not getting any of that jewelry! And neither are you! Not the jewelry AND the painting."

Edgar stepped silently, like a cat burglar, to a position behind Eunice and Livia. He gave Uncle Thomas a confidential, manly nod and a surreptitious thumbs-up as he raised his glass of white wine. Uncle Thomas made his move. "All right, Eunice, it happens that I am an art lover and that painting just does something for me. I helped Winifred hang it after she brought it back from her first trip to Europe without William. I'm going to take it and put it in my living room, along with the big-screen TV you took out of here last week...oh yes, I know about that...in exchange you can have all the jewelry in the house and you won't hear another word about it from me."

Eunice and Livia exchanged glances. The last part of Uncle Thomas' offer sounded too good to be true. Livia turned to hide a smirk, pretending to examine the painting. Eunice, worn down by the battle, sighed, turning to take a last look at the beautiful painting. "All right," she said, "have it your way. But just for the record, I took Winnie's TV out of here because she asked me to bring it to the hospital for her so she could watch her soaps. You know her eyesight was failing, and she couldn't see that tiny TV the hospital provided. You can come pick it up tomorrow."

Edgar was elated. The cancelled stock certificates he would trade to Uncle Thomas were worthless. The painting, however, had been appraised at $12,000 at the first gathering in Aunt Winifred's house three days before by his cousin, an art dealer from New York.

Gary, Gilbert and Dinah retired to the basement

with a blenderful of whiskey sours. Gary sighed, "No wonder there are so many stories about dead people and ghouls. Did you hear those people up there? I want this. I want that. Aunt Winifred wanted me to have this. I'll let you have the jewelry for one painting and the color TV. Hey Gilbert, let's not you and I get into that."

"I'm with you. Let's just take whatever's left over."

Later, when Gary went back up to the kitchen to make a tray of sandwiches, he heard Uncle Thomas in the dining room. "$5,480? That's quite a chunk of change! I agreed the funeral expenses should come right off the top of Winifred's estate, but that didn't give those two carte blanche to spend whatever they wanted. I vote we allot $2,000 from the estate and leave it to them to come up with the difference. It's only fair to the rest of us."

Gary grabbed the sandwiches and hurried to get out of the kitchen unnoticed. He knew that despite the wily Edgar's encouragement, Uncle Thomas would be unable to convince the others to go along with his motion.

CHAPTER 3

Gary finished cleaning the winter's rust off his hibachi, thankful that this time he wasn't interrupted by a death in the family. Gilbert loaded the hibachi with coals, piling them in a perfect pyramid. He soaked them with charcoal lighter fluid, pulled a kitchen match from his shirt pocket, lit it with his fingernail, and threw it on the coals. Instantly, the hibachi erupted in a ball of flame.

"You know," Gilbert said, "we really did get ripped off on that funeral. If we had cremated her, it would have cost less. No coffin, no plot of land, no gravestone, and a cute little urn, to boot."

"Yeah Gil, you're right. I really feel like an ass. We should have checked with the old folks. Maybe they wouldn't have minded a cremation, who knows?"

"I'm sure everyone who has ever buried someone thinks the same thing," Gilbert observed. "Problem is, they think it, they don't say it. Cremation, that's got to be the wave of the future. This burying people is getting out of hand. The urban sprawl in this area hasn't left much land for cemeteries. We were lucky to get that spot for Aunt Winifred without having to drive thirty miles to the country. There's got to be a better way."

"Yeah, there's got to be a better way," Gary sighed, "but Devine isn't going to come up with it. The status quo is being too good to him. The bastard!"

Staring into the flaming hibachi, Gary continued,

"But the problem with cremation is that people are squeamish about it. They figure it might hurt or something. Or, what if God wants to resurrect the body? What the hell's he going to do with a handful of ashes?"

"Well, if God can resurrect a dead body, he can do anything he damn well pleases," Gilbert argued. "A handful of ashes wouldn't be any more difficult to resurrect."

"Yes, I agree with you, but people don't think like that. Maybe they want to give God every advantage they can. We should open a funeral parlor right next to Devine," Gary said idly. "We'll call it Acme Cut Rate Funerals."

Gilbert poked at the flaming coals with a stick, musing, "We've always wanted to start our own business ever since we had that hot dog stand in high school. And Dinah's a smart lady, she could help too."

Gary's eyes widened as he thought out loud, "How much could a basic, no-nonsense funeral cost? If customers are hell-bent on a viewing, we'll just keep the guys in an icebox during the day and bring them out for a few hours at night so people can see them. We don't need all that embalming."

"Yeah," Gilbert agreed, tossing away his stick, looking brightly at Gary. "And we could have one nice casket that they can rent for the viewing. After that, we'll use a pine box to bury them, like in the westerns."

Gary thought a moment, then said with disappointment, "Yeah, but then we're still stuck with cemeteries and gravestones."

Gilbert chimed, "How 'bout if we just keep them in the freezer forever."

Gary raised his eyebrows and nodded. "Yeah, that way people from out of town wouldn't have to take time off work and rush to the funeral. We could just take them inside the freezer for a viewing. Unlimited funerals. That could be a selling point."

"Damn good idea, Gary. We could look into cryobiological freezing, like they do with sperm and stuff."

"You're right. They're doing that with whole humans now. I read about it. Only the people aren't dead, just almost dead. When science comes up with a cure for whatever they got, they get thawed out and fixed up and live for another twenty years or so."

"Maybe we could offer a complete line of cryobiological freezing services in case the people aren't sure whether they're really dead, or just having an out-of-body experience."

Gary snapped his fingers, and pointed at Gilbert. "But even if they're not dead," he said, "eventually they'll need a funeral. There's always going to be a market."

"You know, we can save money on the freezing part if we just embalm them real good to begin with. Those Egyptian mummies have been around for centuries and they still look good as new. I'm sure with modern science we can come up with an even better way, something where they don't have to wear rags over their faces. People wouldn't come from out of town to see someone with rags on their face."

Gary paced excitedly back and forth across the patio, regarding Gilbert's comments. He wondered why the ancient Egyptians had no objections to putting rags over their faces. He wondered about the statues in hundreds of parks, and what the reaction would be if they had been hewn and molded with rags on their faces. Of course, those rags would serve no purpose, the stone or bronze underneath wouldn't need rags. Only once-living flesh would need rags. Like the rags Mr. Wiggins, the old funeral director turned taxidermist, dramatically pulled off the deer head and rack he and Gilbert bought from a successful hunter years ago. Mr. Wiggins, the cranky old buzzard, pulled the rags off such with a proud flourish, like he was unveiling a statue. Mr. Wiggins. The old funeral director turned taxidermist.

"You don't suppose," Gary hesitantly ventured, "that Mr. Wiggins might want to get back into operating a funeral home? And he might have some ideas about how we can keep the rags off people's faces. Remember how he was always experimenting with new forms of taxidermy?"

"Mr. Wiggins? Working with us?" Gilbert nodded. "Mr. Wiggins. Working with us," he repeated. "Yeah, I like it."

Gary clapped his hands together loudly, and said, "I'm going to give him a call right now. Just to see how he's doing. Feel him out on this. Watch the coals."

Gary ran into the house and fished through his old telephone directory. The binding broke and several pages fell to the floor. Among the fallen pages was a dog-eared, yellowed business card with Mr. Wiggins' phone number. Gary dialed.

"Hello, is this Mr. Wiggins? ... Gary Colbert. ... Fine, fine. You? ... I'm sorry to hear that, Mr. Wiggins. ... Hey, that's rough. ... Yeah, I know, you got to watch those bastards. ... Yes, Mr. Wiggins. ... Mr. Wiggins? ... Yes, Mr. Wiggins. The reason I'm calling is..."

CHAPTER 4

G&G's Funeral Home was located just a quarter mile from Devine Funeral Home, in an old house on a busy side street in a bustling part of town newly rezoned for small business. Phone service and utilities were hooked up, and the proper permits, care of Mr. Wiggins, hung on the wall in the office.

On a crisp Saturday morning the dew on the grass in front of G&G's put a shine on Gary's shoes as he walked over and shook hands with the work crew that had placed the big sign on the lawn. "It looks great!" Gary said. "Good job."

The crew chief stepped back, admiring his work. "G&G's Funeral Home," he read. "Looks OK."

The chief held a brown clipboard before Gary. "If you just sign the delivery receipt, we'll be off," he said, offering Gary a well-chewed ballpoint pen.

Gary pretended not to notice the chief's ballpoint, and withdrew a gold pen from his shirt pocket and signed with a proud flourish, underlining his name with such force that the pen ripped the top copy of the receipt.

As the chief tore the bottom copy from the clipboard and handed it to Gary, he said, "Remember, we give a discount on removal of signs we install. Good luck to you, sir."

Gary replaced his pen, silently damning the chief for his curse. Remove the sign? A discount? I'll give you a discount...on a funeral. Gary looked down at the receipt in his hands, and tore it in half, then in quarters. He crumbled it into a little ball and buried it in the soft earth at the base of the G&G's sign.

Satisfied the chief's curse had been countermanded, he strode confidently up the front walk and opened the door, noting its clean, fresh paint. He walked past the spacious, bare living room, into the office to join Dinah, who sat at one of the two desks preparing a newspaper ad.

"The sign looks great, Dinah. How's the ad coming?"

"I can't wait to see it. The sign," she answered, smiling at Gary. "And I have some great ideas for the ad. It'll be important our first ad be really good to get us off on the right foot. We have to mention how we're different from other funeral homes. Fair prices, no consultation fees, and most importantly, our twist."

"Makes sense," Gary said, taking a seat at the other desk, propping his feet up. "Isn't it great old Mr. Wiggins is working with us?" he mused. "He seems quite excited to be in the business again; kind of like this is his chance to get back at the big funeral home operators who put him out of business. We should bring some of his taxidermy stuff to display. He has a barn owl that would look great right in the front hall. Make that the first thing people see when they come in. It'll give them the impression they're making a wise choice."

Dinah looked up from her work. "For the ad," she said, "how about in big letters, 'G&G's Funeral Home,' then in smaller letters underneath, 'Display Your Loved Ones in a Permanent Way for all Eternity.' We should print some pamphlets, too. After all, we do have kind of a radical concept here. We have to present it right so it'll catch on."

Gary placed his hands behind his head and leaned back. "A pamphlet," he said, staring at the ceiling, using it as a backdrop to envision the project.

"We'll collaborate," Dinah said. "You and Gilbert put the words together, and I'll do the artwork."

Over the next few days, the pamphlet took shape. The front of it read:

The New Concept in Funeral Arrangements
only at
G&G's FUNERAL HOME

*No Burial Expense
*Unlimited Viewing
*Perpetual Display

The pamphlet opened to show Dinah's depiction of a typical funeral at G&G's. She was proud of the sketch; it was the most creative and original piece of art she had produced since graduating cum laude from the Academy of Creative Arts. A gathering of men, women and children stood with bowed heads as a black-robed minister spoke, one hand holding a large book, the other gesturing benevolently toward a figure standing beside him with uplifted eyes, and hands clasped reverently in prayer. At first, she had trouble indicating that the standing, praying figure was the deceased. Just to get started on the problem, she tried writing-in the word 'deceased,' with a little arrow pointing toward the figure, but the effect was cartoonish. Then she tried putting little x's in his eyes, but the effect was even more cartoonish. Finally, she removed the label and arrow, redrew the eyes, and added subtle rays emanating from the deceased's head. Immensely satisfied with the result, she only hoped the text would do it justice.

The text read:

The wave of the future is here and now at G&G's Funeral Home. In the old days families were burdened with huge funeral expenses. No more! Exclusively at G&G's Funeral Home you get more service for less.

Special features of a G&G interment include:

* No Burial Expense — Because the deceased is on permanent display at G&G's Funeral Home, gone forever is the terrible waste and expense of buying plots in a cemetery. Gone forever are expensive headstones prone to vandalism. Gone forever are long automobile processions to out-of-the-way cemeteries where row

upon row of mass-produced headstones
can never do justice to the individuality
your loved one exhibited in life.

*   Unlimited Viewing — Out-of-town
family and friends can combine regularly
scheduled holiday travel with funeral
viewing, any time between interment and
eternity.

*   Perpetual Display — Loved ones are
treated to the one and only G&G process,
which keeps them looking fresh and
young. Derived from age-old techniques,
the G&G process is a blend of ancient art
and modern science. Your loved one can
be permanently fixed in his or her most
favored setting—in a favorite rocker, in an
action pose reminiscent of a lifetime trade
or profession, even resting peacefully in a
soft easy chair.

Dinah informed the newspaper of the opening of
G&G's Funeral Home. The newspaper sent a reporter,
but when he arrived, he was disappointed. "When you
get a customer," he said, with forced, condescending
patience, "give me a call and I'll come running back.
You got something different, but I don't see it as news
until someone actually goes for it."

Following the dismal opening, Gary, Gilbert and
Dinah distributed the pamphlets door to door and
Dinah's quarter-page newspaper ad appeared on

consecutive Sundays.

Still no customers, and the only inquiry came from a woman asking if she could bring her Plume in, crying that no other funeral home would take a Pekingese. Gilbert took the call and considered it briefly before nixing the idea as gently as possible to the distraught woman. He mentioned the request later to Gary, explaining why he had rejected the job. "We don't want to get that kind of coverage for our first customer. Remember what the newspaper man said. He'll be covering the first G&G's funeral. If we're known for burying dogs, we'll be the laughing stock of the funeral business. No way!"

Gary nodded silently. He stroked his chin and ran a finger first under one eye, then the other. "This does present a strategy to get the business going, though," he said. "The first customer. That's the key. It has to be someone big and important. Someone whose judgment and class is beyond question. Maybe someone foreign. Like, say, the beloved philanthropist prince of the Republic of Surinam."

"How can we get him?" Gilbert asked. "Where's Surinam? Is it a republic? How do you know it has a beloved prince? Is he in town? How do you know he's going to die?"

Gary paused. The devious glint in his eyes spawned a devilish look that spread across his face. Gilbert knew the look and glanced over his shoulder to make sure Dinah wasn't nearby. He leaned forward, fascinated at the sudden transformation that took place on Gary's face, wary and skeptical because he had seen it before. From chubby cheeked and friendly to ruthless and demonic, he had seen it before. He had seen it back when they were in high school, the time when Gary replaced a sparkplug with a duck call in the fourth cylinder of his much-hated trigonometry teacher's car after being made to stay after school the day the lovely Mary Ellen Lindstrom agreed to meet him at the gazebo in the park. Mary Ellen never forgave him for not showing, and Gary never forgave his teacher. Gilbert recalled how he had reluctantly helped Gary carry out the scheme of revenge. And it worked! After a little difficulty starting the engine, the hapless teacher jumped out of the car peering here and there, trying to find the source of his car's rough idle and the muted, but audible quacking.

Or the time four, or was it five, years ago, when, after a spat with Dinah over an ugly brass-plated floorlamp she paid too much for at a flea market, Gary used Gilbert's basement to disassemble the lamp, installing a clever, but diabolical spring-loaded firing device that struck a primer cap from a .45 bullet. Gilbert cringed remembering the patch of steel-wool Gary stuffed into the bulb receptacle. When poor Dinah switched on her lamp, the primer exploded, and the steel-wool shorted the lamp, sending smoke and embers in all directions. Dinah put the flea-market lamp at the curb and never bought another electrical appliance secondhand.

To his credit, though, Gilbert noted, Gary was

ashamed afterward, and bought Dinah a brand new floor lamp. But while he was rigging Dinah's lamp, the devilish glint never faded for a moment from Gary's eyes. And of all the, though fortunately infrequent, hell-inspired tricks Gary pulled, they all worked! Gilbert was loath to hear this latest idea, but found himself, much against his will, anxiously awaiting. Gary readied to speak, turning his demonic stare directly on Gilbert. Gilbert swallowed hard and braced himself.

"I'm going to get us a beloved prince," Gary began slowly. "Or a former undersecretary for foreign affairs. Or something. We can work out who he is later."

Gilbert was puzzled, but didn't interrupt. He knew that somehow Gary would get a beloved prince. He only worried what role Gary had planned for him.

Gary snapped his fingers and grabbed Gilbert by the lapel with manic fury. "I'll tell you what I'm going to do..."

Dinah entered the office, and Gary loosened his grip on Gilbert's lapel and softened his voice. "Dinah," he called, "come here. We've got our first customer."

Gilbert was shocked. 'No. No, Gary,' he thought, 'don't tell Dinah. Whatever it is, she's much too nice.'

"Who is it?" Dinah asked hopefully.

"We've got our first customer," Gary repeated, "and he's at the Rose Terrace Hotel downtown. You guys don't know about Rose Terrace, but when I worked for the State Social Services Department, I visited it once in a while checking up on cases. It was like an elephant burial ground. Old indigents, derelicts and crazies...they all flocked there through some instinct to die. You'd die too, incidentally; it's a rat-infested hell hole. I'll go down there, talk to an old buddy of mine who knows all the gossip at Rose Terrace, find out who's about to die and snatch him up and bring him straight to Wiggins' place for processing."

Gilbert's neck twitched involuntarily. He looked briefly at poor Dinah standing there in disbelief. Obviously, Gary had managed to hide this side of himself from her. Snatching bodies, rat-infested hell holes, the old and helpless dying...the possibilities for misdeed were endless, and Gary would consider every one of them. Gilbert felt sorry for Dinah, having to finally realize the depths to which her husband was capable of sinking. He looked back at Gary, amazed that through eight years of marriage he had been able to prevent his wife from seeing the truth. Gilbert lowered his eyes and took a deep breath, preparing to speak.

"Gilbert," Gary continued, "your part in this will be to help come up with a convincing cover story for our first customer. We'll write a press release for the newspaper, then invite everyone we know to a formal wake after Wiggins gets him ready. Don't tell anyone we invite the whole truth, just tell them to come to the wake of someone important and pretend they knew him. Tell them we'll have a newspaper reporter attending, and we'll have to put on a bit of a show."

Dinah's jaw dropped. Unable to speak, she made unintelligible gurgling sounds. Gilbert interpreted. "Gary, you can't just snatch a body like that! What about relatives? What about the law?"

"There won't be any relatives and there won't be any law," Gary snapped. Composing himself, he explained in a gentler tone, "Most of the people who end up at Rose Terrace don't have any family. Or at least no family that cares. And the law will be no problem, leave that to me."

Gary chuckled briefly before continuing. "I'm not literally going to snatch someone. If I'm lucky, I'll find someone near death who can still sign a contract to be buried at our funeral home. Everything will be legal and above board. You two can start thinking of a convincing story we can tell people so he sounds like a respectable, worldly man who would choose only the best for his funeral."

Dinah and Gilbert stared in silence.

"Damn it, guys," Gary added bruskly, "we have to do something to get the business rolling. Can either of you come up with a better idea? Or any idea?" Gary paused, turning first to Gilbert, then to Dinah. Neither said a word. Gary continued, "I know the plan might sound strange, but damn it, we'll pull it off. Just wait, you'll see."

"As long as you keep it all legal," Dinah hesitantly agreed. "I guess it might be OK to stretch the truth a little writing his obit and getting our friends to attend the funeral...just as background to help the reporter write a good story."

"Gilbert?" Gary asked, "Do you have a better idea?"

"No." Gilbert said quietly, surprised at Dinah's acquiescence.

"Good," Gary said, pounding his fist into his palm, "then it's all settled."

CHAPTER 5

Gary stood looking up at the crumbling red brick building. Chiseled into the dingy cement lintel were the words 'Rose Terrace.' Above that was a bas-relief rose blossom with cracked, peeling, faded red paint set precariously in dried, crumbling mortar. Debris littered the sidewalk, rusted abandoned cars lined the street, and a few tattered, weary men sat on the curb drinking from paper cups. Shadowy figures of unkempt men and women, old and young, congregated in groups of three and four in doorways of boarded-up stores up and down the street.

Gary noticed that the little grocery store that used to be across the street had finally given up on the neighborhood and the destitute masses who haunted it. The store's large double doorwell provided a sleeping couple in worn battle fatigues a perilous refuge. The party store at the corner and the store-front chapel next to it were the only businesses still operating. Though their names changed regularly, they would always be there. Looking back at the front entrance of Rose Terrace, Gary felt its day was coming, and it too would be boarded up and left for the city to condemn. Jolted by the thought, he bounded up the stairs before it was too late.

The lobby was filled with cigarette smoke, tinged an eerie blue by the glow from a black and white television playing to a silent audience. Transfixed by the flickering motion, none bothered to adjust the old

TV's vertical hold.

The television gallery turned in unison to see who had entered. Two got up and retreated down the dark corridor beyond the lobby, disappearing behind frail, wooden doors. The rest stared coldly, silently. Gary looked them over, using the moment to plant his feet firmly and open his overcoat slightly to reveal his coat and tie beneath. Despite the constant haze of blue smoke that had been their environment for years, they all looked months, some even years, from death.

He approached the building manager, who sat behind a wooden counter held together by nearly a century's worth of caked varnish. The manager strained to read a newspaper, his only illumination a 40 watt bulb suspended above his head from the ceiling.

"Good afternoon. I'm Gary Colbert from the Department of Social Services," Gary said quickly, reaching for his wallet, flashing the employee ID card he had kept as a souvenir. "Just doing routine verification checks today. Shouldn't take long. I need to see your list of tenants." Inquiring in a friendlier tone, he added, "What happened to Chet, the old manager?"

The new manager looked up and shrugged. "Chet? Oh, he's 'round somewhere takin' a three-martini lunch...a three-day three-martini lunch...you know how that go. I'm just filling in while he's out." The manager chuckled loudly at some secret joke while he reached into a drawer for a sheaf of papers.

Gary tried to fathom the joke, wondering if the inmates had taken over the asylum, and what they had done with Chet. It didn't matter. The list mattered. One name on the list mattered. Gary took the papers and scanned. A smile came to his face. He stopped reading. "Ah, Ed Hammond, my old buddy," he chuckled, "glad to see he's still around. How's he doing? He had a bit of gangrene on his foot last time I was here."

"Ed? Oh, Ed's doing all right. He ain't got no more gang-green no more. He ain't got no left foot no more, neither." The manager laughed. "Yep, the hospital cut him up real good short time back. Ain't seen him three, four day now, though. He don't get around so good...you know, the foot and all."

"I better pop up and see him, then. I don't want Ed thinking I forgot about him."

"Suit yerself," the manager said, returning to his newspaper.

Gary took one last disappointed look at the crowd watching television. They had lost interest in him and had returned to watching the hypnotic flickering on the TV screen.

Gary turned and focused his eyes on the stairway behind the manager's desk. Peeling, dirty paint, carpet runner worn to the backing, gray light filtering through the unwashed window at the top of the stairs...it was all the same, only a little worse than the last time he had visited. The only thing new was a hand-lettered sign on the banister, which read: DONT LEEN ON BANSTER.

Up the stairs, around one turn, up another set of
stairs to the second floor, where the fire door had been
propped open with a crushed, empty soup can, either
for ventilation or the tenants' convenience, Gary
couldn't tell which. Up the next flight of stairs to the
third floor, where the fire door was propped open with
an overflowing trash can. Gary went through the door
and turned left toward apartment 3-G, which faced the
alley in back of Rose Terrace. The door was closed, but
Gary could hear voices. Putting his ear to the door, he
could hear the radio broadcasting a baseball game. He
paused before knocking on Ed's door. He smiled to
himself, remembering what one of Ed's neighbors once
said about him. It was a day much like today, the chilly
weather was the same, the wary, almost hostile stares
in the lobby were the same, Ed was listening to a ball
game on the radio. The neighbor exited the communal
bathroom at the end of the hall and commented as he
passed, "Don't believe half what that crazy bastard
tells you. He thinks he's a broadcaster on the radio the
way he goes around talking 'bout everybody."

Gary's smile broadened. His mission was going
well. Ed, the broadcaster, would know who at
Rose Terrace was about to die. With Ed's help, Gary
would be well on his way to securing a prince for
G&G's Funeral Home. Encouraged and emboldened
by a renewed sense of mission, Gary knocked loudly
on Ed's door. "Ed? Ed Hammond? It's me, Gary
Colbert from the Department of Social Services."

No answer. Gary knocked again, announcing

himself louder. Still no answer. Gary put his ear to the door, alert for sounds of rustling inside. No one rustled, but he did hear of a rhubarb developing at the ballpark over the second knock-down pitch that inning. Gary pulled out his state ID card and tried slipping the lock, knowing it was hopeless; he had helped Ed install a deadbolt after one of the other tenants broke into his apartment looking for loose change for a bottle of wine. Gary pounded on the door. "Ed? Ed? Are you in there?"

No answer. Both benches had emptied, and the umpire was ejecting the batter who charged the mound. Gary listened closer, then, remembering what the manager said about not seeing Ed for a few days, bounded down the stairs to the lobby.

"Get your pass key and come with me," he shouted at the manager. "Ed's in trouble."

"Pass key? I don't have no pass key. Least ways none I know of."

"Never mind. Follow me."

Gary rushed back up the stairs, grabbing the banister, using it to pivot around the first turn. The banister creaked and swayed. The manager followed with slow, painful steps, hugging the wall, staying clear of the rickety banister. He paused, looking up at Gary, "You go on, Sonny. I can't run like that anymore."

Gary scrambled up the stairs and down the hall, knocking once more on Ed's door. No answer. He looked down the hall for the manager to appear.

Hearing him creak up the stairs to the second floor, Gary leaned back and kicked the door just above the door knob. The brittle, dry wood splintered and gave an inch, the lock still holding, anchored to its clasp by the fragmented trim around the door. The manager arrived, a worried look on his face. He stumbled over, looked at the damage and the man from the state. Shrugging, he stood aside as Gary slammed into the door with his shoulder. The door flew open and a horrible stench wafted into the hallway.

Ed lay on the bed covered with ragged, dirty blankets from neck to toe, except for his left leg, which was a bloody, ulcerated stump of caked yellow sores running from the ankle, where the leg had been cut, to just below the knee. A heavy feverish sweat covered Ed's face. A dank glow illuminated the room from the drawn window shade, browned and mottled with age. Clothes and a mound of soiled toilet paper lay discarded on either side of the bed.

Gary turned his face away, took a deep breath and rushed into the room, tearing away the window shade, working furiously to open the locked window before he had to breathe again. Face turning red, he slowly expelled the air in his lungs, banging on the window sill, pushing on the window frame, worried it might break under the stress, shattering the glass, lacerating his arms, exposing his bloodstream to an environment so concentrated with germs he could almost see them crawling up the walls and across the floor, swarming in dense clouds throughout the room. At the last instant before giving up and fleeing the room for air, the window gave, opening fully with a screeching sound. Gary stuck his head out and breathed deeply through the blackened, tattered screen.

A foul ball flew up over the backstop at the stadium, bouncing off the roof of the broadcast booth, producing a loud crashing noise heard over the radio. "Wow! That was close! And the count goes to oh and two on Gibson, batting here in the ninth in this most bizarre game of the season."

The apartment manager stood gaping in the doorway, holding the sleeve of his sweater over his mouth and nose. "Look at this mess. Man oh man! Ol' Ed done die in his sleep."

Ed's dry, pale lips parted slightly, and his head turned toward the stream of cool, fresh air from the window. He made snorting, wheezing sounds and mumbled something. His eyelids opened, revealing moist, jaundiced eyes which starred blankly at the ceiling.

"Call an ambulance," Gary ordered.

"OK, I'll call. Tell Ed to hold on," the manager said breathlessly, taking another look at Ed to confirm he was still alive before turning and disappearing down the hallway.

Gary held his breath and looked briefly at Ed before rushing out of the room to the bathroom down the hall to fetch Ed a glass of water. In the bathroom, exposed pipes running between the ceiling joists dripped steadily onto a section of moldy plaster that had fallen to the floor. A tenant groaned and let loose a noisy stream of diarrhea from one of the toilet stalls. Not seeing any cups, Gary grabbed a roll of toilet paper from the unoccupied stall and saturated it under the tap in the lone sink, noting the ugly patterns formed by its worn porcelain, rust stains and the scum oozing from a blackened sliver of hand soap.

He rushed back to Ed's room, hyperventilating on the way, holding his breath before entering. Ed's head turned and his lips moved, but produced no sound. Gary held the saturated roll of toilet paper over Ed's mouth and let a trickle of water drip down. Ed took in the water and swallowed. He sighed and breathed deeply once and stared into Gary's face. The gratitude in Ed's stare made Gary feel petty and snobbish for holding his breath in Ed's presence. He forced himself to look at the exposed, milky-colored leg and took his first breath in Ed's room.

Gary said, "Ed. Ed, it's me. Gary Colbert. I came to see you, Ed."

Ed's arm moved under the blankets, struggling, maneuvering to get untangled from the layers and folds. Gary saw the maneuver and was horrified. He thought, 'No, Ed. Don't do that. Don't Ed. Please.' Ed's arm emerged from under the blankets and he reached out and clasped Gary's hand. 'Oh, Ed, I asked you not to do that.'

Looking over his shoulder, Gary reached into his coat pocket with his free hand and pulled out a funeral contract. "Ed, quick, sign this."

Gary handed Ed a cheap ballpoint and folded the contract, holding it in his palm, making a surface for Ed to write on. Ed mumbled feebly, "Gary. State. Forms." He put a shaky signature on the form, dropped the pen and smiled weakly up at Gary.

Gary looked over his shoulder again, pocketed the contract and smiled broadly, relieved. He gingerly picked up the pen and tossed it out of sight under the bed onto a pile of caked toilet paper. "Ed, old buddy," he said soothingly, "don't worry. I'm going to take good care of you. You just lay back and rest."

Gary walked down the hall to the bathroom and began washing his hands with the blackened, soft sliver of soap. He looked around for another bar of soap to wash off the first. He looked for a paper towel to dry his hands, but saw only a limp, threadbare cloth towel spread across the dusty, rust-encrusted radiator. He flicked his hands toward the towel, sprinkling it with flying droplets of water.

The stench in the bathroom was different than in Ed's room, but just as overpowering in its own way. Gary propped the door open a few inches, wedging the section of damp, fallen plaster between the door and door jam. The occupant in the stall called out, "Hey, buddy. I'm all out of toilet paper in here. Hand me the roll from the other stall."

Gary wiped his hands on his pants and made a pretense of looking in the other stall. "I'm sorry. Looks like some damn fool stole it."

"Oh sheeeit! What am I supposed to do now?"

Gary reached for the towel, picking it up between his thumb and forefinger as if it were a dead rat. He slung it over the stall door. "Here, might as well use this."

"Gee, thanks. I feel like a rich man wiping my ass with a real towel. 'Course, a real rich man wipes his ass with hundred dollar bills. I know that for a fact. I heard about it from Ed. You know Ed?"

"Sure I know Ed. You know Ed?" Gary answered, sticking his nose into the hallway to breathe.

"Everyone knows Ed," the man answered through the stall door. "Haven't seen him much lately, though. Not since I helped him take off that damn bandage they put on him."

"Ed took his bandage off? Why'd he do that?"

"Said he didn't need it. Said the doctors don't know nothin'. A cut like they cut him needs air to heal right. They was just tryin' to get him sick agin so they could get him back in the hospital and finish their experiments."

Gary pushed the door open wider with his elbow, holding it with his foot, breathing once more. "Experiments?" he asked.

The jingle of a belt buckle came from the stall. "Yeah, Ed said they did experiments on him after they gave him the annie-stetic. Said there's no way he's going back there."

Gary hurried to leave before the man finished buckling his trousers, afraid he might emerge from the stall with towel in hand. As an afterthought, he turned and said, "They did experiments on me too. They implanted radioactive isotopes in my cock to see if I could light up the nurses. I'm going back again tomorrow for some more."

"Wow! Really?"

Gary walked back to Ed's room, a wide, satisfied grin on his face. He entered, pleased to find the stench dissipated. He walked over to the window, carelessly stepping on Ed's clothing on the floor. He looked out the window into the alley below. A garbage dumpster overflowed onto a discarded sofa. Beyond, litter and weeds, the burnt shell of a house, empty lots, and boarded buildings were all he could see. He turned toward Ed with a chilling thought. "Ed, you got to help me make G&G's work or else I might end up down here."

Ed gasped and wheezed, and his hands twitched involuntarily, as if in response to the sound of an ambulance siren homing in on Rose Terrace. The ambulance screeched to a halt out front. Gary heard a rush of activity in the lobby, voices, and the clattering of a collapsible stretcher. He went into the hall to the top of the stairs to direct the paramedics to Ed's room. The stretcher banged against the wall in the lobby, and even from three floors up, Gary could hear the falling plaster. He heard the stretcher bang against the wooden banister and the manager cry out as the wood split and the banister fell, its slats and railing entangling the legs of the stretcher.

Gary shivered, sensing an unseen spirit force

throwing every obstacle in the way of the paramedics, preventing them from reaching Ed, delaying the medical attention that might keep him alive, aiding in the formation of G&G's Funeral Home. He shook off the feeling, not wanting to be indebted to such sinister spirits, trying to convince himself that it was the natural orchestration of fate that Ed was near death and deranged into removing his bandage, that Ed, and himself, and the pokey manager, and the clumsy paramedics, and Rose Terrace itself were all here together this day.

The paramedics freed the stretcher and rushed up the stairs. Gary pointed toward Ed's room and grabbed a corner of the stretcher, helping carry it into Ed's room, getting out of the way as the paramedics set it next to the bed and fixed its legs in place. He found himself strangely ambivalent to the disgusted look on the paramedics' faces as they surveyed the soiled toilet paper and filth of the room, and the discarded bandage, brown with dried blood and yellowed from the festering sores it once covered. Gary felt his body and mind seem to drift apart, making the scene being played out in front of him unreal. The paramedics gently lifted Ed onto the stretcher and wheeled him out the door into the hallway. Gary collected himself and rushed after, lest his chance for finding G&G's prince should escape.

"I'm Gary Colbert," he called after the paramedics as they maneuvered the stretcher down the stairs. "I'll follow you to the hospital."

"Suit yourself," said one of the paramedics, not looking up, concentrating on keeping the stretcher level.

'Suit yourself,' Gary repeated to himself. 'I will. Those will be my watchwords for the day. I'm going to suit myself and stick near Ed until he dies. Then I'm going to grab his body before anyone knows what's happening.'

Rushing through the lobby after the paramedics, Gary overheard the manager arguing with the tenants watching TV. "No. You know the rules. No one gets Ed's things until he's dead for sure."

Gary arrived at the hospital ten minutes after the ambulance. He checked in with the administrator on duty in the emergency room and waited. An hour-and-a-half later, she informed him that Ed was DOA, and he could present his paperwork to the morgue attendant before transporting the body for funeral services.

"Thank God he's still fresh," Mr. Wiggins said. "I can fix him up, no problem. They really messed up his innards with their autopsy, though. And I'll have to fashion another foot for him out of wire and plaster."

"Sorry about the foot, Mr. Wiggins," Gary apologized. "And I didn't know about the autopsy, the hospital just went ahead and did it on their own. Just do the best you can and we'll take care of the rest. If this works out, you'll have a full-time business again real soon."

Mr. Wiggins, wearing a tattered, but clean laboratory smock, scratched his head and ran his fingers through his long white hair. He poked twice at Ed's cheek to test for resiliency, then lifted Ed's limp arm, cradling Ed's elbow in his palm. "How do you want him posed?" he asked.

"I'll leave that to you, Mr. Wiggins. Whatever is easiest for you."

Mr. Wiggins nodded thoughtfully. "I'll come up with something. Why don't you go on home, Sonny? It's already late, and you look like you've been through the wringer."

Gary smiled, breathing a long sigh of relief. His mission was over and it had been a complete success. Looking around Mr. Wiggins' basement workshop, at the equipment, the stuffed trophies, the tools and materials, he relaxed, feeling confident in Mr. Wiggins' ability. He looked around the basement again, remembering the hard rain that started falling the first night he met Mr. Wiggins. He recalled Mr. Wiggins' hospitality and penchant for fine liquor and talk. After that first night, Gary always thought of Mr. Wiggins as Captain Kangaroo's demented brother—playful and lovable, yet prone to off-color remarks and bizarre behavior. Like the stuffed crow stacking contest he initiated that night. Or the proud and graphic presentation of his collection of squirrels and other small game mating in a variety of unnatural ways. "Thanks, Mr. Wiggins," Gary said, smiling. "It has been quite a day. Call me tomorrow and let me know how it's going."

"I'll do that. Now get out of here and let a man get to work."

Gary drove out of Mr. Wiggins' loose-stone driveway, down the unpaved country road, finally onto the highway headed to the city, and home, all the while knowing in his head that indeed the mission was over, but feeling in his heart that there was yet one more thing left to be done.

At home, he shook the feeling off as irrational, and took a long, hot shower, shampooing and scrubbing Ivory soap over his body, letting the lather soak into his skin. He dried himself with a clean towel and joined Dinah, who was sleeping peacefully.

CHAPTER 6

The next morning at breakfast, Gary relayed the news to Dinah. "We got our first customer. He's at Wiggins' now."

"So soon? Who is he?"

"An old welfare case of mine. I planned to ask him who in the neighborhood might be needing a free funeral soon. But it turns out he was on his deathbed himself, and he practically begged me to give the free service to him. He said he didn't want anybody performing experiments on him after he died."

"Experiments? What kind of experiments?" Dinah asked, stirring her coffee.

"Who knows? Someone must have told him they do experiments on indigents."

Dinah stopped stirring her coffee and looked at Gary, disapproval in her eyes. "Gary, you didn't tell that poor old man they would do experiments on him, did you?"

"No. Of course not," Gary answered indignantly. "But when he started begging me to take him, what could I do?"

Dinah continued stirring her coffee, slowly. "So, what's his name?"

Gary thought a moment. "Never mind his name. We'll have to come up with a new name, anyway. I want you to know him only by his new name."

"Well then, what does he look like?"

"I'm not sure what he's going to look like after

Wiggins gets through with him. He was in pretty bad shape. Poor old guy had his foot amputated a few weeks ago, and the whole damn leg became infected."

Dinah stopped stirring her coffee again and set the spoon down deliberately. "So he only has one foot?" she asked. "How are we going to explain that?"

"We won't have to. Wiggins will fix him up with another. He's a genius; he can do anything."

"Fix him up with another? You mean like Frankenstein?"

"No," Gary answered, irked at Dinah's incessant objections, "not like Frankenstein. Like by using a wire frame and plaster. It's just his foot. Don't worry, Wiggins will take care of it."

Later that morning, at the office of G&G's, Gary told Gilbert of his success, while Dinah sat with arms folded and said nothing. "...so sticking him in the trunk was the only problem," Gary finished, "the morgue attendants didn't like doing that. But from now on, Wiggins will pick them up in his Step-Van, and we're in business!"

"And it's all legal and above board?" Gilbert asked.

"It's all legal. Above board? I don't know exactly what that means. But from here on we'll have to play it real smart if this is going to work. We can't have a penniless bum be our first customer. We'll have to embellish his life story a bit."

Gary leaned forward and continued, "I've been

thinking about this. What I suggest is, because I think this guy looks kind of Mediterranean, and he has a worn and weathered face from living on the streets most of his life, we'll make him from Malta. A retired sea captain from Malta." Gary closed his eyes in concentration, thinking of the press release. "And he was old. He was instrumental in helping the Allied forces establish Malta as a base of air operations during World War Two." Gary opened his eyes and with a satisfied smile, added, "As a result of his actions, he was awarded the George Cross from Britain."

The phone rang. Gary jumped then quickly answered it. "Oh, hello Mr. Wiggins. ... Ready tonight? Great!" He nodded and gave an 'OK' signal to Gilbert and Dinah. "... It did? ... You did?" Gary paused, thinking. "OK, Mr. Wiggins, I know you did all you could. Don't worry about it, we'll take care of it here. ... Yes. ... OK. ... Thanks, Mr. Wiggins. ... Right, see you tonight."

Gilbert and Dinah looked at Gary anxiously. Gilbert asked, "What? What will we take care of?"

Gary stared into his coffee cup, deep in thought. Finally he said, "Remember how this guy was a World War Two hero? Well, he got his leg blown off by a German mortar. Wiggins said it was so badly decayed it fell off halfway through the process. He stuck a peg leg on him."

Dinah held her face in her hands. Gilbert lowered his shoulders and stared wide-eyed at Gary. "A peg leg?" he asked. "Who's going to believe that? What are we going to do, put him in a striped shirt and give him an eyepatch and say he was a famous pirate? Captain Kidd, G&G's first customer."

"Never mind the peg leg," Gary said irritably, "it happens all the time. It doesn't make any difference. I wish you'd stop complaining; I had a hard time getting this guy, and now it's time for you to start helping. Both of you," he said, turning to Dinah. "We're going to write a press release and send it out by the end of the day. Wiggins will deliver him tonight. We have lots to do, and there's no turning back, so let's get started."

They named their hero Anton Olivier. Dinah found a picture of a group of Maltese longshoremen helping move war materiel and picked one of the men to be Anton. The press release was set on letterhead bearing a Maltese Cross. Gilbert signed it Borg Giorgio Buttigieg, Director of the Maltese Consulate. It looked good.

Late that night, when Mr. Wiggins delivered Anton, Gary and Gilbert carried him into the funeral home. Anton had been molded to a sitting position, the foot of his peg leg extending beyond his tightly rolled pant leg. He fit perfectly into a wicker rocker inherited from Aunt Winifred. They set an old globe next to Anton's rocker. An aged framed seafaring print hung on the wall behind him.

The newspaper reporter was called the next day, and Gary, Gilbert and Dinah's closest friends and relatives were summoned to play their parts. Gilbert disguised himself and played the part of Borg Giorgio Buttigieg, the Maltese consul general. He affected a thick accent to frustrate the reporter and keep him from asking too many questions.

The day after Anton's funeral, this story ran in the paper:

NEW-STYLE FUNERAL HOME OPENS
1st Interee is Maltese War Hero
Daily Daily Special Feature — G&G's Funeral Home, located north of the Miracle Mile Shopping Center, interred Anton Olivier last night by preserving his body and setting it for display on the Maltese war hero's favorite rocking chair.

G&G's director, Gary Colbert, says he expects the novel form of interment to catch on quickly. "It makes perfect sense in today's world. It's cheaper than the old funerals and doesn't take up any valuable land resources."

Interees at G&G's are on permanent display and can be posed in an unlimited number of ways. A few of the deceased favorite possessions can be displayed nearby.

According to Colbert, in addition to the land and cost savings, the new burial concept allows friends and relatives to come pay respects any time they wish, especially important for out-of-towners.

Reaction to the novel burial concept was mostly positive among those in attendance at last night's service for Mr. Olivier. Mr. Borg Giorgio Buttigieg, Maltese consul general and close friend of Mr. Olivier, said, "It very (good). Anton very (smart) man."

Other funeral homes in the area voiced surprise and outrage at the new concept. John Devine, director of Devine Funeral Home said, "It's a dark day for the funeral home industry. At Devine, such treatment would be unheard of."

Despite objections from other funeral home operators, Colbert plans to expand his existing facilities and possibly open another home on the west side by the end of the year. Colbert said, "We've had a number of inquiries and a favorable response from the community. We expected the other funeral homes in the area to object, because we're laying to rest the needless expense and waste associated with funerals. G&G's is ushering in a new day."

The morning after Anton's funeral, the coffee was served with real cream and fresh croissants in the kitchen of G&G's Funeral Home. Gilbert lifted his cup to Gary and Dinah, "This is to our successful first funeral at G&G's."

"And a good write-up in the paper," Gary added. "You made a convincing Maltese consul general, Gilbert. And you did a great job getting the publicity together, Dinah."

"Thanks," Dinah said. "Everything went smoothly. And no one even noticed that Anton's peg leg was really an old leg from a table Mr. Wiggins found in his barn. I thought the claw-and-ball foot would be a sure giveaway. But, you know, it bugs me that the reporter went out and talked to Devine. 'It's a dark day for the funeral home industry.' We don't need that."

"Don't worry about that," Gilbert said. "I think it's good the story mentioned an objection. It makes the reporting sound objective. I'm sure there are some people out there who won't flip and do cartwheels over what we're doing. We'll have to capture their hearts and minds gradually. And when we get going, Devine and his ilk are going to breathe their last."

CHAPTER 7

In the days following Anton's funeral, Gary, Gilbert and Dinah busied themselves with plans and preparations.

"Better call Wiggins and tell him to get a patent on his preservation process," Gilbert said hopefully. "We got to sew up the market before everyone jumps on the bandwagon. And I've been thinking, Gary, you know how Devine has a room filled with casket choices? We could have a room filled with manikins for pose choices."

"Good idea," Gary responded. "Now you're talking. All the poses will cost the same, not like those damn coffins at Devine's."

So they bought the entire allotment of manikins from a clothing retail outlet that had closed. Thirty-two in all: some women, some men, even a few children. They debated about displaying the child manikins, then decided to go ahead, based on the abbreviated child's casket Devine had in his showroom.

Dinah scoured the local thrift shops for clothing, and dressed and posed the manikins in one of the bedrooms, upstairs. Women dressed in evening gowns sipping champagne, men in business suits, a woman sitting knitting, a sportsman casting a fly rod, kids chasing butterflies suspended from the ceiling, or playing with a frisky pup. As curious prospects trickled in, Gilbert took them upstairs and explained that the choice of poses was unlimited and the manikins on display were only there to excite the imagination and offer ideas.

One of the wire services picked up the story from the *Daily Daily* and ran it nationwide. Dinah took calls from across the country requesting more information on G&G's. Most of the callers focused their questions on price, procedure, and the meaning of perpetual display.

One call went like this:

Caller: This is Jeremy Westlaw, and I'm doing a story on the funeral home business for *Actual Fact Magazine*. I heard about your new way of burying people and I'd like to ask a few questions about it. First, is it true you don't bury them, you put them on display?

Dinah: Yes, that's right. All those interred at G&G's Funeral Home are carefully preserved by a special process, then set in a pose of their choice or one chosen by the next of kin. Following the service, friends and family of G&G interees are free to visit and pay respects at any time.

Caller: Is this form of burial sanctioned by the leaders of any of the major religions.

Dinah: Strictly speaking, we feel the religious leaders are more concerned with sanctioning how their respective flocks live

than with how they choose to be buried, be it conventional burial, cremation, being put in orbit by a spaceship,
or whatever.

Caller: How do people go about making
arrangements with you? Do they come
in beforehand, or do the relatives make
the decisions after.

Dinah: Either way. Same as any funeral home.

Caller: Doesn't the idea of putting the dead on
display seem, well, kind of strange?
I'm not sure I'd like to be put on display.

Dinah: (with a slight laugh) Well, I'm sure the
first cavemen who witnessed a burial
must have thought it was kind of
strange. Once people think about it,
though, they'll like the idea. After all, at
one time only the wealthiest pharaohs
could afford this kind of attention and
perpetual honor. And it's cheaper than
any conventional burial.

Caller: Would you like to be buried this way?

Dinah: I will be. In a chiffon dress, with my
grandmother's pearl necklace, and a
copy of Shakespeare's *Romeo and Juliet*
in my lap.

Caller: Next time I'm in town, can I pay G&G's
a visit, just to look around, maybe take
some pictures.

Dinah: All visitors are most welcome.
Caller: Just one more thing: Aren't you afraid
          of ghosts working in a place like that?
Dinah: (slight laugh) Oh, I'm sure ghosts have
          far more important things to do. Don't
          you worry at all, drop in any time.

The first paying customer was Amos T. Wentloff. Amos was born and raised during the Great Depression. Times were tough during his childhood and his parents made do with very little. His first job, outside of helping his father peddle apples, was with the U.S. Army, fighting in Korea.

Upon his return stateside, Amos quit the army and became an advertising salesman. He soon found himself successfully selling advertising on the burgeoning phenomenon of television. Driven by memories of his deprived childhood, he vowed never to be without again. He was married, with two children.

Amos lay in Room 337, Bed B, at Wayne Memorial Hospital, dying of liver and ulcer problems. His wife called G&G's asking for the director. Dinah put her through to Gary.

"Hello, this is Gary Colbert, director of G&G's Funeral Home. May I help you?"

"Yes, it's my husband. He read about you in the paper and wanted me to arrange something for him. It could be any day now. He wanted to make sure everything was taken care of. First, though, he wants to know if you really mean perpetual display? Does that mean forever, or just all the time?"

Gary scratched his head. "Our perpetual display means your husband will be treated better than the Egyptian pharaohs till the end of time. You can have him posed any way you choose. If you like, you can inter him with a few personal mementos, a favorite painting, his best loved book, whatever best exemplifies his personality while he favored this earth. Would you like to pay us a visit and get some ideas for your husband?"

She did, and she did. Her husband was impressed with what he heard. For him it would be a taste of immortality, the crowning glory on a life spent running from anonymity and poverty.

Mr. Wentloff went on display just in time for the arrival of a film crew from one of the networks. He was on the evening news the following day, images of his preserved remains being beamed toward the outer reaches of the universe in an immortality he had never even considered. The news story, Gary, Gilbert and Dinah agreed, was frank and objective, with just enough hype to make it good advertising.

The next day, a small group came to G&G's and formed a picket line out front. Their placards read, 'Stop the Abomination,' and 'Leave Town.'

Gary and Dinah were already busy in the office sipping coffee when the protesters arrived. Gilbert saw them as he drove into the parking lot.

"Hey Gary," he asked, entering the office, "who are those people out there?"

"What people?"

"There are people with signs saying they don't like us."

Gary and Dinah rushed to the front window and saw the group marching like a funeral procession, carrying their pickets up and down in a circle on the sidewalk in front of G&G's. "We don't need this," Gary said, "not when we're starting to get paying customers. Hey Gilbert!" he yelled, "go out and talk to them."

"I'm not going to talk to them," Gilbert yelled back from the office. "You talk to them."

"I'm not going to talk to them," Gary yelled. "Dinah, you talk to them."

"Hey, wait a minute, let's think this thing through," Dinah advised. "Maybe they'll go away. Let's wait and see. Anyway, I have to go make another pot of coffee."

While Dinah made coffee in the kitchen, and Gilbert hid in the office, Gary kept a lookout at the window. The protesters kept marching silently. Occasionally a few would stop to rest and chat. Gary grew tired maintaining the vigil. He paced distractedly around the room, then stopped in front of Anton, sitting by the far wall, opposite the window. Gary remembered the book he had brought from his basement, and walked to the office to get it. "Still hiding, Gilbert?" he asked. "Come on, get some balls."

"I got balls," Gilbert said, "and I want to keep

them."

"Quit worrying," Gary said, picking up the copy of *The Maltese Falcon*. "Here, go put this on the table next to Anton. It'll make a good prop. I'm going to join Dinah for a cup of fresh coffee."

Gilbert took the book and ventured into the living room, peaking out the window at the protesters. He placed the book on the table beside Anton, and, on a whim, opened it to the title page and autographed it:

To my good friend Anton Olivier, for all your help in the writing of this book.
  Best regards,
  Dashiell Hammett

The doorbell rang. "They're here," Gilbert shouted. He ran to the kitchen. "What'll we do?" he asked, dancing around nervously. "They're here! They're here! They're coming to get us!"

"Get hold of yourself, Gilbert," Gary said. "What can they do? Lynch us?"

"Yeah, Gilbert, take it easy," Dinah said. "We're not the Frankensteins. Are we, Gary?"

Gary looked at his wife and frowned. Gilbert ran to the back door and scanned out the window. The doorbell rang again.

"It's all clear back here," Gilbert said. "You guys answer the door, and I'll do an end run. We'll meet tonight at my place."

"No one's going to do an end run," Gary said.

"Sheesh, Gilbert, would you calm down? Dinah and I will answer the door. You wait here and get hold of yourself. Sheesh!"

Gary and Dinah left Gilbert standing by the back door while they went to answer the front. Gary took a deep breath and touched Dinah's hand. "I'm sure it will be OK," he whispered.

Gary opened the door. A balding, happy-faced man carrying a briefcase and a camera said, "Hi. I'm Jeremy Westlaw, from *Actual Fact Magazine*. I called and talked with Dinah. It looks like a good story brewing here. Mind if I come in?"

Gary looked past Mr. Westlaw to the protesters. A couple of them had stopped marching and were looking up the front walk. Gary said, "Come right in, Mr. Westlaw."

"Jeremy, please."

"Gary. Gary Colbert. Good to meet you. And this is Dinah."

Dinah shook Mr. Westlaw's hand. "Oh, yes, Mr. Westlaw. I remember. I didn't realize you'd be visiting so soon."

Mr. Westlaw looked past Dinah, into the living room. Carpet, bare walls and Anton's elbow resting on the arm of the wicker rocker were all that was visible. "Yes, well," he said, "I thought it best to beat my competition."

Mr. Westlaw again looked past Dinah, at Gilbert approaching from the kitchen. Gary introduced, "And this is Gilbert Jackson.

"Gilbert, meet Jeremy Westlaw from *Actual Fact Magazine*."

Gilbert shook Mr. Westlaw's hand and nodded, saying nothing.

Gary and Dinah took Mr. Westlaw on a tour of the facilities. While they were upstairs with the manikins, Gilbert snuck over to Anton and opened the book to the page he had autographed.

After the tour, Dinah ushered Mr. Westlaw into the kitchen for a cup of coffee. "Well, this is really some place you got here," Mr. Westlaw said. "Gary, Dinah, Gilbert...this is really some place you got here. I'd like to meet the man who does the excellent preservation work on your, uh, clients."

Gilbert answered, "I'm afraid he's a little shy. His patent for the process is still pending and he's been kind of testy lately. I'll be able to explain anything you need to know."

Gary tried to change the subject, "Jeremy, did you talk with the group outside? We're trying to think of what we can do for them."

"Yes, I talked with them briefly. If you get me an interview with your preservation man, I'll let you in on a few tidbits I learned."

Gary was worried. Mr. Wiggins wasn't trained in PR. He might blow it. "Let me have a word with Gilbert and maybe we can work something out." He motioned Gilbert into the hall.

"I don't want this guy talking to Wiggins," Gilbert said. "The public doesn't need to know about his process."

"Yeah, but I'd sure like to know what those protesters are saying. It'd help to have some idea what
we're in for when we go out to talk to them. Maybe
he'll settle for a telephone interview."

"Whatever we do, we don't want that camera in
Wiggins' workshop."

"Right."

Mr. Westlaw was disappointed with the offer, but
didn't press the matter. "All right," he agreed, "a
private telephone interview it is."

Gary and Gilbert ushered Mr. Westlaw into the
office and dialed Mr. Wiggins at his home. Before
leaving, Gilbert offered Mr. Westlaw some of the
pamphlets G&G's had printed. While his hands were
fumbling in the desk drawer for the pamphlets, Gilbert
turned on a small recorder he carried to record ideas
for G&G's on the way to work in his car. He closed and
locked the drawer, hoping the recorder would pick up
at least one side of the conversation. "Oh, I'm so sorry
Jeremy," he apologized. "There don't seem to be any
more pamphlets. I'll forward one to you as soon as we
get more."

A few minutes later, Mr. Westlaw emerged from
the office. "I see what you mean about him being testy.
I'm afraid I didn't get much."

"Well, like Gilbert mentioned, there's a patent
pending and all," a relieved Gary said.

"Still, I'd sure like to know how he does it. The
skin stays so elastic. It's like no other taxidermy I've

ever seen."

"Mr. Westlaw," Gilbert said irritably, "I think it would be best if you concentrated more on the opportunity we're providing for an alternative to expensive, wasteful funerals. The main point of your story should be that those funerals aren't the only way to go anymore. If Mr. Wiggins doesn't want to talk about his process, we're just going to have to respect that. Now, what did you learn from the people outside?"

Mr. Westlaw flinched as if hating to be told what the main point of his story should be. However, like any journalist, he always allowed those he interviewed to blow up when they've had enough. There was a good story here and it was important to stay on good terms with the people who would provide it. "That's an interesting crowd you got out front," Mr. Westlaw finally said. "I told them I was writing a story on you and they practically mobbed me for information. They're objecting mostly on religious grounds. Seems one of the other funeral homes in the area has been spreading rumors about you, about how you're tied in with the devil and how you use the bodies for cabalistic rituals late at night."

Gary, Gilbert and Dinah stood, mouths gaping, looking at each other with the same thought, "Devine."

Gary spoke, "We'll have to put an end to that. Cabalistic rituals? That's the furthest thing from our minds. Who was this other funeral home?"

"I'd rather not say till I've had a chance to talk

with them myself, although I doubt I'll get anything from them. That's slanderous talk. Believe me, I know."

"Whoever they are, they probably know more about devils than we do," Gary spluttered. "Well, I guess I'll have to go talk to these people and set them straight before this snowballs. Want to come, Mr. Westlaw?"

Outside, the mid-morning sun was hot and the marchers were tired and wet with sweat. Gary took a step off the porch, paused and called loudly for Dinah to bring pitchers of ice water and lots of cups. Walking down the front walk, with Mr. Westlaw following, he couldn't make out that anyone was in charge of the protest, and the marchers didn't seem aware he was director of the business they were picketing. Gary let a burly ox-man pass and addressed an elderly woman. "Hi. What's all the commotion?"

"We think this place is an abomination to all decency. What they do to people, my! It's an outrage. Haven't you been watching the news?"

"I think I saw a story or two."

Two protesters stood off to the side, resting. Gary asked for a placard and took a position marching behind the elderly woman. Mr. Westlaw stood back, admiring Gary's tactics.

"If there's anything untoward going on here, I want to know about it. What have you heard?" Gary asked the elderly woman.

"Well, first they perform some type of black mass

over the people. Then they do all manner of unspeakable things to the body. After that, they put them on display and worship them as gods. It's pure blasphemy. Our dead were meant to be treated with respect and rejoined to the blessed earth. We're going to put an end to what's happening here."

Dinah came out with the ice water and paper cups. Gary started pouring and handing them out, and soon the entire procession stopped marching and gathered around him. "I read the stories in the papers," he said, "but I didn't see anything about any problems here. Where did you find out about this place?"

The ox-man said, "They're doing stuff in there, and we don't like it."

Someone else said, "We have to protect our children."

Another said, "First they do this stuff with the dead, then they start on the living. Where will it end?"

Gary repeated, "Yeah, but where did you hear about them doing this stuff?"

Mr. Westlaw took out his camera and snapped a picture of the elderly woman as she answered, "We just heard it around, that's all."

Gary decided to lay his cards on the table. He knew he had to make it good. "There's nothing strange going on here," he began, speaking clearly and convincingly. "It's just a normal funeral home with normal people. I'm Gary Colbert, director of G&G's Funeral Home. I don't know what sort of person would spread those rumors about my funeral home,

Gary Freeman

but I'm glad for this opportunity to put your minds at rest...at ease. There's nothing associated with the black arts going on here, I can assure you. Our only wish is to offer good people, such as yourselves, an alternative to the needless high cost of dying. Why, you practically have to go into debt. Am I right?" A few people nodded. Gary continued, "The G&G method, which is highly spiritual in every sense of the term, not only ends the immoral practice of shamelessly putting a huge financial burden on people when they're most susceptible to a sales pitch from a slick-talking operator, it also gives people the chance to celebrate their God-given time on Earth through our perpetual display. Please don't be misled by rumors started by a few slick funeral home operators in the area. Believe me, they don't have your best interests at heart. It's only in their interest to close down an upright home such as ours. I'll gladly offer all of you a tour of our facilities so you can judge for yourselves. Please, follow me."

He led them up the walk to the front door, and motioned them inside. "To your right is our Main Viewing Room. As you can see, we have on display the honorable Anton Olivier, World War Two hero and former ship's captain. And next to him is Amos T. Wentloff, television pioneer and successful business-man. Both are situated in natural poses among familiar possessions. Don't they look good?"

A few people nodded, peering nervously from over the shoulders of those in front. The group tread lightly further into the Main Viewing Room. One woman said, "They look so healthy and vibrant, like you expect them to get up and start talking. Do you do any restorative surgery on them?"

"As a rule, we don't have to," Gary answered. "The G&G process alone takes ten years off."

The ox-man, the elderly woman, and a few others were warily looking around the room, as if expecting to find the pentagrams and bloodstains that would confirm the charges of demonic practices. But everything looked normal, like anybody's living room.

A man asked, "What if the family wants a regular service?"

"This is just like any other funeral home. Services are performed according to any format the family desires," Gary answered. "Mr. Olivier's family, for instance, plans to have a second service later in the year for family members overseas who couldn't make the first one. We at G&G's can afford to be very obliging. Since we don't have to clear the room to make way for the next interee, there's absolutely no time limit. Why, I was at a funeral home down the street, I forget the name of the place, and I hate to mention this, but it's so common at these other homes, but I overheard a couple of the directors saying at the end of the service, 'Let's turn off the air conditioner so nobody hangs around too long. We got to get that other stiff set up.' There's none of that at G&G's. You take your time and do it your way."

A voice from the back asked, "I'd like to be buried

playing the piano. Is that possible?"

"We have a motto at G&G's: If It's Not Possible, We'll Make It Possible."

Mr. Westlaw, standing behind the crowd, smiled broadly and held his hands high in the air, making clapping motions. He looked at Gary and silently mouthed, "Bravo!"

Gilbert and Dinah had been listening from the hallway. Gilbert prompted Dinah to join Gary by gently pushing her into the Main Viewing Room. She stumbled slightly and turned to give Gilbert a furious look. Sensing the group's attention had turned to her, she smiled, looking homespun and demure.

Gary introduced, "This is my lovely wife and assistant director at G&G's, Dinah."

Dinah blushed. "We're so glad to have you here."

The ox-man said, "Everything looks OK here." He asked the elderly woman, "Mumsy, why did that man tell us those things about this place?"

"I don't know. Maybe it's like Mr. Colbert said, they don't want the competition." To Gary she said, "I don't know what to say. Everything looks so nice here. I'm not sure it's what I would want, but I guess it's OK for some people. I'm so sorry about everything. But, well, you can understand our concern when we started hearing stories."

"It's good to get any misunderstandings cleared up," Gary said. "We're very grateful that you good citizens are keeping an eye on the neighborhood. As for whoever misled you, well, I can only say thank goodness they haven't pulled the wool over your eyes."

Dinah passed out pamphlets as the people left. As they disbanded outside, she called out cheerfully, "Come back anytime and see us. We're always happy to receive visitors."

When the last protester left, Gary closed the door and leaned on it with a sigh of relief. "I'm going to have a big glass of cold lemonade, and gin. That was tight."

Mr. Westlaw shook Gary's hand. "Mr. Colbert, that was magnificent. I couldn't have done better myself. I think you're going to be a big success. I'm going to run out and try to catch some of those people for some concluding remarks. See 'ya later."

Gary handed him a pamphlet, saying, "Here. I guess Dinah had some stashed away. Good-bye."

Gilbert entered. "Gary, that was the greatest job I've ever seen. You were great! That recording of Westlaw talking with Wiggins came out great too. Want to hear it?"

"In a second," Gary answered, wiping his brow, walking to the kitchen. With lemonade and gin in hand, Gary joined Gilbert in the office. He wished he had picked some mint for his drink as he leaned back in his chair relishing Mr. Westlaw's frustration.

"Hello. This is Jeremy Westlaw. I'm writing a story about the funeral home industry and I've been talking to Gary Colbert at G&G's Funeral Home. Hello? Hello?"

CHAPTER 8

More customers came. Jim Willis, lifelong factory rat, chose to be interred in the bathtub, upstairs. He liked to sing in the tub; he was famous for it throughout every neighborhood he ever lived.

Jim sat amongst tastefully placed plastic soap bubbles floating on a realistic plastic food wrap surface, with arms outstretched expansively, hitting a high note. Wiggins rose to the challenge of making permanent bubbles, finding the perfect solution in a decoupage kit for making filmy plastic flowers. He had great fun calculating where the bubbles were needed most. A smooth-worn bar of soap in Jim's hand was a finishing touch supplied by Gilbert.

G&G's received a bonus from the owner of a tool and die shop who had worked his way up from apprentice in dungarees and oily blue workshirt to executive in three-piece suit. Lester B. Atterly made the arrangements himself. He wanted his large desk moved into G&G's own office. There, Lester could sit like an executive portrait. The bonus compensated for rearranging the office furniture to make room.

Shortly after Lester, came G&G's first female customer, Jain C'mor. Jain had operated a metaphysical bookshop with her lifelong friend and confidant, Madam Kitty. Together they gave readings and plotted astrological charts in the back room of the bookshop. It was Madam Kitty who brought Jain to G&G's for interment, hoping to keep in touch with Jain's clientele by having them keep in touch with their beloved Jain.

Jain sat opposite Anton, by the front window in the Main Viewing Room. She was bedecked in gaudy jewelry, a stylish scarf, which bundled her flame-orange hair, and a flowing satin robe with sequins, quarter moons and ankhs, and luckily, no pentagrams.

At Jain's service, Dinah commented to Madam Kitty that Jain and Anton made an interesting pair. Madam Kitty replied, "I should think they will soon be engaging in metaphysical discussions of the highest order."

Jain's service attracted a large gathering of her former clients. They were an unusual lot, and they took a keen interest in G&G's and the other interees. One had heard about the man in the bathtub and asked to see. Dinah escorted her upstairs, and soon the entire assembly was headed upstairs, then into the office to see the executive at work. Several inquired about making arrangements in advance for themselves. Gary and Gilbert scheduled several appointments.

Jain's service attracted more media attention. Madam Kitty had called the TV stations and the newspapers. One of the stations sent a film crew. When air time came, twenty seconds worth of free advertising for Kitty and G&G's was shown. The local papers also ran stories. With pictures.

Business skyrocketed. Over the next several months, room became scarce at G&G's. The home took on a party atmosphere, with ladies in fancy gowns, men in sports clothes swinging nine irons, even an old man sitting at the wheel of his '36 Cord in the remodeled garage.

And of course, there was Anton sitting in his favorite rocker taking in all the excitement. As senior interee at G&G's, he held an importance and prestige that had escaped him in life.

Gary, Gilbert and Dinah found they couldn't keep up with the maintenance and housework the new business brought. "If we could at least hire some high school kids part-time to help keep things clean," Dinah urged.

Gary was reluctant. "Do you think high school kids could handle this? I mean, sometimes we have to lift these people up to dust and vacuum underneath. They might have nightmares. And what about their parents? We don't need any more protests."

"Well we do need more help, Gary. I just can't keep up with everything."

"She's right," Gilbert said, "we will have to take on some help. Especially if we're going to open another outlet across town. What about the twins? They're getting to be 19...20? They'd probably be happy to start learning a profession. What do you say I talk to Ken about it?"

"It might be a good idea to keep this in the family," Gary agreed. "How is your brother, anyway? I haven't seen him since Anton's funeral."

CHAPTER 9

That evening at home, Gilbert ate a light dinner of sliced Spam and cabbage fillet, cooked to steamy perfection after 60 seconds in the microwave. While it cooked, Gilbert noted with amusement how the dirty dishes stacked in his sink were beginning to look like the skyline of New York City.

After eating, the single plate he used for that night's dinner became a revolving restaurant balanced atop the United Nations Building. Torrential acid rain beat through the city streets and battered the glass and steel structures of his little city, cleansing them bit by bit of the layers of pollution and grime. Satisfied that New York would survive for another day, Gilbert turned off the faucet and replaced the dish sprayer in its cradle.

"Ken, Ken, Ken," he sighed, leaving the kitchen, walking the few short paces to his living room, oblivious to the stacks of old movie posters mounted on cardboard leaning against the walls. "Ken, Ken, Ken," he repeated, plopping himself in a chair, staring at a poster for a sci-fi flick that had bombed at his old theater, seeming to notice it for the first time. *The Beast with Two Heads.* "So Ken, we're going to get Rick and Ron working at G&G's. Well, well, well."

Gilbert reached over and picked up the phone on the table beside him. He dialed Ken, and while the phone rang, recalled Gary and Dinah's wedding. At the reception, he had taken Rick and Ron aside, handing them a mislabeled copy of "They're Coming to Take Me Away," instructing them to sneak it into the DJ's stack of CDs. Rick and Ron had pulled it off perfectly. The two twelve-year-olds even played a good job acting as surprised as everyone else when the DJ played the record.

To this day, neither Gary nor Dinah, nor Ken for that matter, had been able to pin the prank on anyone. Gilbert hoped the twins had forgotten the incident, worried they might inadvertently let the details slip in front of Gary or Dinah. It was a joke Dinah hadn't appreciated.

Ken answered the phone. "Hello."

"Ken? Gilbert. How is everything?"

"How is everything? You tell me. How's business?"

"Going great. Once we got our first customer, things have been hopping. We're running out of room, in fact. You should see the people we got."

"I hear there's quite a few crazies."

"No, I wouldn't say that. Not officially. They're just looking for an alternative, taking advantage of our new system."

"So, that's the official word, huh? Well between you and me, Gilbert, I say there's one born every minute, right?"

"And for every one that's born, there's gunna be one that dies."

"Shrewd, Gilbert. Very shrewd."

"Yes, thank you, Ken. But the reason I'm calling is

that things are going so well at G&G's, we're going to need some help. Maintenance, keeping things clean, that sort of thing. Do you think the twins would want the job?"

Gilbert held the silent phone to his ear, trying to ascertain Ken's thoughts by the length and depth of the pause. "Ken? You there?" he asked. Not hearing any response, he continued, worried Ken might hang up abruptly. "The reason we want them is mainly because they're young, and we can more easily mold them into what we're going to really need in the future: administrative help, sales, energy, ideas. They could make a career out of it."

The phone remained silent. Gilbert imagined Ken standing there in his living room on perpetual display with a telephone to his ear. "Ken? Are you still there?"

"I'm still here, Gilbert. And I got to tell you, little brother, you got yourself a deal! This is just what those two need. Discipline, hard work and some responsibilities. I tell you, Jan and I were really getting worried about those two. Running with the drinking crowd, sleeping in till noon. This is really a godsend, Gilbert.

"Oh, and Gilbert, I'd like you to make them fill out job applications and be interviewed for the position...just to make it a better learning experience for them."

"Can do, Ken. I'll send them applications. Get them cleaned up and ready for an interview. And, uh, Ken, do me a favor and read them the riot act before they come here. This business is my bread and butter.

Do you know what I mean?"

"I understand. Don't worry, if they screw up I'll let them know they'll answer to me."

With that assurance, Gilbert slept soundly that night.

Rick and Ron handed their applications to Dinah, in the kitchen at G&G's. Dinah looked over the applications quickly; the illegible handwriting and dirty smudges didn't invite her interest. "I'll pass these in to Gary and Gilbert. Have a seat. I'll be right back."

Dinah knocked once on the office door and entered. "The twins are here. Here are their applications," she said, handing one to Gary and the other to Gilbert. "Gilbert," she asked, "are they literate? I can't make out anything from their handwriting."

"The high school graduated them," Gilbert answered.

"I think this is Rick's," Gary said, looking over the application Dinah had handed him. "I can make out an 'R' at the beginning of his name."

"Wait," Gilbert said, looking over the other application, "This one has an 'R' too. That could be either Rick or Ron."

"No, wait," Gary said, "I think this is a 'k' at the end of his name. Dinah, is this a 'k'?"

Dinah stood in the doorway and shook her head. "They're your blood relatives, guys. You figure it out. I just hope they can handle a broom and dustpan."

Dinah turned around and closed the office door,

leaving Gary and Gilbert turning the applications this way and that, holding them side-by-side, trying to decipher whose was whose. Rejoining Rick and Ron in the kitchen, Dinah offered, "Let me get you boys some orange juice. Gary and Gilbert are working on an enigma at the moment. They'll be right with you."

"An enigma?" Ron asked, horrified. "Here? On themselves or a customer? I thought you had some old man who did that kind of stuff for you."

Dinah handed the boys their orange juice. "No, Ron," she sighed, "not that kind of enigma."

Dinah leaned against the counter. She closed her eyes and took a deep breath while the boys gulped their juice. "So," she said, waiting for the boys to finish swallowing, "you guys are all through with school?"

"Yeah. We graduated last year," Rick said.

"Yeah. *School's out for-ever*," Ron sang, beating a drum measure on Rick's arm.

"Do you plan to go to college?"

"What for?" Rick answered, slapping Ron back, "we don't need the hassle."

"Yeah. We were going to fix up Dad's old van and drive cross-country. But if you got a job, I guess we'll do that instead."

"You know," Dinah said, "if you're hired, you'll have to wear dark pants, a white shirt and a tie."

"A tie? What for? I thought we were just going to clean up. What do we need a tie for?"

"For presentation," Dinah answered sternly. "A lot of people come here for very solemn services and they don't want to see a couple of grease monkeys hanging around. You're going to do your work and treat everybody with the utmost respect. This is a funeral parlor. Do you understand?"

Rick and Ron looked at each other and slouched in their chairs. "We know. Dad told us all about it," Rick said.

"Yeah. He lectured us about not causing any trouble," Ron added.

"Did you listen to him?"

"Yes ma'am."

"Yes ma'am."

Gilbert stuck his head in the kitchen. "Rick. Ron. Why don't you come into the office for a minute."

Gary sat on the edge of his desk, holding both applications. Gilbert took a seat at his desk, motioning for Rick and Ron to sit at the two chairs in front of Lester's desk. The twins approached hesitantly, looking at Lester sitting behind his desk returning their stares. They pulled the chairs away from Lester and sat down.

"This is Lester," Gilbert began. "He doesn't say much, but we've come to appreciate his presence nonetheless."

Gary glanced over at Lester, seeking inspiration. "We've been looking over your applications," Gary said. "I see you both worked at the same McDonald's last year. Is that correct?"

"Yeah," Rick said, "they're always desperate for help."

"What did you do there?"

"We mostly kept the floor clean and the tables clean."

"One night they had me doing the fries when the regular fry guy didn't come," Ron said proudly.

Gilbert asked, "What did you learn from working at McDonald's?"

"To show up for work on time and to call if you can't make it."

"And to keep everything clean."

Gilbert continued, "What about working together with the other people there? How did you get along with your supervisor?"

"The supervisor was a jerk," Rick blurted. "Sometimes he'd ask you to do something and then after you already did it he'd keep asking you if you did it yet."

"Yeah, the supervisor was a jerk," Ron agreed, "but we got along with him fine."

Gilbert winced. Gary took over. "At G&G's the business is just like McDonald's, only more so. We have to make everything nice and clean for the customers and keep everybody happy. People come here for a very important reason: to bury their loved ones. Sometimes people don't have it all together when they come for services or whatever. It's our job to understand that."

Gary paused and looked first at Rick then at Ron. Satisfied he had made himself clear, he continued, "At first, your duties will be to help Dinah with the day-to-day operations. That means keeping the front lawn cut, the windows washed, the floors vacuumed, that sort of thing. Then later, if you learn the ropes, maybe you can start helping with some of the administrative duties. G&G's is growing, and we here at G&G's are proud. We're depending on you two to grow with us. Gilbert and myself are going to be pretty busy for the next couple of months opening another home on the other side of town. When things are ready, we'll have you working at both places.

"For now, though," Gary continued, hopefully, "we'd like to get you started making the first G&G's a sort of showcase. Twenty years from now, when you two are directors of your own G&G outlets, you'll be able to drive by this home and tell people you were in on it from the beginning."

"That's true," Gilbert said. "We have high hopes for you two. And as you can tell by looking around our funeral home, we have good reason for having high hopes for G&G's, too. The G&G empire. And you two will be a part of it. And by starting at the bottom you'll learn everything there is to know.

"If you can start Monday," Gilbert continued, "we need you to give the outside of the garage a facelift. We had to hire professional builders to do the inside of it. That's how fast G&G's is growing; we have to use the bloody garage to lay people out. Your job is to paint it to match the house. Also, Dinah will be going to the nursery for some shrubs to plant around the garage. After that, there's going to be plenty more to do. Any questions?"

The twins fidgeted.

"You'll be making minimum wage to start out, same as at McDonald's," Gary said.

"But we got 65 cents an hour over minimum at McDonald's," Rick protested.

Gary checked with Gilbert, who nodded. "OK, fair enough—65 cents an hour over minimum. All set then? See you Monday. Good luck, gentlemen."

CHAPTER 10

Dinah kept Rick and Ron busy. By the end of the first week they had reluctantly accepted her discipline and even began showing up for work eagerly each morning. Gary and Gilbert were satisfied with their progress painting the garage and left their complete supervision to Dinah as they spent more and more time looking at buildings for the second G&G's.

Most of their offers were laughed at. They just couldn't afford the places they were seeing. It had been a long, hot week.

"What a week," Gary sighed, driving up to G&G's. "We must have looked at a dozen places. You know, I feel the hand of Devine interfering in that lease property on Ridgeway Park."

"I think so too, but not the Devine you're thinking of. It was divine providence. A lease isn't going to do us any good. We'll have to buy another place. Just think of the trouble the real Devine could make if we leased. What would we do with everybody if Devine bought the building and we lost the lease? And the parking was great, just like the agent said. But that's because half the businesses on the street were boarded up. I say we were damn lucky we didn't get it."

They entered the back door at G&G's, after checking the new shrubbery around the garage. Dinah was in the office talking on the phone, and Rick and Ron were in the kitchen making themselves sandwiches.

Gary plopped down at the kitchen table while

Gilbert got a bottle of cold tonic water from the refrigerator. The twins ate conscientiously, being careful not to drop any crumbs on the floor. Pouring drinks, Gilbert addressed the boys over his shoulder. "How've you guys been doing?" he asked. "The garage looks pretty good. Dinah been treating you OK?"

"Yeah, OK," Ron answered. "We finished painting and planting the plants like she told us to."

"It was a hot week. I got sunburned yesterday," Rick added.

"Yeah, well, you gotta watch that sun."

Dinah entered. "I was just talking to the family of the man with the Cord. They say they were over yesterday and the car had a lot of dust on it. They were pretty irritated. They said they want the car kept spotless."

Gary said to Rick and Ron, "You got a new duty. Keep the Cord spotless."

"Also, the insurance man visited," Dinah continued. "That car is worth a lot of money; our insurance isn't going to cover it. We'll have to take out additional coverage on everything people bring in here. He took an inventory. This place is turning into a museum. He said that autographed copy of *The Maltese Falcon* is worth a small fortune itself. And then there's the watches and jewelry, and gowns on the ladies. It all adds up. His estimate is in your office."

Gary rose and motioned for Gilbert to follow. "We'll take a look."

Gary examined the insurance man's figures and sank back in his chair. He asked, "Why did you have to autograph that book? We can't tell the insurance man it's a fake. There are people out to get us; they'd have a field day with that."

"Hey, I didn't know it would cause any problems. It seemed like a good idea at the time."

"Well check with me first if you come up with any more good ideas."

Gary turned to Lester, who sat motionless behind his big desk, like an occidental Buddha. It was the first time Gary noticed the inscrutable expression Wiggins had fashioned on Lester's face. "Lester, what would you do? Got any good ideas?"

Gilbert got up to leave. "See you Monday," he said abruptly. Then, to avoid a curt exit, he added unenthusiastically, "Want to get together Sunday for a barbecue or something?"

"No. Dinah wants to go somewhere. See you Monday."

After Gilbert left, Gary wedged a pen between Lester's fingers and placed a blank memo pad on his desk.

Sunday morning, Gary asked Dinah, "Do you want to go out for some pancakes and then maybe take a drive? I feel like going somewhere today."

"Pancakes would be great. Where do you want to drive to?"

"I don't know. Just a drive in the country for a

couple hours."

After strawberry crepes for Dinah and Belgian waffles for Gary, and extra coffee to go, they were on the interstate heading north, sipping coffee, listening to the radio, enjoying the scenery.

Gary saw a sign 'C38 to Mancelona Next Right.' He liked the sound of it. C38 to Mancelona. He imagined a big bingo tournament being held there. He wondered what there was to see on 38. He imagined himself an infantryman in Italy heading for a rendezvous with his unit at grid coordinate C-38. Dinah became his Italian lover in a war-ravaged countryside.

On C38, three miles outside Mancelona, he saw a teetering, abandoned farmhouse providing cover for a squad of Axis paratroopers. Their mission was to meet up with the Third Panzer Division in an all-out blitzkrieg on the Allied munitions depot in town. The Third Division never made it, cut to pieces by unrelenting air attacks out of Malta. The squad in the farmhouse was planning a quick-strike suicide mission on the ammo dump. But they would never leave the farmhouse alive.

Gary made his way to a cluster of trees 20 yards from the house and let loose with a captured RPG. Then, while the survivors were still in shock from the concussion, he single-handedly stormed the remains of the shelter, blasting his way from room to room with his Thompson. He would receive a medal and a footnote in history books, and C38 would become known as 'Gary's Road to Glory.'

Mancelona was closed, except for a weather-beaten bar with a satellite dish on the roof. The Allied Command Com Center. They drove by a few rows of small peasant houses, then past an automobile junkyard filled with rusting, twisted hulks—the charred remains of the Third Panzer Division. The town had been spared destruction, for one more day.

On the other side of Mancelona, Gary pulled into the parking lot of a dilapidated motel featuring a dozen small cabins. "Let's hole up here a while," he said to Dinah.

After registering, Gary escorted Dinah to Cabin 12. The cabin smelled musty and unclean. The bed sagged and the sheets were stained. Gary mounted his war prize against the wall.

"How 'ya doing, Gilbert? Have a good weekend?" Gary asked cheerfully.

"Huh? Oh yeah, great. I checked out the newspaper for new listings. Here's a couple we should look at," he said, handing Gary three pieces of paper with newspaper clippings stapled in the upper left corners.

"Hmm, looks good. Did you call?"

"No. I thought they might be good ideas, so I thought I'd check with you first."

"Oh hell, knock it off, Gil."

In the kitchen, Dinah poured Rick and Ron orange juice as she gave them their week's assignments. "You guys did a great job on the garage last week. Thanks.

But listen, we're having more and more visitors come in to look around. The insurance man wants someone in the lobby at all times to keep an eye on things. He's worried some of the jewelry might get stolen. And I'm going to need one of you in the basement painting the floor and walls with mildew resistant paint. I don't care how you work it out, but whoever is in the lobby has to be dressed neatly in a shirt and tie. Oh, and will one of you dust off the Cord? Also, I had some more pamphlets printed. I'm going to put them by the front door. When people leave, I want whoever is there to turn his head so people don't feel uncomfortable about taking one. And say 'yes sir' and 'yes ma'am' and don't answer any questions."

Dinah joined Gary and Gilbert in the office, leaving the boys to decide who would take which chores. "I'm having the twins man the lobby and fix up the basement," she said. "We're really going to need the extra room. And remember, Mr. Wiggins is bringing over that...that other one this afternoon. Don't forget the service this evening."

"Oh, yes, him," Gary said. "Gilbert and I were just on our way out to look at a couple of places, but we'll be back in time. Don't worry about him."

Gilbert drummed his fingers on his desk. "I just hope Wiggins followed our instructions. To the letter."

Gary changed the subject. "Hey Dinah, check with Wiggins to see if the moisture in the basement will be any problem," he said. "We might have to put in a dehumidifier."

At their first appointment, Gary and Gilbert waited an hour for the agent to show. They gave up and had lunch before going to a 1:30 appointment.

When they pulled their car to the curb in front of the 1:30 building on the west side of town they couldn't believe their eyes. The building was freshly painted and had a large, paved parking lot. They could still make out the outline of letters that had been removed from the building's facade. Detart Architecture. It was perfect.

The agent showed up on time and after a tour of the building, Gary and Gilbert were prepared to make an offer. "It's not exactly what we had in mind," Gary told the agent. "The paint is the wrong color and the parking lot isn't big enough."

"But it does have some good points," Gilbert said, handing the agent a piece of paper. "Here's our offer."

The agent looked at the paper and said, "I think we can do business."

Gary and Gilbert went straight to the liquor store and bought a pint of sloe gin. They drove to a nearby riverfront park strewn with broken bottles and tall weeds, where they cracked open the bottle and passed it back and forth while surveying their new neighborhood. They were in high spirits, making up toasts and bantering about ideas on the future of G&G's Funeral Homes.

"Here's to Detart Architecture for leaving us such a fine building," Gary said, taking another gentlemanly sip from the bottle, offering it to Gilbert.

"And her's to us for finding it," Gilbert slurred, the effects of the sweet gin beginning to take hold.

Gary laughed and mimicked, "And her's to Dinah for being such a good partner."

Gilbert turned his head and chuckled. "Her's to the future of G&G's: may the franchise gods smile on us."

"Speaking of the future," Gary said, taking a deep swig, wiping his mouth with the back of his hand, "We should get back and help Dinah. Remember who we have to bury tonight."

"Why'd you hafta remind me," Gilbert said, grabbing the bottle from Gary's hand. He paused briefly to construct an appropriate toast. "Her's to organized crime," he said, emptying the bottle into his mouth.

The service that evening was short and to the point. The gathering of business associates of one Anthony William (Tony Bill) Malone followed Gilbert silently through the Main Viewing Room, upstairs to the newly named Richelieu Room. Gilbert stood off to the side with Gary and Dinah.

The associates stood in rank while one of their fellows eulogized with one sentence. "Let no one forget Tony Bill." He then removed the sheet that had been draped over their former comrade. Tony Bill had been shot twice in the forehead and several times around the mouth with small caliber bullets. Gilbert shivered, remembering what the associates had said about the arrangements. "He's gonna have some facial scars around his face. Leave 'em there. What we're doin' is makin' Tony Bill a kinda monument to what happens when you have an overloud mouth. Know what I mean?"

Tony Bill had been posed kneeling saying his prayers. The bullet holes in his face made him look a pitiable sight. The associates paused briefly, then silently filed out of the room, down the stairs and out the front door. As soon as they were gone, Dinah and Gary moved the macabre display into a corner, then joined Gilbert in the kitchen for a drink, turning off the lights in the funeral home as they went.

Gary poured two tall, cool glasses of tonic and gin. "Here's to Tony Bill," he said, handing one to Dinah.

"Oh, Gary. Don't joke about it," Dinah scolded. "It...it's creepy."

"I'm sorry, Dinah," Gary consoled. "It's all over now."

Gary looked at Gilbert, sitting at the kitchen table, eyes starring blearily into the empty shot glass in front of him. Dinah sat down wearily next to him, resting her face in her hands. Gary pulled out a chair opposite her, and said in a loud, cheerful voice, "Well, Dinah, what do you think of the building we found?"

Dinah raised her head and peeped through her fingers at Gary. "It sounds perfect," she finally said. "Do you really think we'll get it?"

"It looks good," Gary answered, raising his glass.

"The agent said, 'I think we can do business.'"

Gilbert blinked and turned to Dinah. "We should know for sure in a couple days," he said, straightening in his chair. "Until then, we could start making up a new pamphlet and a new ad campaign for our expansion."

Dinah raised her glass saying, "I've come up with a few ideas. I'll show them to you in the morning."

"What did Wiggins say about using the basement?" Gary asked.

"I couldn't figure it out," Dinah answered. "He just said something about humidity isn't what we have to worry about. He wasn't very talkative."

Gary and Gilbert looked at each other, frozen by Wiggins' cryptic warning.

In the Main Viewing Room, the moonlight shown on Anton's face. The faint olive-colored outline around his mouth gave the impression of a frown.

That night, Gilbert had a bad dream. A blinding dust storm blew from the west. He was being chased by a band of green-skinned Arabians brandishing scimitars and surgical scissors. Gilbert tried to flee, but his limbs felt hollow, and gave under his weight. He was buried up to his neck in desert sand. The Arabians sped by in big shiny antique convertibles shouting and whooping as they swung their weapons. A huge buzzard circled and landed in front of him, crowing, "It isn't the dust storm you have to worry about."

He awoke before dawn. That didn't happen often,

but when it did, he rarely had any trouble going back to sleep. Today was different. He tossed and turned and did his best to get more sleep, but it was hopeless. The shadow of a forked branch moving outside his window startled him. Traces of his dream returned, and he made the first priority of the work day a visit to Wiggins.

Gilbert arrived at G&G's at eight thirty and made a pot of coffee. While it brewed, he went into the office and sat at his desk, thinking. He couldn't focus on any one thought until he looked over at Lester and the blank memo pad in front of him. Gilbert took the pen from Lester's hand and wrote the first thing that came to his mind. 'When in the course of human events…'

He wandered into the Main Viewing Room. Remembering with a chill the forked branch that had startled him earlier, he hesitated to make sure everything in the room was still. He stepped carefully over to Anton and without thinking spun the globe that sat next to the senior interee. Gilbert focused his eyes on one section of the globe, its shapes and colors spinning by in a hypnotizing blur. When it stopped, he read 'Mali.' Looking closer he read 'Timbuktu.' "Have you ever been to Timbuktu?" he asked Anton.

The slight olive tinge around Anton's mouth created the illusion that he was about to speak. There was a noise, and Gilbert jumped back, raising his hands in fists.

"The coffee's ready. Gilbert must be here."

Gilbert relaxed and quickly walked to the kitchen,

glad he was no longer alone. "Good morning, Dinah."

"Good morning, Gilbert. You're here early."

"I woke up early, so I decided to come in. Where's Gary?"

"He went back to the car to get my file on the new ad campaign. You look tired. Didn't you sleep well?"

"No. I slept lousy. I woke up at four-thirty and couldn't get back to sleep."

"Here, have some coffee," she said, putting her hand on his arm. "Do you want me to fix you something to eat?"

"No, that's OK, nothing for me. I had toast at home."

Gary came in, carrying Dinah's file. "Hey Gilbert, you're here early. Man, you look like hell! Come on, we have to go in the office. I got something I want to talk to you about," he said, grabbing the cup of coffee Dinah had poured for Gilbert. "Dinah, get Rick and Ron set when they come, then come show Gilbert your ideas for the new brochure."

Since putting the memo pad in front of Lester, Gary was in the habit of checking it first thing every morning. "'When in the course of human events.' Did you write that?"

"Huh?" Gilbert said, rubbing his eyes and yawning. "Yeah. It seemed like something Lester might say."

In a low voice, Gary asked, "I wonder what Lester would say to Wiggins. Have you noticed Anton lately?"

"Yeah, I was just looking at him this morning. It's starting to happen."

"I know. I hope Wiggins has come up with something. I'm sure he has. He's pretty smart when he puts his mind to it. You and me are going over to see him this morning."

"Good. I was thinking of doing that anyway," Gilbert mumbled.

"Do you think anyone else has noticed Anton yet?" Gary asked.

"No, I don't think so. It's not that noticeable unless you know what to look for. Not yet, anyway."

Rick and Ron arrived, arguing and joking about the women wrestlers they had seen at the arena the night before. They seemed quite at home at G&G's now. Dinah told them that a group from the Contemporary History Society was coming to visit and they would both have to wear ties and look professional. Rick and Ron said their 'yes ma'ams' and after Dinah left, went back to talking about the women wrestlers.

Dinah brought her file and a cup of coffee into the office and sat in a chair next to Lester's desk. She handed the file to Gilbert, saying, "Look these over and tell me what you think."

While Gilbert thumbed through the sheaf of papers, Gary asked Dinah, "What was this about the Contemporary History Society? Who are they?"

"Oh, they just want to look around. I don't think

they plan any trouble. One of them said the family who lived here a few years ago was active in the local chapter and they were curious to see what we did."

"No problem. Pass out lots of brochures, they sound like good prospects," Gary said. "Gilbert, how do you like Dinah's new brochure?"

"Looks good," Gilbert said, looking up. "But the first thing we got to do is put a sign on the second G&G's and get a good picture of it for the new brochure. But instead of putting the pictures of our places one above the other like you have here, Dinah, we should put them side by side. We don't want to give the impression that one is better than the other. The new wording for the brochure is OK, but I think we should get some testimonials from satisfied customers. I could whip up something from Anton's relatives.

"And we should have a slogan," he continued, "something like 'At G&G's We Do Your Dead Ones Proud' or 'Come to G&G's, for a Visit or a Stay.' Something catchy like that."

Dinah said skeptically, "Gary and I will put our heads together and try to come up with a slogan. Are you sure you won't let me pour you a cup of coffee?"

Gary said to Dinah, "As soon as the deal on the new place goes through, give that writer a call. What was his name? Westworld? Westinghouse? German name... Jerry Westheimer..."

"Jeremy Westlaw," Dinah said. "I'll do that. But there's something about that guy..."

"What?" Gary asked.

"I don't know..."

"Just don't let him find Wiggins. Speaking of whom, Gilbert, we have to get going. Remember? He wanted to talk to us about buying some new lab equipment."

Gilbert looked surprised, but then quickly added, "Yeah. Right. We're keeping him pretty busy and he needs some bigger beakers. Shall we go, Gary?"

CHAPTER 11

Gary and Gilbert turned onto Wiggins' dirt road on the outskirts of town, where the city started becoming the country. Wiggins' house stood a quarter mile down the road, surrounded by a rotting wooden fence, the kind that didn't keep people out, but didn't invite them in. A half dozen untended crab trees shaded the front yard. A dried, dead oak straddled the driveway. The acreage in back belonged to a farming family down the road. It was planted with rows of corn. A flock of crows rested on the dilapidated barn that served as Wiggins' garage, sunning themselves after a good breakfast. Wiggins' front door was nailed shut with 2x4s, and the broken panes of glass in the living room windows were covered with sheets of clear plastic.

Gary gave two short beeps on his horn as he turned into the gravel driveway. He parked in back, between Wiggins' Step-Van and a rusted tractor that looked like it hadn't moved since Elvis sang on *Ed Sullivan*. Wiggins came out the back door dressed in blue work pants and a dirty lab coat. "Good morning, gents. Like some coffee?"

"No thanks, Mr. Wiggins," Gary said. "Hey, you should do something about that oak tree out front. A good storm will blow it right onto your roof."

"That's what the fella down the road says," Mr. Wiggins answered. "He wanted to cut it down last winter. He was going to charge me for it then haul the

wood off for his fireplace. I told him to forget it. I told
him if it's going to fall, it'll fall the other way. So we
have a bet going."

A rustling among the crows caught Wiggins'
attention. "Want to see something funny?" he asked,
picking up a rock. "Watch this."

He threw the rock as hard as he could. It struck the
roof of the barn, startling the crows into flight. The
rock ricocheted upwards into the mass of flying birds,
nicking one in the tail feather. Wiggins chuckled. "I got
that down pretty good now. Hit the roof, get the birds
flying, then the rock keeps going right through them.
Nine times out of ten, you hit something. Took me
years to come up with that…I used to use two rocks."

Mr. Wiggins ushered Gary and Gilbert into the
house. The kitchen was littered with dirty pots and
pans. The refrigerator made a clanking racket.
Numerous stuffed crows hung from the walls and
ceiling.

They went directly to the basement workroom.
Hundreds of animals of all shapes and sizes greeted
them with glass-eyed stares. Mr. Wiggins had
mentioned more than once how he loved the variety
nature provided. He had bears with fangs ready to
clamp shut, peacocks in full bloom, ducks by the
dozen, bobcats, kitty cats, a baby elephant with a dried,
broken trunk, an alpaca with a stupid look on its face,
and a hundred other creatures from all over the world.

Gilbert was drawn to a shelf holding a three-foot
montage of small creatures mounted on a plank of

polished maple. He hadn't noticed the display before, and looked intently at the detail. A cat pawed playfully at a mouse hiding beneath a pile of varnished twigs. A hummingbird sucked at a bright, blooming flower. A small garden snake slithered around the flower's stem. Peering from out of a burrow was a vole. A large housefly sat at the burrow's entrance. Gilbert looked more closely at the vole stalking the housefly, absorbed in the display's intricate detail. The fly took off, buzzing Gilbert's nose. Gilbert jumped back with a curse, swinging his arms wildly.

He quickly joined Mr. Wiggins and Gary, who stooped over a workbench, examining a diagram Mr. Wiggins had drawn. Gilbert rested his arm on the alpaca's head and peered over Mr. Wiggins' shoulder. "So you see, Sonny," Mr. Wiggins explained, stepping aside so Gilbert could see, "that's how I figured it should work. Now in normal taxidermy, we generally gut them and wrap the preserved skin around a wire frame, or else we stuff them with excelsior."

Gary asked, "Excelsior? You mean the stuff the Three Stooges used to squirt at each other?"

"No. That was seltzer."

Gilbert asked, "Excelsior? Wasn't that what that guy ran through the streets yelling after he discovered gravity?"

"That was 'eureka.' And it was Archimedes who said it, not Newton."

"I thought excelsior was some kind of magic potion you drink to live forever," Gary said.

"That's 'elixir.'"

"I know where I heard of excelsior," Gilbert stated confidently. "That's the name of the Sword in the Stone."

"That's 'Excalibur'! Gentlemen, gentlemen, please," Mr. Wiggins pleaded. "Excelsior is something quite different and not nearly so exciting, I'm afraid. Excelsior is just wood shavings used for packing, and sometimes in taxidermy."

"Wood shavings?" said Gary, disappointed. "Excelsior is wood shavings?"

"Excelsior is wood shavings," Mr. Wiggins repeated. "I'm sorry to disappoint you, but it's the truth."

"But I always thought excelsior was something great," Gary protested.

"Oh! Why yes of course, dear boy. If you use it that way, excelsior means 'ever higher.' I guess that's why people use it as a toast sometimes."

Gilbert idly scratched the stupid alpaca between the ears. "Toast?" he asked. "I had some toast this morning that tasted like excelsior. I'm all out of butter, and I don't have any jam."

Mr. Wiggins stepped a little further to the side, raising his hand to his ear, using his index finger to make small circling motions. Gary shook his head slowly and coughed. "Anyway," he said, "let's get back to business. We all knew from the beginning there might be a problem. How close are you to a solution, Mr. Wiggins?"

"I haven't found anything definite yet. I need

more time. The smears I took from Anton yesterday will be very helpful, but they're still in culture dishes. It'll be a few days until I know exactly what I'm dealing with. And it'll be a while longer before I can come up with an answer that'll work. In the meantime, I suggest you get Anton out of view. Once it starts, it won't stop," Mr. Wiggins said, adding, "and keep an eye on the others while you're at it."

"Getting Anton out of view won't be any problem," Gary said. "There's no one to raise a fuss if he disappears. What worries me is hiding the paying customers. We promised perpetual display."

"Hey don't worry, Gary," Gilbert said. "If it comes to that, we can always say they're out for maintenance. Anyway, how many relatives have we got coming back once the service is over?"

"Not many," Gary agreed. "Still, it sets up a big potential for problems and I don't like it. We need an answer fast, Mr. Wiggins. How much time are we talking about?"

"Not long, not long, I assure you. And just in case it is long, I'm working on some excellent ideas for quick fixes. I'll perfect them while I wait for Anton's cultures to grow."

As they headed back upstairs, Gilbert noticed a faint light coming from the porthole of a metal door on the far side of Mr. Wiggins' basement. The porthole had heavy rubber seals around it and was covered with condensation. He wiped away the condensation and peered inside. His bloodcurdling scream froze

Mr. Wiggins and Gary in their tracks.

Gilbert pushed them out of the way as he ran full tilt up the stairs. Mr. Wiggins regained his balance and shouted after him, "Don't be afraid, Sonny, that's just Mrs. Stoner. She won't hurt you."

Mr. Wiggins chuckled all the way up the stairs and into the kitchen, where he broke out in a hearty laugh. "Are you boys hungry?" he asked. "Gilbert, perhaps you'd like to look in my refrigerator."

CHAPTER 12

While Gary and Gilbert were visiting Mr. Wiggins, Dinah prepared for the Contemporary History Society's visit. She had Rick and Ron vacuum the entire house while she dusted and laid out pamphlets. By 11:00 a.m. everything was ready. She inspected Rick and Ron, straightening Rick's tie and fixing the back of Ron's collar.

The doorbell rang and the group entered, timidly at first, but warming quickly to Dinah's charm. "Please come in. We're so happy to have a visit from an intellectual organization. There's certainly a lot of contemporary history to study these days, isn't there?"

A big busted woman with poorly-tinted hair answered enthusiastically, "Oh yes! And we do try to stay on top of things. I'm Dorothea Revere, president and founder of the local chapter of the Contemporary History Society. I brought along a leaflet telling a little about the Society. We're all very proud of our shared interests. We're especially proud of the Society's motto and seal," she said, pointing to the top of the leaflet. "It was designed by our own Betty Roth. Betty, come here and take credit for your work."

Betty Roth greeted Dinah, explaining that the seal was a silhouette of Paul Revere riding his horse, carrying a lantern in one hand and an American flag in the other, the reins clenched between his teeth. "The motto is from the famous poem by Longfellow," she explained. "It symbolizes our feeling that history is a living thing for all generations to enjoy."

Dinah read, "'Listen, my children, and you shall hear.' Very nice. I couldn't agree more. Let me give you a little tour of our home, and maybe someday G&G's can have its own little place in history."

Dinah received a brief history lesson on Grant's tomb and the cemetery at Gettysburg as she led the procession slowly through the Main Viewing Room, then into the office to see Lester, then out to the garage. "As you can see," she said proudly, "the lovely Annex is dominated by Mr. Justinian Brown at the wheel of his beloved antique car."

"Where's the man in the bathtub?" asked a man in the back.

"We have more viewing rooms on the Upper Level. Would you like to see?" she asked, herding the group back inside.

"Dinah, you got a phone call."

"OK, Ron. I'll take it. Would you show the Society the Upper Level? This is Dorothea Revere, the local chapter's president and founder. Dorothea, this is Ron, one of our young helpers."

"It's very nice to meet you, young man."

"Nice to meet you, ma'am."

Ron brought the group upstairs and into the Richelieu Room. Rick sat motionless on a chair, next to the assassinated gangster. Betty Roth said, "Oh my! Look at that poor young man. Such a tragedy."

Ron pursed his lips and gave Rick a hard stare. "It's really not that bad," he told Betty. "That guy was a delinquent who was killed falling from the roof of a house he was breaking into. Maybe you heard about it. Anyway, the police brought him here because he didn't have any family and no one wanted to spend a lot of money on a real funeral."

Dorothea said, "How interesting. Well, I guess it was the right thing to do. They should save the taxpayers' money, especially if he was a ruffian."

A man standing next to Dorothea asked, "Why is that other one kneeling in the corner?"

"He's there because he talked too much," Ron answered, then quickly pointed the group out of the room and down the hall toward the bathroom. The last person to leave the Richelieu Room was a white-haired lady who walked unsteadily on a three-pronged aluminum cane. Rick, still seated, winked at her and smiled. The lady did a double take and hurried into the hallway.

Ron closed the door to the Richelieu Room and waited at the top of the stairs while the Society visited the bathroom. Filing out, Dorothea said to Betty Roth, "That man looked so happy singing in his bathtub. I always wished I could sing."

"I wonder if they ever have to change the water?"

"Oh no, dear. I don't think that was real water. Young man, is that real water?"

"Yes ma'am," Ron answered seriously. "But they treated it to the G&G process so it won't evaporate. That's why it doesn't look real."

Dorothea shrugged and led the group downstairs.

The lady with the three-pronged cane was last. She peaked warily at the closed door to the Richelieu Room before taking the handrail and making her way down the stairs, refusing Ron's offer of help.

Dinah rejoined the group in the Main Viewing Room. "I'm so sorry to be called away like that. Did you enjoy your tour?"

Dorothea said, "Oh yes. It was the most interesting field trip we've had in months. What you're doing here is so...contemporarily historical. And I'm all in favor of your motives. Why, when I buried my dear Henry I was aghast at the cost. Something should be done, and you're certainly doing something. On behalf of the Contemporary History Society, I'd like to invite you to one of our meetings. Our schedule is printed on the back of our leaflet. You're most welcome to attend."

"Thank you very much, Dorothea. I hope to be there."

"And bring your young helper. After all, our history will be his legacy."

"That's very thoughtful, Dorothea. Bye bye."

"How did it go with the Contemporary History Society this morning?" Gary asked.

"Very well. They're a bunch of sweethearts. They invited me to one of their meetings."

"Might not be a bad idea to go. You never know when we might need allies."

"Or customers," Gilbert added.

"Oh, while you were away, Mrs. Stoner's son

called. He was going through some of her things and found an organ transplant card. He was wondering if you could send some of her organs to the hospital. He gave me a list over the phone."

"No way!" Gary said. "Wiggins is putting her through the process. Those organs are deadly now. Anyway, you got to transplant organs right away. You can't wait to do it. I'll give Mrs. Stoner's son a call."

"OK, thanks," Dinah said. "What's new with Mr. Wiggins?"

"Nothing!" Gilbert exclaimed.

"What about the new lab equipment?" Dinah asked.

"Oh yeah," Gary answered quickly. "He wanted some more equipment. We looked around and agreed. No big deal. I'm ready for lunch."

Dinah took a step back, her brow furling involuntarily. She looked at Gilbert, then back at Gary. Finally she said, "The boys and I have already eaten. There's some soup left. I'll get you some. Gilbert, do you want some lunch?"

"Nothing for me, thanks," Gilbert answered, holding his hand to his stomach. "I'm not hungry."

While Dinah warmed Gary's soup in the kitchen, Gary and Gilbert conferred around Anton. "He's getting worse," Gary noted, relieving the itch under his eye. "We should have had him out of here before the History Society visited this morning. We're damn lucky no one noticed."

"What are you going to tell Dinah?"

"I don't know. I might have to tell her the truth."

"It'll be a lot easier for us if she knows. I think you should find a way to tell her, after all, she is your wife."

"I know. But she'll be mad I didn't tell her before."

"If Wiggins doesn't come up with an answer soon, she'll find out for herself and be even madder. Tell her."

"OK," Gary said. "Tonight at home. At least it'll clear the air about moving Anton. Can you meet me here around nine tonight? We'll move Anton and rearrange things so it won't look like anyone's missing."

"Where can we move him?"

"The attic."

Gilbert shuddered. "I was going out tonight," he said. "Can't we do it tomorrow morning, in the daylight?"

"You can still go out. It'll only take an hour. I want to get it done tonight because Wiggins will be here first thing tomorrow to deliver Mrs. Stoner for a morning service. There won't be time."

That evening, after dinner, Gary said to Dinah, "We can leave the dishes for later, dear. Let's sit down in the living room for a while."

Dinah's face went cold and blank. "What have you done? It's not like last time, is it?"

"No. Absolutely nothing like that. I haven't even looked at anyone else. And I never even hardly looked at her. It was just an innocent mistake. I told you that. Anyway, this is about business. Something's come up that you should know about."

Dinah walked silently past Gary into the living room. Gary took a deep breath and followed. He sat down in the love seat, resting his arm on the back of the couch, motioning Dinah to sit beside him. Dinah took a seat in the matching armchair, opposite Gary. She sat straight and stiff, waiting for Gary to begin.

Gary cleared his throat. "Do you remember when we first started the business and Mr. Wiggins was going to patent his process?" he asked hesitantly. "Well, he never did. He never even applied. It seems there were some details he hadn't worked out yet. We thought he would have them taken care of in no time, so we didn't bother you about them. You were so busy with the promotion and stuff. By the way, you really did a great job."

"Cut the crap, Gary."

"OK. OK. Sorry. What's going on is Wiggins' people aren't as perfectly preserved as we thought they'd be. It seems that after a few months something happens and they start to...to...sort of...decompose."

"Oh no, Gary!" Dinah shouted. "How could you? Decompose? You mean they're going to rot and fall apart?"

"No, they'll never completely rot and fall apart. They'll just sort of...partially decompose."

"What do you mean, partially decompose."

"Not all the way. It's just that their skin will start

turning a different shade."

"What shade, Gary?"

"Sort of...green."

"Honestly, Gary. I don't know whether you're a lunatic or a moron. And now you got plans for another G&G's across town?"

Gary smiled sheepishly and averted his eyes, staring briefly at the carpet in front of Dinah's feet, noticing the smooth lines of her calves, wishing he could comment on how they turned him on, praising her, making her forget her anger.

Dinah lifted herself from the chair just enough to adjust her dress, pulling it downward, over her knees. "How confident are you that Wiggins can come up with an answer?" she asked icily.

"If anyone can, Wiggins can."

Dinah stared hard at Gary, biting the inside of her lip. "Didn't you once say you had a cousin living in Fiji?" she asked.

"Yes. Why?"

"I want you to write him a nice letter telling him how much you would like to see him. Then get all the papers on the house and all the bank accounts together and make sure your passport hasn't expired. Then get a bag packed. Just in case. We'll do everything we can to straighten this out, but I want to be ready to take a long trip in case the shit ever hits the fan. Do you understand me, Gary?"

"Yes dear."

The night air had turned cold and damp, and a harsh wind screamed like an omen through the forked branches of the trees in front of G&G's. Gary and Gilbert met at the back door.

Turning on just enough lights to see, they silently made their way to the Main Viewing Room. From there they carried Anton's globe, his book, the small table the book rested on, and the seafaring painting upstairs. Gary opened the attic door and flicked the light switch. Nothing happened. The full moon shone brightly through the dusty cobwebs covering the attic window. "Come on," Gary said, "we can see OK."

"I've never been up here," Gilbert whispered. "I don't know my way around. I don't want to fall through the floor."

"There's a good floor up here, Gilbert. You won't fall through. And there's nothing to trip over. There's nothing up here at all."

Gary boldly led the way, carrying Anton's table and book. The wooden steps creaked when Gary put his weight on them, and again when he lifted his weight off. At the top, he stopped. "We'll put Anton's stuff over here," he said, pointing to a spot near the center of the attic. "Come on."

Gilbert slowly followed and set Anton's globe and painting next to where Gary had placed the table. He could see a clear path across the attic floor to the window on the other side. The rest of the attic was studded with bare posts. The slant of the roof disappeared into pitch blackness. From the darkest corners he thought he saw piercing, fiery red eyes glowering at him. He stood, silent and still, afraid to move. Mrs. Stoner's face appeared directly in front of him, hanging and bobbing in a dance of the dead. Creaking footsteps echoed through the attic, and he spun quickly, punching the air. Gary was already halfway down the stairs, rushing to leave and lock the door, condemning him to spend the rest of his life wandering the dark attic to be eaten alive every evening by hideous ghouls.

Gilbert ran to the stairs, stumbling over Anton's table, sending it and Anton's book tumbling across the floor. He scrambled down the stairs, three at a time, focusing on the door as if it were his only portal to life. As he crossed through it into the artificial light of the hallway, his fears vanished and he could not understand why he had panicked. He brushed himself off and pretended he had lost his balance on the dark attic stairway.

"Don't worry, I'll carry Anton up myself," Gary said. "They don't weigh anything after Wiggins puts them through the process. You start rearranging the others downstairs so it doesn't look like anyone's missing."

"Hey Gary," Gilbert asked, his racing heart not yet returned to normal, "did you tell Dinah?"

"Yeah. I told her after dinner."

"How did she take it? Was she mad?"

"Yes, you could say that." Gary answered, adding, "She said if Wiggins doesn't come up with something fast and people find out what's going on, we'd better be prepared to leave everything and go on the lam. People would skin us alive."

"Hmm. Smart lady."

Mr. Wiggins' blue Step-Van pulled into the drive at G&G's just as the morning street lights out front flickered off for another day. Gary came out to meet him. Mr. Wiggins opened the rear door of his van and set the aluminum ramp in place. Together they maneuvered a large cardboard box marked 'office furniture' onto a dolly and rolled it inside to one of the Upper Level rooms. "Sure is getting crowded around here," Mr. Wiggins said.

"I know. We got people all over the place. It'll be a while before our new home opens. Until then, we'll try to get the basement ready. If we fix it up with fresh paint and lots of bright lights and maybe some Astroturf and potted palms, people won't mind burying their dead down there."

"Grow lights. You're going to need grow lights," advised Mr. Wiggins. "They simulate the sun's own light, the whole spectrum. Good for plants, natural looking, too. Put in a little waterfall while you're at it. I'll bring you some of my stuffed birds. You can stick them on the potted palms. It'll look kinda like the Garden of Eden."

"We'll do that. Great idea, Mr. Wiggins."

After removing Mrs. Stoner from the office furniture box and placing her burial accessories around her,

Gary and Mr. Wiggins relaxed around the kitchen table with a cup of coffee. "Mr. Wiggins, would you like to see Anton?" Gary asked. "Gilbert and I moved him to the attic last night."

"No need. I already seen him last time. Strange what's happening. I can't figure it out. It has all the earmarks of a bacterium, but after my process, no bacteria on earth would want to live in one of my bodies. I'll find the answer, though. Don't worry. In the meantime, you should get together some cosmetics and see what you can do. We'll fix things up, by hook or by crook," Mr. Wiggins said confidently. "Uh...besides you, me and Gilbert," he asked, "who else knows what's happening?"

"I told Dinah last night."

"Oh? You told your wife?"

"Yeah, after all, she is a partner in this."

"Was she mad?"

"A little."

"Well, I'm going to be moseying along, then. Got lots to do. Call me later and tell me how the cosmetics worked out."

"So long, Mr. Wiggins. Talk to you later."

Gilbert detoured on the way to work to pick up Dinah. They arrived ten minutes after Mr. Wiggins left, as Gary was finishing a bowl of oatmeal. Mrs. Stoner's service was scheduled for nine o'clock and there were still preparations to be made.

"Good morning, Gary. Wiggins get here OK?"

Gilbert asked.

"Yep. Everything's set up in the bedroom up-stairs."

"The Richelieu Room on the Upper Level," Dinah corrected. "We've got to start using the names, even when we talk among ourselves. We can't afford any slip ups," she added.

Gary walked on eggshells to the sink and washed his bowl. "Everything's set upstairs, Dinah...in the Richelieu Room upstairs...on the Upper Level," he stammered. "Me and Wiggins arranged Mrs. Stoner's shawl around her shoulders and put her knitting basket beside her chair."

"Good," Dinah said, "I'll see to the music and coffee."

Mrs. Stoner's service went off almost perfectly. A minor hitch developed when one of her friends arrived from the convalescent home in a wheelchair. But Gary and Gilbert managed to carry her up the stairs, wheelchair and all.

There was no minister to officiate, so Gary donned a black suitcoat and coaxed the gathered flock through several Bible readings and a brief generic statement about the love and joy Mrs. Stoner had brought to those around her. After the service, the convalescent home vice-administrator presented Gary with a check for $500, explaining, "The family asked me to give you this. Mrs. Stoner stipulated that the minister at her funeral service should receive this sum as a gratuity. It was a beautiful ceremony, Mr. Colbert. So simple and uncomplicated. There's just one thing Mr. Reilly, our administrator, wanted me to mention," she said, searching for the right words. "If you want to leave some of your brochures with him, that would be all right. But he doesn't think it's appropriate to distribute them directly to our residents."

"Oh, yes, sorry," Gary said, slipping the check into his shirt pocket. "I can see how that might have been a mistake. It's our new marketing department. I'll speak to them. Tell Mr. Reilly everything will be taken care of."

After Mrs. Stoner's guests left, Gary danced around, hugging Dinah and slapping Gilbert on the back. "Look at this. FIVE HUNDRED DOLLARS! Just for acting like a minister."

"Five hundred dollars? What for?" asked Gilbert.

"She wanted it: The minister at her service gets FIVE HUNDRED DOLLARS!"

"Hey, not bad for a morning's work," Dinah said. "Where are you going to take us for dinner tonight?"

"The Skewer and Brand. Steaks for everyone."

Gary danced and sang through the rest of the day, answering the phone cheerfully, skipping up and down the stairs, tipping heavily and happily at the Skewer and Brand.

CHAPTER 13

The afternoon was cold and damp. The first leaves of autumn had fallen, forming wet clusters on the walk leading to G&G's front door. A squirrel paused briefly on the lawn to fix his grip on a nut. At the sound of a barking dog, he raced around the side of the building, trying to keep his furry underbelly off the wet grass, not caring, not even aware that Gary and Gilbert were at that moment signing the purchase agreement on the new G&G's across town.

After a solemn drive back to the first G&G's, they entered the front door, stopping briefly to wipe their shoes while appraising the Main Viewing Room, now crowded with familiar faces. Dinah was in the office using half of Lester's desk to sort debits and credits.

"Are we solvent?" Gary joked.

"Actually, things are looking pretty good."

"Where's Rick and Ron?" Gilbert asked.

"Cleaning the basement. We can have it looking presentable in about a week. Mr. Wiggins called. He said he's bringing over some tropical birds when he delivers Mr. Peterson tomorrow."

"Great," Gary said. "We'll have that basement looking really good. What are we going to call it?"

Dinah put down her paperwork a moment. "I don't know," she said. "The Subterranean Chamber. The Lower Level. Rock Bottom."

"The Last Resort. The Bottom Falls Out. The Lost Paradise. Paradise on a Stick," Gilbert offered.

"It'll have a garden theme," Gary said. "Lots of plants and natural stuff. The Garden of Eden."

"Too presumptuous," Dinah objected.

"The Garden at the End of the Rainbow. Marvin's Gardens," Gilbert suggested.

"Let's just call it The Garden," Gary proposed. "Maybe make it plural, The Gardens. Which is better, Dinah?"

"The Garden. Mr. Peterson can be found in The Garden," she said, trying it out. "No. People might go outside looking for Mr. Peterson. The Downstairs Garden. The Lower Garden."

"No. We shouldn't say anything about down or lower," Gilbert advised. "How about the Perpetual Garden."

"That's it! The Perpetual Garden!" Gary exclaimed. "Gilbert, you're a genius! People will know it's not outside, especially in winter. And it ties in with perpetual display. The Perpetual Garden."

"Sounds good," Gilbert agreed.

"It'll work," Dinah concurred. "Oh, by the way, Mr. Peterson's son is coming at three to go over the arrangements."

"Does he have a minister?" Gary asked.

"'fraid so," Dinah said, going back to her debits and credits.

Gary sat down at his desk, leaning back comfortably in the chair. "You know, Gilbert, we're doing OK here at the first G&G's, but what if we've already saturated the market? What if the only people interested in perpetual display have already come in? What if this is just something people do because it's different, and after the novelty wears off, nobody comes?"

"I've been tossing and turning every night thinking of that," Gilbert answered, taking a seat at his desk. "The only way to be sure of more business is through marketing and publicity. I've been so worried that last week I subscribed to the *Morbidity and Mortality Weekly Report*, put out by the Centers for Disease Control. They got some great information in there. Last issue they had an article on Swine Flu. They predict it'll be coming back this winter and deaths will be high because people won't believe the warnings. I'm just paraphrasing, mind you. Here's the article," Gilbert said, reaching into his desk drawer, handing Gary the local library's copy of the magazine, folded into a pocket-size wad.

"This could be our lucky break," Gary said, nodding appreciatively at Gilbert's initiative. "We can run a Swine Flu Special. Maybe even open a whole room dedicated to Swine Flu victims."

Gilbert jumped to his feet, speaking excitedly and carelessly. "That's exactly what I had in mind. And as a public service jester, we can print leaflets telling people to get their shots. Nobody will, of course, but our name will be right there at the bottom and people will think we have a special place in our hearts for Swine Flu cases, and they'll bring their dead relatives to us." Gilbert snapped his fingers and raised clenched fists high above his head. "We'll be the Kings of Swine Flu!" he shouted.

"Now Gilbert," Dinah laughed, "you know what we said about your good ideas."

"Aw, Mom, you never let me have any fun!"

"Mind if I hang around for the service?" Mr. Wiggins asked, as he wheeled in the office furniture box containing Mr. Peterson. "It's been years since I've been involved in the nuts and bolts of funeral homin'."

"Sure, Mr. Wiggins," Gary answered. "Maybe you can come up with some ideas."

"You're talking to the right man. I'm full of ideas. Even when I can't get any solid ideas, I find I can at least get some foggy ones."

"I know that for a fact, Mr. Wiggins. Afterwards, let's go down the basement...the Perpetual Garden...and you can look around down there. We hope to have it finished soon.

"Oh, and Mr. Wiggins," Gary added, "I think you should get yourself a new office furniture box. This one is looking pretty tattered."

Mr. Peterson was interred next to Mrs. Stoner in the Richelieu Room on the Upper Level. He was a widower who had buried his wife long ago back in England. Mr. Peterson's son remarked to Gary before the service that his mother used to knit all the time also, and although she bore no resemblance to Mrs. Stoner, it seemed comforting to see his father next to her. "It would have been nice to have the both of them here," he said. "But at least we know we can always come visit Father whenever we want to. He was always full of stories, especially about what it was like to raise a family in London after the war. I'm planning to write a book based on his stories, you know."

"A book?" Gary asked. "What an excellent idea. I wish I could write."

"You can. Anyone can."

"I don't know," Gary said, unconvinced. "I did help write some ads and a pamphlet for the funeral home."

"There you go. See, you can do it. Why don't you write a book about G&G's Funeral Home?"

Gary thought a moment, eyeing Mr. Peterson's son to see if he was putting him on. Musing over the book idea, Gary had a vision of fame and fortune, signing autographs, chatting with the rich and famous, striking multi-million dollar deals, marketing T-shirts and Anton dolls, explaining who Anton was and where he came from, dodging questions about the green problem, landing in jail, disgraced and penniless. Gary cleared his throat. "I don't think a book about G&G's would be that interesting; what we do here is all pretty routine. But good luck on your book."

When the service was over and the guests left, Gary and Gilbert took Mr. Wiggins to the Perpetual Garden. The light in the stairwell was bad and Mr. Wiggins walked slowly and carefully. "You know," he said, "you'll have to improve the lighting here, and maybe add some flora to the stairwell to help set the mood."

Mr. Wiggins groped and felt his way down the stairs, using the time to strike up a conversation. "You know, the service this morning brought back old memories of my own little funeral parlor years ago. We didn't have anything elaborate, but it was a small community and people didn't seem to mind. We got along OK," he said, pausing a moment. "Then the interstate came through and our little town began to bustle. I've always kinda regretted that I didn't try harder to keep pace with things. That's when I lost the business."

Gary and Gilbert weren't listening. They had already heard the story a hundred times.

"Yup, lost the business," Mr. Wiggins continued, wistfully. "My own fault. Big operators from the city came in with their fancy Cadillac hearses and snappy funeral director's suits. And the flowers! My God, they seemed able to get their customers an endless supply of flowers. More than the local florist could provide. I always wondered where they got them. Folks got to feeling shamed if they didn't have lots of flowers at a funeral. I couldn't compete."

As Mr. Wiggins reached the last step leading down to the Perpetual Garden, Gary extended his arm in a proud sweeping gesture, beckoning Mr. Wiggins to take a look. "And this is our Perpetual Garden," Gary said, waving Rick and Ron over.

The twins had just finished laying the final piece of Astroturf. "Rick and Ron. You remember Mr. Wiggins," Gary introduced.

Rick and Ron shook hands with Mr. Wiggins. "How do you like it, sir?" Rick asked.

"Step inside and take a look," Ron said.

But Mr. Wiggins just gazed around the basement with a dreamy look. Finally, he said, "Yes. This is shaping up real fine. You know what would be nice? Pipe in some sound effects. Birds chirping and squirrels talking, that sort of thing."

"I have a CD of the 'Songs of the Humpback Whale,'" Gilbert offered.

Mr. Wiggins didn't hear.

One week later, the Perpetual Garden opened for business with its first occupants. It was also G&G's first double funeral.

Billy Quince and Minerva Williams carried out their suicide pact, dying of carbon monoxide poisoning in Billy's rusty and dented subcompact.

Nothing ever went right for the unfortunate couple. And whenever they did get a break, something would always take it away. It was all there in the suicide note they left beside them on the front seat of Billy's car. Also in the note was their request for perpetual display at G&G's. "...so all the ungrateful creeps who done us wrong will have something to apologize to."

Mini's mother granted the last request. "Billy was

no good from day one," she spat, looking from Gary to Lester and back again. "And that girl might have been my daughter, but she was like a vampire, sucking the lifeblood out of everything around her. Serves them right to be buried this way."

"Yes ma'am," Gary answered. "I understand. There was nothing in their statement about interment pose. Perhaps you could help us with that. Would you like to look around and get some ideas?"

"I don't have to look around. I read about you in the papers. You can make people stand or sit or lay in a bathtub, or...this," she said, pointing at Lester. "I want you to make them sit on the front seat of that...that car. I sold the rest of it to the junkyard."

"We can do that. Certainly," Gary said, pausing to think of some way to pacify Mrs. Williams. "We'd like to make things as easy as possible for you," he continued. "And I'm sure your lovely daughter is among the saints right now doing her best, too."

Mrs. Williams spluttered, "If she's with the saints, then those saints are in the wrong place. And I hope she is watching. I'll give her a perpetual display she'll never forget. Using my own garage to kill herself. Why, the firemen almost choked to death getting her and that...that Billy out. You just bury them like I told you to."

"Yes, Mrs. Williams. Now, for the service, wouldn't it be nice if..."

"No service. No nothing," Mrs. Williams said, angrily. "You just tell me when they're ready and I'll come over to make sure it's right. Then you'll get your money."

Billy and Mini were interred according to their wishes. The story appeared on page three of the *Daily Daily*.

Suicides End Up at G&G's Funeral Home

Jeremy Westlaw, Special Writer — Last week's tragic double suicide victims, Billy Quince and Minerva Williams, were put on perpetual display in the new Perpetual Garden room at G&G's Funeral Home. The pair were interred at G&G's according to wishes stated in a suicide note found in the car they killed themselves in by carbon monoxide poisoning. Clara Williams, Minerva Williams' mother, carried out the request, stating that, "Mini never knew what she was doing. I hope this makes her happy."

Mr. Quince and Ms. Williams were interred sitting on the salvaged front seat of Mr. Quince's automobile. They became the first interees in G&G's newly finished Perpetual Garden.

Gary Colbert, co-founder and spokesman for G&G's, said of the double burial, "We at G&G's are proud. Proud to be there to serve the public in whatever way we can. Perpetual display was the dying wish of this unfortunate couple. We trust they have found a peaceful resting place in accordance with their wishes."

Interested parties can visit G&G's Perpetual Garden during normal business hours Monday through Friday.

The next day, Mr. Westlaw had trouble finding a parking place at G&G's. When he entered the front door, Rick directed him to the Perpetual Garden, pointing out the Main Viewing Room, and mentioning the rooms on the Upper Level and in the Annex.

"I'm here to see Mr. Colbert. Jeremy Westlaw."

"Oh, yes, sorry, Mr. Westlaw. Right this way."

Rick led him through the crowd to the office, knocking twice on the door before opening it. Gilbert smiled and said, "Come in Mr. Westlaw. Quick, shut the door."

Gary added, "That story of yours has caused quite a stir around here. I'm almost sorry I asked you to add that part about visitors being welcome."

"It's not Mr. Westlaw's fault," Gilbert said. "Heck, we're in business to be seen. The exposure is great. People are going to the Upper Level and out to the Annex. I hope they're thinking about how they want to be posed."

"I'm sorry the story was edited so badly," Mr. Westlaw apologized. "I couldn't get the paper to run the part about your lower funeral costs."

"That's OK, Mr. Westlaw," Gary assured him. "You did your best. Now come over here and we'll give you the scoop on our second home across town. It will be located in the former offices...the beautiful former offices...of Detart Architecture. Here, take a look at the floor plan."

Gary pointed to the drawing spread across his desk. "The building is a two story white colonial with plenty of parking," he explained. "Next week we'll have a professional remodeling crew start on our custom renovations. Scheduled grand opening is the middle of next month."

"We should have some type of grand opening celebration," Gilbert suggested. "Maybe put up a display explaining the G&G process."

"People aren't interested in the process, Gilbert," Gary said sharply.

"Oh, I think they'd be fascinated," Mr. Westlaw said, leaning forward. "I could help put it together."

"No, a display isn't necessary," Gary said emphatically. "You don't see other funeral homes putting up displays of their processes. But you know, Gilbert, maybe some sort of grand opening ceremony wouldn't be a bad idea. Will you be in town then, Mr. Westlaw?"

"I'll be here."

"Good. I hope we can interest you in covering the grand opening."

"I'll be there."

After Mr. Westlaw left, Gary formed a hard fist and hit Gilbert hard on the arm. "What were you thinking of, bringing up the process? Don't ever mention the process again in front of anyone, especially Westlaw!"

"You're right. Hey, ouch, that hurt! Sorry. I don't know what I was thinking of. I guess I was thinking of Westlaw as part of the team."

"Well he's not. We're using him for publicity and he's using us for writing material. We have a mutually parasitic relationship. That's different from being on the same team."

"You two did a great job on the Perpetual Garden."

"Thanks Uncle Gilbert," Ron said.

"Your next project is going to be of even greater historic importance for G&G's. Preparing our first expansion outlet."

Rick and Ron straightened up in their chairs opposite Gary and Gilbert in the office. Gilbert pulled out the floor plan of the new G&G's and spread it across his desk, motioning Rick and Ron to take a closer look. "Not much needs to be done, really," he said. "The paint is good, but the carpets need to be cleaned after those damn remodelers got through with the place. I want you to start by putting up the nameplates for the different rooms. Do it according to what we wrote on this floor plan. Don't get the names mixed up; we spent a lot of time coming up with names to fit the mood of each room. For example, this room on the First Level facing east, the Sunrise Room, don't get it mixed up with this one on the Upper Level facing west, the Sunset Room. Got it?"

"Yes sir."

"Yes sir."

Gilbert continued, "After you get the nameplates up, we'll rent a truck and you can get the furniture Dinah is out buying at the fire sale downtown. The floor plan shows where everything goes."

Gary added, "After your fine job on the Perpetual Garden, and if you get the new place looking just as good, Gilbert and I are going to start training you in administrative duties. Needless to say, you'll be in line for promotions and a raise."

After Rick and Ron left for the second G&G's, Gary pulled a small paper bag out of his bottom drawer. "Let's go," he said to Gilbert.

One by one they went to each interee in the Main Viewing Room, applying a bit of lipstick to one and a brush of skin toner to another. "Don't put it on too thick," Gary advised. "Just enough to cover any green patches. We don't want the makeup to be too obvious."

"I hope this works. Good thing the newer people on the Upper Level aren't turning bad yet, this stuff is hard to put on. How do women do it?"

"Just keep working, Gilbert."

Across town, in a dimly lit, run down bar and grill a quarter mile from the second G&G's, a grisly faced customer wearing a tattered goose down hunting jacket listened with indifference to the man two stools down talking into his phone. "Yes. I'm sure. I've seen the floor plan. And those two kids just went in carrying a box and some tools. They're planning some sort of grand opening soon. ... I don't know, but I'm sure the public will be invited. ... No, I still can't track down where their man, Wiggins, does his work, but I got a lead. ... Yes sir. Thank you, sir. I'll talk to you later, Mr. Devine."

During the two weeks it took Rick and Ron to prepare the second G&G's, business continued booming at the first. A constant stream of visitors came to see the suicide couple on the front seat of their car. Word of the other displays spread too. The man praying in the corner, the man in the Cord, and the man singing in the bathtub were all very popular.

Two more suicides chose G&G's perpetual display. "We're starting to get a reputation," Gary said seriously. "It's not the kind of image we want. People are starting to say we're enticing people to commit suicide. It's going to be very important that our first customer for the grand opening across town be upstanding and of sound mind."

Gilbert suggested, "Another Anton?"

"No more Antons. That worked once because we were unknown and there was nobody asking too many questions. It won't work again."

"Well then, who do we know that's OK and about to die?" Gilbert thought aloud.

Dinah offered, "We don't need a customer for the grand opening. We can keep stacking the suicides in the first G&G's and wait until we get someone right for the second. The grand opening can just be to show people the building."

Gary nodded slowly, thoughtfully. He looked at Dinah, grateful for her good advice and contributions to the business. "That's what we'll do," he said at last.

Gilbert commented, "Great idea, Dinah."

Taking a deep breath of relief, Gary said, "Now let's look over the artwork on the grand opening invitation one more time."

Dinah picked up the large yellow envelope leaning against Lester's desk and handed it to Gary. "I think we overdid the writing on this," she said. "It's too spectacular."

"You're right," Gary agreed. "We have to tone it down. Change this part 'Grand Opening Celebration!' to 'Grand Opening Ceremony.' And for God's sake, get rid of the exclamation point! We can keep the part about serving sparkling wine and hors d'oeuvres, but we should add a line about a minister saying some auspicious words or something."

"Don't you want to do that yourself?" Gilbert asked.

"No. We should have someone real do it. A real minister. Dinah, see if you can find somebody. Also, Gilbert, you were right — we should have some kind of motto we can add to the invitation. Something that states plain and clear our philosophy. G&G's Funeral Homes — Where Memory Lives in Beauty."

"Too conventional," Gilbert objected. "Cemeteries have been using that line since the Middle Ages.

G&G's—Death with a Difference."

"No."

Dinah offered, "G&G's Funeral Homes—Funerals that last a lifetime."

"No."

"I know," she protested, "I'm just thinking out loud. How about G&G's—Dignity that Lasts."

"Maybe. It's on the right track."

Gilbert's brow furled and his lips pursed. "To tell you the truth, I can't think of anything dignified to say about us. And why do people demand dignity when they die?"

"So they'll be remembered fondly," Gary answered.

"How they're buried doesn't have anything to do with that. It's how they lived that determines how they'll be remembered. What about in a war when someone gets vaporized by a bomb? There's nothing left of him, but do you think people can't have dignified memories of him?"

Dinah leaned forward toward Gilbert and said softly, "Of course you're right, Gilbert. For some people. But what about the others who need to know that someone is out here offering these services, for when their time comes."

Gilbert stared deeply into the swirl of a knot in Lester's oak desk. In a slow, quiet monotone he said, "When I go, just donate my organs to the hospital and burn the rest. It doesn't matter." He jumped to his feet and turned for the door. "Fix the invitation any way you want, I'm going to the kitchen for a drink."

Dinah turned to Gary with a silent, steady stare. After a moment she said quietly, "Gilbert has a point. We're preying on people's fear of being forgotten after they die. Just like Mr. Devine. And even if we don't put the surviving relatives into debt, we're still fostering the notion that earthly remains are somehow important."

"Not you too, Dinah. Look, it's all there in black and white in a dozen sociological studies—funerals aren't for the dead, they're for those left behind."

"Still, the people left behind think they have to treat a dead body like it was still alive. A pine box won't do, you need a varnished mahogany coffin with satin pillows. Why do we even need any kind of box at all? We're supposed to turn from ash to ash, dust to dust. Those protesters had a point too—trying to preserve dead bodies is blasphemy." Dinah stood abruptly, pushing away the invitation artwork.

"And with the suicides and Mr. Wiggins' problem with his process..." she continued, shaking her head, "and your patchwork makeup job...and now we have to stage a grand opening ceremony at a second G&G's? It's all getting to be a bit much, Gary. I'm sorry to say it, but I'm beginning to have serious doubts about what we're doing."

Dinah turned and joined Gilbert in the kitchen.

Gary banged his fist on his desk. "Damn it!" he said loudly. Out of the corner of his eye, he saw Lester. Remembering the serene countenance that had always comforted him, he turned fully toward Lester. But now the serene countenance only made him envious. "Damn it!" he repeated. He rose from his chair, picking up the invitation artwork, then throwing it back down. "Damn it all, those two," he muttered as he stormed out of the office into the kitchen.

When he entered, Gilbert and Dinah broke their hushed conversation in mid-sentence. Gary grabbed a glass from the counter and sat down at the table, in front of the bottle of tonic water. He said, "OK. You guys might be right, but what are we going to do? We've got all our money invested in this business and a lot of people counting on us. We can't quit now."

Dinah said, "Nobody said anything about quitting. Of course we have to go on. We have no choice. It's just that Gilbert and I are starting to feel kind of funny about it."

"If we go on," Gary grumbled, "you two will have to keep up a good front. You've got to at least show you're behind G&G's, especially with the grand opening next week. There'll be lots of people asking questions and scrutinizing the answers. You'll have to be sharp. We'll all have to be sharp."

Gilbert inhaled deeply and raised his glass to his mouth. He paused, then filled his mouth and swallowed hard. "I know my livelihood depends on it and I have no choice," he said, staring straight ahead. "Maybe," he said, taking a smaller sip, looking away toward the hallway leading to the office, "maybe I just need a vacation."

Dinah toyed with the glass in front of her, moving it from side to side, swirling it round and round, making a vortex of the tonic water inside. "We have no choice. I know that," she said. "But there are so many problems. Money invested, public image, our people turning green...I'm going to need a vacation too after we get the new place open."

"Just put out a good effort for the next couple weeks, then we can take a few days off and go somewhere," Gary promised.

CHAPTER 14

"It looks real good," Gary said, reading the half-page public invitation in the *Daily Daily* spread across his desk. "Ten hours to zero hour, all systems go."

"I am kind of excited, Gary," said Dinah. "I have visions of spotlights and movie stars and crystal chandeliers. I hope we have lots of people."

"That's the spirit. We'll have lots of people. Free eats and drinks always attracts a crowd." Turning to Gilbert, Gary asked, "You going to be OK?"

Gilbert gently rocked back and forth in his chair. His eyes crossed and he started making low humming sounds. The humming sounds grew in intensity and his rocking motions increased in violence. His hands gripped the arm rests of his chair and his whole body shook in a final palsy. He closed his eyes and assumed a deathly calm.

He jerked his head toward Gary and opened his eyes. In a rapid-fire staccato, he said, "Hey, I'm just in this for the money, like everyone else. I'm going to get out there and sell sell sell. Everyone who comes tonight gets a selling job from me. And I'm going to push push push it till they drop from exhaustion. Nobody gets out without signing up and leaving me a deposit."

Gilbert stood and began pacing the office, scolding Lester, admonishing him for his do-nothing attitude, ordering him to bring his whole family and his secretary and his coworkers and his dog into the G&G

gallery.

The phone rang. Dinah took Gilbert gently by the arm, guiding him out of the office. As she shut the door behind her, Gary stared after her, then at the newspaper ad, then at the ringing telephone. He picked it up slowly. "Good morning, G&G's Funeral Home," he greeted. "Mr. Westlaw, hello. Did the editor OK a piece about our grand opening? ... He did? OK, that's good. ... No, everything's fine. I just have a bit of a cold. I'm a bit under the weather. ... Thank you. ... No photographer? Oh well, try to work in the address and a good description of the building. And mention the parking. ... Oh, sorry, yes of course, Mr. Westlaw. Just write it as you see it. ... Of course, Mr. Westlaw. ... Good. ... Good. ... See you at seven."

Gary got up to check on Gilbert and tell Dinah that Mr. Westlaw's story got the go-ahead from the editor. He found Dinah sitting in the Main Viewing Room, next to Jain. "Westlaw's story is a go. Where's Gilbert?"

"I don't know. He just rushed upstairs saying he had to meet with someone. I heard the attic door open. You don't suppose he's talking to Anton, do you?"

"Not Gilbert. He's afraid of the attic. But I'll go take a look."

As Gary bounded up the stairs, Dinah called after him, "Be careful."

Gary was surprised to see the attic door ajar. He heard voices coming from atop the stairs. He quietly walked up. Gilbert was pacing in front of Anton, whose face was now noticeably wrinkled and green. "And another thing, Anton, you can't be lollygagging around up here anymore. You're in this up to your oversized red and green eyeballs. I don't want to hear any more about you just sitting here doing nothing. Get out there in the spirit world and sell sell sell!"

Gilbert ceased his wild animations while he adopted Anton's part. "Yes sir, Mr. Gilbert. I'll get on it right away. G&G's is the best thing to happen to funerals since people started dying. You're absolutely right, Mr. Gilbert. I'll get all my spirit friends to work on it right away."

Gilbert resumed his pacing, shaking his finger in Anton's face. "And another thing: if any of your spirit friends don't like what we're doing, you tell them we don't need any self righteous foggy apparitions telling us what to do. Got it?"

He skipped and danced around Anton, then broke into a song, singing in a squeaky falsetto, "I'm a foggy apparition in an onion patch, an onion patch, an onion patch. I'm a foggy apparition in an onion patch..."

Gary cleared his throat. "Hey Gilbert, are you OK?"

"I'm better than OK, I'm great!" Gilbert shouted, still skipping and dancing. "I'm the greatest funeral salesman in the world. In the whole world. In this world and the next. I got connections. Ask Anton."

"Did Anton tell you that this type of business requires a soft sell?"

"He told me. I'm going to soft sell those bastards

till they turn to putty in my hands," he said, making wild pantomime motions of shaping putty. His pantomimes became more exaggerated. He violently pounded and stretched the putty, throwing it on the floor, stomping on it, jumping up and down on it like he was killing a giant cockroach. "Everybody's going to be buried at G&G's. No exceptions, no excuses," he cried in a hoarse, manic scream. "And damn their souls to hell if they go anywhere else."

Gary looked across the attic, then from one corner to the other, then at Anton, at Gilbert, at the vast empty space around them. Although it was daytime, the attic was dark, and it invited uninhibited behavior. On an impulse, Gary bounded over and stomped on the putty. "Take that you sinful wretches," he shouted, letting himself get caught up in Gilbert's hysteria. "Be buried by us or be damned."

Gilbert took hold of Gary's hands and they played ring around the rosey, singing, "We're foggy apparitions, filled with great ambitions. Ashes, ashes, green skin and all."

They danced up and down the attic, leaping and pirouetting, venturing into the darkest corners of the attic, defying the spirits to do their worst, laughing at them, taunting them, finally falling to the dusty floor, exhausted.

After catching their breath, Gary and Gilbert looked at Anton then at each other, then let out a hearty laugh. They rose, dusted themselves off, smoothed their hair with their hands, and, looking abnormally normal, went back downstairs and rejoined Dinah in the Main Viewing Room.

Dinah studied them with concern. But Gary and Gilbert paid her no heed. She hadn't been exorcised.

People started arriving shortly after seven. First Mr. Westlaw. Then friends and relatives. When Rick and Ron's mother and father arrived, Rick poured them drinks while Ron offered a bowl of nuts. Gary approached, all smiles and handshakes. "Ken. Jan. Your two sons here have been instrumental in our success. They're really doing a great job. Dinah will have to start training them in more important duties, what with two homes to run and all."

Ken said, "We're glad you gave them a chance." He turned to his twin sons, putting his arm around Jan. "You two kids have done a great job fixing up this place. It really looks good. If you learn all you can here, you'll go far."

Real guests started to arrive. First, a few hungry and thirsty passersby who tried to hide the reason they had come by asking simple questions. "How long have you been in business? How many people have you got? Aren't you afraid of ghosts?"

A few relatives of people interred at the first G&G's arrived. Madam Kitty came, along with a legion of Jain's followers. Relatives of the man in the bathtub announced to all they met who they were. A florist walked in delivering a beautiful heart-shaped wreath with 'Best of Luck, Congratulations' spelled out in rose buds. The card was signed by the associates of Tony Bill. It said, "We like your style. Hope to do business with you again soon."

Gary stood in the middle of the crowd, toasting frequently with well-wishers, bantering with friends and relatives, smiling and joking, enjoying the success of the grand opening.

Then, in an instant, his smile faded, and he froze, his heart jumping to his throat. He watched in horror as, on the other side of the room, an old man wearing a thirty-year-old suit emptied a glass of sparkling wine into his mouth. Gary excused himself and searched the room for Gilbert, spotting him talking expansively to a pretty follower of Jain. Gary tried to motion to him, but couldn't get his attention. He approached from the girl's blind side, catching Gilbert's eye.

"Ahh, here's Mr. Colbert, the real brains behind G&G's," Gilbert said. "Gary, meet Aura Lee, a friend of Jain."

Gary stood speechless for a moment. The large crystal earrings peeking from between wisps of Aura Lee's long, ash blond hair reflected the brilliant purple haze from her sequined poncho. The effect was stunning. "I'm very pleased to meet you, Aura Lee," he stammered. "Jain is a favorite of ours at G&G's."

"Gilbert was just telling me you plan to dedicate a room to Jain so her friends can be near her when they pass," she said in a soft, even voice.

Gary coughed. "Yes, well, it was Gilbert's idea. But we want it to be something special. That's why we won't offer the Jain C'mor Room until everything's just right. It may take some time. Excuse me," he said, turning to Gilbert. "Gilbert, the president of the local Chamber of Commerce wants to get his picture with both of us. Could I drag you away for a moment?" Turning back to Aura Lee, he apologized, "This will only take a minute."

When they were out of earshot, Gary whispered, "Hey Gilbert, cute chick!"

"Yeah, isn't she something?"

"Yeah, she sure is," Gary said, turning to take another look at her. "But get your mind back on business. Did you know Wiggins is here?"

"I asked her out," Gilbert said, "but she said no, the time isn't right."

"Gilbert. Did you hear me? Wiggins is here!"

"What? Wiggins? Here?" Gilbert said, his eyes darting around the room. "He must have seen the invitation in the paper. I didn't invite him. Where is he?"

"He's over by the wine table. We got to keep an eye on him. Make sure he doesn't say anything. Make sure he doesn't get drunk. Make sure he knows about Westlaw."

Gary turned, straight into Mr. Westlaw's path. "Ah, and here are the two entrepreneurial geniuses themselves," Mr. Westlaw said. "You certainly got a good turnout tonight. I'd like just a couple more details for the story. My editor likes me to sprinkle in a few facts now and then," he chuckled.

Gary looked past Westlaw's head to check on Mr. Wiggins. He didn't like what he saw. Mr. Wiggins was talking to a much younger man, whose pale, somber face, dark blue tailor-made three-piece suit, and stiff, correct manner bore all the indications of a mortician. Gary said to Mr. Westlaw, "Gilbert can fill you in on everything. He's handled most of the arrangements for the second G&G's."

But before Gary could excuse himself, Mr. Westlaw said, "But I have questions about both the first and the second G&G's. Just a few details and something quotable from each of you. First, how long have you been in business? How many people do you got? Don't you worry about ghosts?"

Gary watched as the mortician leaned toward Mr. Wiggins, putting his hand on Mr. Wiggins' back, whispering something to him. Whatever he said made Mr. Wiggins jump back with a start before taking a half step back toward the mortician to hear more. Gary said, "Please Mr. Westlaw, I was just on my way to the pantry to check the temperature of the next case of wine. And from the looks of things, we're going to need it soon. Gilbert knows all these details much better than I do. I'll be back in just a minute. That'll give me some time to think of something really quotable for your story."

Gary saw the mortician insert a business card inside a napkin, which he left on the table in front of Mr. Wiggins. Mr. Wiggins looked over his shoulder and picked up the napkin, using it to wipe the base of his wine glass. He stuffed his hand into his pants pocket, napkin and all. The mortician nodded discreetly and silently moved away, dancing through the crowd toward the front door. Like an angel of death, he seemed to leave a dark trail that lingered long after he disappeared.

Mr. Westlaw stretched a crick in his neck, just far enough to see that Mr. Wiggins was standing alone. "Whatever you like, Mr. Colbert. I'll be here for another ten minutes or so, then I have to get the story to the editor."

Gary took his leave and approached Mr. Wiggins, who seemed absorbed eyeballing Gilbert's new acquaintance. Gary said, "Mr. Wiggins. Good to see you."

Mr. Wiggins jumped. If there had been any wine left in his glass, it would have spilled. "Oh, hi. I'm just standing here enjoying the spread. These are tasty hors d'oeuvres. Who's that girl standing over there?"

"Her name is Aura Lee. She's a follower of Jain. I'll introduce you to her if you like."

"By all means."

"First, though," Gary said, scratching his eye, "I'd like to apologize for not calling with an invitation for tonight's grand opening. It was kind of a last minute thing. We're very glad you could make it, though."

"Oh that's all right, Sonny," Mr. Wiggins smiled. "I thought it was kind of classy how you did let me know, getting the newspaper with the invitation announcement delivered right to my door. When I saw the paper on my porch, though, I got to tell you, I thought it was a mistake." Mr. Wiggins chuckled. "I haven't subscribed to a newspaper in ages. That Brenda Starr in the comics is still one nice cookie. Uh...did you get me a paid subscription for the rest of the year?"

Gary hesitated. "Yes. Yes, we did. If there's any problem with the subscription, let me know. Uh, Mr. Wiggins, I thought I recognized that man you were just talking to. I can't place him, though. Who was he?"

Mr. Wiggins stammered, "Who? What man? The one I was just talking to? I don't know. I never saw him before in my life. He just said he was an old friend of the family. I don't know his name. Maybe Gilbert would know."

"I'll go check," Gary said coolly. He nodded stiffly and left. Mr. Wiggins hadn't answered well enough to receive an introduction to Aura Lee.

Gary walked bruskly through the crowd to Dinah, who was at the door greeting people. Taking over her post, he told her, "Go keep Wiggins busy. Try to find out who he was talking to. That guy in the fancy suit. Did you see him?"

"He looked like a mortician. Do you want me to ask Mr. Wiggins?"

"No, don't do that. I just asked. Wiggins lied. Just go check him out. Take him in the back and try to get him drunk. He has a business card in his pants pocket I'd like to see. Tell him he can spend the night at our place. Pick his pocket if you can."

"I'm not going to pick his pocket, Gary."

"All right. Just do whatever you can."

Mr. Wiggins smiled warmly as Dinah approached. He immediately began talking, dominating the conversation with disjointed comments about the weather, the hors d'oeuvres, the county road commission, anything trivial. In desperation, Dinah picked up a cracker, dipped it in sour cream, and dropped it in the cuff of Wiggins' pants. "Oh, I'm so sorry, Mr. Wiggins. Hurry, come quickly into the back and take your pants off. I'll wash that spot out before it sets. I'm so sorry."

Mr. Wiggins patted Dinah's shoulder. "Oh that's all right, honey," he said. "This is just an old suit. I'm going to have to get a much better one soon. I really must be going now, anyway. I've got another suicide waiting for processing tonight. Good night, and thanks for the party." Seeing Gary stationed at the front door, he added, "Dinah dear, I'd like to go out the back and measure the rear entrance one more time. I've got to get the right size packing crates for deliveries."

"Why of course, Mr. Wiggins. Right this way," Dinah sighed, escorting Mr. Wiggins through the crowd to the back door. "Mr. Wiggins, you don't need to buy a new suit," she said, pulling the cuff of his coat, slipping behind him to measure the width of his shoulders. "I could refit this one for you. It wouldn't be difficult at all. And your pants just need a little tightening here in the pocket area," she said, slipping her hand into his pocket, pretending to gauge how big a tuck it would need, grasping the paper napkin with her fingertips.

Mr. Wiggins turned quickly. He slapped his hand over his pocket, holding it tightly, leaving just enough slack to allow Dinah's hand to emerge empty. "No, no, no, Dinah, dear," he laughed. "I'm afraid this old suit just isn't worth all that trouble. Just look at how worn and baggy it is. Thanks anyway. Good night, hon."

When everyone had left, and Rick and Ron were busy cleaning up, Gary, Gilbert and Dinah held their first business meeting in the office of the second G&G's. Gilbert asked, "Well, what's going on with Wiggins?"

"I don't know," Gary answered. "But he was acting pretty strange. Neither of you sent him a newspaper subscription, did you?"

"No."

"No."

"Someone did. That's how he found out about the grand opening ceremony tonight. What did you find out, Dinah?"

"Nothing. He was evasive. Sorry I couldn't get that card from his pocket. I tried. He did say something strange, though. He said he would be getting a new suit soon. What in the world would someone like Mr. Wiggins need a new suit for?"

"The one he was wearing must have been left over from when he was a funeral home operator," Gary noted.

Gilbert observed, "Remember when he was over to see the Perpetual Garden? He mentioned that he missed the funeral home business. Do you suppose he's up to something?"

Gary frowned. Dinah raised her eyebrow. Gilbert stared into the swirl of a knot in the office door.

Back at the first G&G's the next morning Gary, Gilbert and Dinah pored through the newspaper. Gary read the first section and the business section, Gilbert read the entertainment and sports sections, Dinah read the fashion and editorial sections. They traded sections. They traded sections again. The story of their grand opening was nowhere.

Gary stood up angrily, hurling the fashion section across the office. "Not one word! Nothing! All that trouble and no newspaper coverage. What do they think this is? I'm going to call that rag and find out why they didn't run our story."

Gary got the number for the city desk from the masthead on page three. As he was dialing, Gilbert said, "Don't make it sound like we're begging for coverage. Be cool about it, don't make us sound desperate."

"Don't worry, I'll handle it."

Halfway through the fourth ring, a harried voice answered, "*Daily Daily*. City."

"Yes, is this the editor of the city desk?"

"The editor is busy. Can I help you?"

"Maybe. I was at a party last night for the grand

opening of G&G's second funeral home. There were a number of important people there and I was wondering why it didn't receive any coverage in your paper this morning."

"Last night? I don't know. I haven't heard anything about it. This is the day shift. The story might have come in on the night shift and I can't say what they decided to do with it. It might have been badly written or it might have been bumped for something more important. We only have so much space. Thanks for calling." Click.

Gary boomed into the dead connection, "Bumped for something more important? Badly written? Since when do you people know what's important? Since when do you care about bad writing? I'm canceling my subscription right now. And cancel Wiggins' too while you're at it. Idiots." Slam.

Dinah said, "Now Gary, don't get so excited. You never know about newspapers. They do things kind of funny. At least we had a good crowd last night and got some exposure that way. The newspaper really doesn't matter that much."

Gary was still fuming. "Maybe Westlaw didn't even write a story. That guy is beginning to bug me. I'm cutting off all contact with him. From now on, if we can't trust someone, we aren't going to do business with them."

Gilbert asked, "Does that include Wiggins?"

CHAPTER 15

The rash of suicides ended and a suitable candi-
date for first interee at the second G&G's was signed,
sealed and delivered. Mr. Wiggins was unusually
chipper as he wheeled the office furniture crate
through the back door and into the room where the
grand opening ceremony had been. He set the crate
down on the exact spot where he had munched hors
d'oeuvres and drank sparkling wine. He was singing
"Zippity do da" as Gary joined him. "Good morning,
Mr. Wiggins. Dinah told me you arrived. I wanted to
help carry our first interee across the threshold."

Mr. Wiggins answered cheerfully, "No problem. I
did that myself."

Dinah joined them, eager to see the new arrival.
"Oh Mr. Wiggins, she's perfect."

"Thank you, ma'am. I thought so, too. Here's her
accessories, I'll leave it to you to arrange them. Mind if
I come back tonight for the first service?"

"Of course not, Mr. Wiggins," Dinah answered
warmly. "You're always welcome. There's coffee in the
office if you'd like to take a break."

"No thank you, ma'am. I got to be on my way. I'll
see you tonight." Turning to Gary, he asked, "Do you
need any help with the service tonight, young man?"

"Well, to tell the truth, the family wants to keep
the service small."

"OK, that's no problem. I'll just stay in the background and pretend I'm the janitor. I just want to

observe a bit. See ya."

That evening, as Gary stood off to the side a respectful distance from the minister, he saw Mr. Wiggins enter and take a seat in the back row. Gary broke into a cold sweat—Westlaw was leaning against the back wall. Gary waited until the minister cued everyone to bow their heads before discreetly exiting to find Dinah.

"Dinah, how did Westlaw get in? Did you or Gilbert tell him about tonight?"

"I didn't tell him. Gilbert might still be at the first G&G's. I'll give him a call."

Gary rejoined the service just as the guests took up hymn books. He took his place off to the side of the minister and clasped his hands and bowed his head as he mouthed the words.

After the hymn, while a close friend of the deceased read a Bible verse, Dinah silently entered the room and signaled to Gary that Gilbert hadn't told Mr. Westlaw about the night's service. She turned her head and acted surprised when her eyes met Westlaw's. Dinah made her way unobtrusively across the room to him and whispered, "Mr. Westlaw, how nice to see you."

"Hi. I read about tonight's service in the obit section of the paper. I read them religiously now. I didn't want to miss this. It's kind of historic, the first interee at the first new branch and all. Anyway, I got some news for you and Gary and Gilbert that I think will be of interest."

"Gilbert is manning the fort at the first, but I'm sure Gary and I will be delighted to see you after the service."

When the service was over, Mr. Wiggins rose and took a step toward Gary. But the minister had already turned to Gary to shake hands and exchange pleasantries. Mr. Wiggins caught Gary's eye and nodded good-night. As he turned to leave, he came face to face with Mr. Westlaw, who quickly turned away, pretending not to know who he was. Gary saw it all.

After the funeral party had left, Gary called from across the room, "Mr. Westlaw. Dinah says you have something important to tell us. Why don't you step into the office; Dinah is waiting there for us."

In the office, Gary pulled a bottle of brandy and two glasses from his bottom desk drawer. He kept one glass and handed the other to Dinah. "Will you join us, Mr. Westlaw?"

"Yes. Thank you."

Gary grudgingly took another glass from the drawer, intentionally smudging the inside rim with his thumb. He set it down in front of Mr. Westlaw. After pouring his and Dinah's drink, Gary set the bottle next to Mr. Westlaw's empty glass. As Mr. Westlaw poured himself a drink, Gary asked, "Mr. Westlaw, there's something I'm curious about. Did you know the newspaper didn't run your story about our grand opening?"

Mr. Westlaw stammered, "Oh, yes. Apparently it

was pulled at the last minute. Oh well, that's the newspaper business. But never mind that. I got something that's really going to interest you. Just yesterday I heard through the grapevine that your competition, Devine Funeral Home, has taken your perpetual display idea and come up with their own version. What they're doing is giving everybody the conventional service, but then they take a holographic picture of the deceased lying in their casket and display it in a special room. They call it the Hall of Holograms."

Gary set his glass on his desk, pausing to think before responding. 'Competition from Devine. Damn. Customers who might hesitate about G&G's form of perpetual display might go for a hologram. Damn. Why didn't I think of it. It has to be cheaper and easier than what we go through. And holograms don't turn green.'

Gary asked, "Is this Hall of Holograms open to the public?"

"Yes. 9 to 5 Monday through Friday. No appointment needed, just walk in."

Gary picked up the bottle of brandy. "This is interesting news, Mr. Westlaw. Can I pour you another drink?"

When Mr. Westlaw left, Gary phoned Gilbert. "Gilbert, Westlaw was just here and he told me that Devine has started his own form of perpetual display. He uses holograms. ... Yes, they're on display right in his funeral home. It's open to the public, same as us. ...

No, I don't care if he recognizes us. He sent someone over here for our grand opening, so we'll go over there and reconnoiter his operation. Dinah wants to check some things at the first, so we'll see you there early tomorrow."

The next morning, Gary felt a sense of ease being back at the first G&G's amid all the familiar faces. While Dinah went to check on things in the Annex, Gary relaxed at his old desk in the office waiting for Gilbert. A copy of the *New York Times* lay open in front of Lester, and Gary imagined Lester grumbling about the national debt and giving offhand tips on good stocks. "Here's a good one for you, Sonny. Xerox is selling at 5 1/8. IBM is at 3 1/4, up a 1/4. Devine Funeral Home is at 68 5/8, up 10 3/8 from yesterday."

Gary rose and aimlessly wandered into the Main Viewing Room, casually checking on who might need fresh makeup. "So what if Devine is at 68 5/8, up 10 3/8 from yesterday," he told Jain. "We still have the Perpetual Garden."

The sound of the back door banging against the wall told Gary that Gilbert had arrived. "We're up the creek if Wiggins turns on us," Gary said, entering the kitchen. "You don't suppose he's found a cure for the green problem and he's holding out on us, do you?"

Gilbert finished pouring a cup of coffee. "Good morning," he said. "It's possible, but let's not get paranoid about it. The makeup seems to be holding OK, so for now let's trust Wiggins to come up with a permanent solution. Maybe we better call him and prod him on a little."

"I'd like to check out Devine first, as soon as Dinah gets in from the Annex. Then we'll talk to Wiggins."

Dinah entered the back door. "The Cord has dust on it again," she stated. "And Mrs. Perkins looks kind of funny around the mouth." Dinah's eyes widened in horror. "Is that what will happen to our people?" she asked.

Gary and Gilbert looked at each other, realizing they had forgotten to put makeup on the interees in the Annex. Gary tried to sound calm. "It's a slow, gradual process, Dinah," he said. "Gilbert and I have it under control—we've been dabbing a little skin toner here, a little blush there. It'll hold till Wiggins comes up with a permanent solution."

Gilbert said, "I'll dust off the Cord and take care of Mrs. Perkins as soon as we get back. Don't worry, Dinah."

Dinah stared wordlessly, first at Gary, then at Gilbert. "I hope you and Mr. Wiggins know what you're doing. Makeup doesn't sound like much of an answer. It sounds like putting a Band Aid on a hemorrhage."

Gary put his arm around her waist. "Don't worry, Gilbert and I are working with Wiggins. We'll find a permanent solution soon."

"Sure we will, Dinah," Gilbert added. "It's only a matter of time."

As Gary and Gilbert drove into the parking lot of Devine Funeral Home, they spotted an attendant putting little magnet-mounted flags on a long line of cars. Gilbert said to Gary, "Good. Devine is busy with a funeral. We can sneak in, check things out, then leave."

"I was kind of hoping to see Devine. He might let something slip."

Walking to the door, Gary called over to the attendant, "One of our friends was buried from here a few days ago. We're from out of town and didn't get a chance to make the service. We understand the family has installed him in the Hall of Holograms. Could you direct us?"

The attendant pointed and said, "Just go in that door over there and up the stairs on the left. You'll see signs."

Gilbert asked the attendant, "This Hall of Holograms, it's something new, isn't it?"

"Brand new. They just started it last week. It's pretty neat."

Gary and Gilbert approached the heavy white door. It opened as Gary reached for the doorknob. The angel of death beckoned them in. "Are you here for the O'Rourk service?"

Gary sensed the angel recognized them. "No. We're interested in seeing the Hall of Holograms."

The angel swallowed hard and shifted his feet. "I'll escort you," he said, motioning another attendant to take the door, whispering something in his ear before leading Gary and Gilbert upstairs. At the top of the stairs he turned and abruptly asked, "How did you hear about the Hall of Holograms? You're in the funeral home business, perhaps?"

"Yes, we're with G&G's Funeral Homes," Gary said, flashing the angel a wide smile. "We always try to stay abreast of what's happening in the industry."

The angel nodded and turned, silently leading Gary and Gilbert to the Hall of Holograms. "Please feel free to look around," he said. "I'll have my father, Mr. John Devine, join you to answer any questions just as soon as the O'Rourk service is over."

The angel bowed politely and walked slowly back downstairs. Gary and Gilbert entered the Hall of Holograms. Before looking around the room, Gilbert said, "That was Devine's son."

"Does that surprise you?"

"Yes. I didn't know Devine had a son. I didn't think he was able. I thought his sperm must be full of formaldehyde or something."

Gary laughed. He had thought the same thing.

Gary and Gilbert turned to soak in the ambience of the Hall of Holograms. The decor of the large, drab room was dominated by a red carpet faded pink by the sun. Several brown stains near the only window marked where pots of flowers used to thrive. The carpet's pile was matted tightly in spots. One pattern of spots indicated where a couch used to set, another, a filing cabinet. The only furniture left in the room were two overstuffed Naugahyde easy chairs and a matching loveseat with broken springs.

The wallpaper was clean, but like the carpet, faded. As yet, only four members had been inducted into the Hall. Each was framed in cheap, bronze-colored aluminum. The quality of the holograms was not good. Gary and Gilbert moved their heads back and forth and to and fro, trying to make out the details and get the 3D effect.

"This is pretty crappy," Gilbert said.

"It doesn't look like much, does it?"

"I wonder how he's marketing it?" Gilbert asked. "I haven't seen any advertisements or news stories. He must be selling it to people as they come in."

"Maybe it's part of the package deal now," Gary guessed.

"Who are these people, anyway? They should have little plaques."

"That's not a bad idea. I mean, for us. A little plaque for everyone at G&G's telling the interee's name and birth and death dates, just like a tombstone."

"We should have thought of that before, Gary. It would be impossible to go through the files and match up the names and faces. Only the relatives know who is who now. Except for a couple, like Lester and Jain. Who is the man in the bathtub, anyway? Do you remember?"

Gary thought for a moment. "I don't know. Maybe Dinah knows."

"I suppose we could at least get Lester one of the things executives put on their desks with their names on them."

"Go ahead."

"Do you want one?"

"I'm not dead yet."

Gary took a last glance around Devine's shoddy Hall of Holograms, preparing to leave, relieved G&G's had less to worry about than he had feared. He made a half turn for the door, but stopped when Gilbert leaned closer, and in a conspiratorial tone whispered, "Hey Gary, I was serious before when I said to donate my organs to someone and burn the rest. I don't want any of this nonsense for me. What about you?"

"I haven't thought about it. I don't know," Gary said, pausing to think. "Donating your organs sounds like a nice idea. At least part of you is still alive."

"I don't care about that," Gilbert said. "When I'm dead, I want to be dead, period. I was just thinking of helping someone else."

"I never knew you to be so altruistic. When did that start?" Gary asked.

"I guess working in this business has given me a new perspective. But do me a favor, don't tell anyone what a good guy I am. I don't want people expecting too much from me."

"If you want your organs transplanted, there's some form you have to fill out. Better check with the secretary of state's office. And don't worry, Gilbert, I'll have you cremated."

Gary's face lit up. "Hey! I'll cremate you and put your ashes in a little jar and display it at G&G's. And we can put up a little plaque saying you were one of the founders of G&G's. It's cheaper than an oil painting."

"No," Gilbert responded. "That would be a bad idea. People would ask why one of the founders chose to be cremated and not perpetually displayed. It would be bad for business."

Gary couldn't dim the devilish glint in his eyes as he tried to suppress the thought of perpetually displaying Gilbert. The more he tried to suppress the idea, and the variety of poses he and Mr. Wiggins could put Gilbert in, the more he felt his face reveal what he was thinking. Gilbert took a step back, and stared blankly at Gary. Gary's face reddened and he broke into a wide, thin smile. Gilbert's horrified reaction forced Gary to tightly purse his lips to keep from laughing out loud. It didn't work. Tiny bursts of air seeped through, making whoopee cushion noises. Gilbert warned, "Remember, you might go first."

"I have Dinah to make sure I don't get put on perpetual display," Gary said, laughing.

Gilbert took another step back, turning his head from side to side, gaping his mouth in frustration. Gary sensed the joke had gone far enough. "Don't worry, Gilbert," he said sincerely, "I promise not to put you on perpetual display. I'll do whatever you want."

Mr. Devine waltzed into the room, his suit coat off, tie loosened and shirt sleeves rolled up. He smiled broadly as he briskly walked up to Gary and Gilbert, extending his hand in an expansive gesture. "I'm happy to have two such esteemed colleagues visit my

Hall of Holograms," he said. "I must admit, I got the idea from your operation. Candidly, what do you think?"

Mr. Devine didn't make any indication that he recognized them as former clients. Gary decided to let sleeping dogs lie. He was caught off guard by Mr. Devine's openness and cheer. While Gary tried to get a bearing on the situation, Gilbert shook Mr. Devine's hand and said, "Thank you very much, Mr. Devine. I'm Gilbert Jackson, and this is Gary Colbert. You've heard of G&G's Funeral Homes?" he asked innocently.

"Yes. Yes of course. And to be frank, I've been following you right from the start. At first, I had reservations about what you were doing. Several of us at the more traditional homes were very concerned that you would reflect badly on the industry. But I think there's been a change in how we feel. After all, who can argue with success?"

Gary was still off guard. He feared Mr. Devine would try to sign them up to join some sort of funeral directors association where they would have to pay dues and attend meetings. "It's been hard, but we're happy with the results so far," he said cautiously. "I think Gilbert and I can understand your initial concern."

"Well then, tell me," Mr. Devine said, gesturing around him, "what do you think of my Hall of Holograms? I have a brother-in-law who does the holograms. Keeps it all in the family that way."

Gilbert had warmed right up to the new Mr. Devine. "This is a great idea," he said. "I think it might catch on. And when it does, I can tell you right now, your trouble will be finding enough wall space."

"It's just at the experimental stage right now," Mr. Devine replied, apologizing for the spartan decor, "at least until we see how the market responds. It's certainly not a large-scale display operation like G&G's, that's for sure." Mr. Devine paused, then added, "I wish I could figure out how you're able to manage your perpetual display magic."

Gary answered, "Well, we all have our little trade secrets."

"Yes, of course." Mr. Devine looked at his watch. "Well, business goes on. I'm glad to have finally met you. Feel free to look around, and maybe, if you don't mind, I'd like to pay G&G's a little visit some time."

Gilbert invited, "Drop in any time. At either G&G's. I'll be spending most of my time at our first home and Gary at the second, but we're usually all together at the first on Friday mornings."

"Thank you very much, Mr. Jackson. Mr. Colbert."

Mr. Devine smiled warmly and walked quickly out the door, rolling down his sleeves as he went.

Gary and Gilbert took one last look around the Hall of Holograms. Gary said, "It looks like crap now, but I think Devine just might pull off something big with this idea. And if it catches on, we're in trouble."

"Remember, we're already in trouble," Gilbert said. "We have another home to fill, payments to make, the green problem, and if we lose Wiggins, we lose everything. I don't know about you, Gary, but I'm worried."

"Wiggins is our biggest worry. The rest of the problems we can deal with ourselves. As soon as we get back to the office, I'm going to give that buzzard a call. We have to find out where he stands."

Mr. Devine smiled happily at Miss Krofchak as he skipped into his office, where he adjusted his tie and suitcoat for a meeting with his lawyer and his CPA.

Gary strode determinedly through the open office door back at the first, with Gilbert close at his heels. The sight of Rick leaning back in Gilbert's chair, with his feet on Gilbert's desk, and a smile across his face made Gary stop in his tracks. Gilbert bumped into him. Gary turned to Gilbert and smiled, nodding toward the daydreaming Rick. "Uhm," Gary coughed.

"Oh, you're back!" Rick said, jumping to his feet. "Dinah went to the second with Ron to meet some lady who wants to be buried there. I've been taking calls while she's gone."

"Anyone call?" asked Gary.

"No."

"OK then, keep up the good work."

Gilbert smiled and walked past Gary, telling Rick, "You better go dust the Cord. Let us know when you're finished."

"Yes sir."

Gary took a seat at his old desk and looked over at Lester, envious once again of his serenity, yet comforted by his presence. Gary sighed and picked up the phone. "Well, what can I say to Wiggins?" he asked Gilbert, turning toward Lester to include him in the conversation. "Any ideas?"

"I don't know," Gilbert answered. "Just tell him the makeup is working fine, for now. But it won't hold forever."

Gary dialed. Wiggins' phone rang once and immediately went into voicemail. Gary hung up. "I don't want to leave him a message unless I have to."

Rick came back looking puzzled. He asked, "There wasn't that much dust on the Cord, but one of the ladies in there is looking kind of spooky. What's wrong with her?"

In unison Gary and Gilbert said, "Nothing."

Gilbert continued, "It must be the lighting in there. We'll check it out later, don't worry about it. You can go get started on the yard work now."

After Rick had left, Gary said to Gilbert, "Stay here with Rick. I'm going over to the second to help Dinah."

"Tell her about Devine. See what she thinks."

"Ok. Remember to fix up the people in the Annex."

"Don't worry, I will."

At the second, Gary told Dinah all about the new Mr. Devine and the crappiness of his Hall of Holograms. Dinah shrugged. "Maybe he's finally accepted G&G's and perpetual display," she suggested. "Maybe he wants to bury the hatchet."

Gary regarded Dinah's comments, then, in an affected Charlie Chan accent, said, "Man may bury hatchet to hide murder weapon."

CHAPTER 16

"Hey Dinah, can you put a head on this?"

"Sure. Gilbert? Can I warm yours?" Dinah asked as she topped off Gary's coffee.

"Yeah, thanks. Damn fine coffee, Dinah."

"So anyway," Gary continued, "it seems we're all agreed that we'll play down the part about visitors welcome in our ads for a while."

"Yeah, I just wish I hadn't told Devine we're all together here Friday mornings. Hey you don't suppose he would come today, do you?" asked Gilbert.

"He might," Gary answered, blowing on his coffee to cool it. "I hope not, though. I'd like to tidy up a bit before we let him see our operation."

Gilbert froze and his face took on a ghostly white pallor. "Oh God. I forgot to fix up the people in the Annex!"

Dinah steadied the coffee carafe with both hands to keep from dropping it. Gary stopped blowing into his cup and was greeted by the distorted reflection of his open mouth as the waves in his coffee subsided. Before either could speak, the sound of the front door opening echoed through to the kitchen area. The sound of Mr. Devine's voice followed. "Good morning. Mister Colbert? Mister Jackson?"

"Quick," Dinah said, "you two go take care of it while I stall him. I'll give him a tour."

"We can't. I can't. The makeup is in our office," Gilbert whispered loudly. He jumped up from the table, knocking over his chair with a loud crash.

"Just do it!" Dinah ordered. She unclenched her fist and turned to intercept Mr. Devine.

"What'll we do?" asked Gilbert. "What if he wants coffee? We should have made more coffee."

"Forget the coffee. Pick up the chair and keep away from the door so he doesn't see you," Gary whispered. "When Dinah gets him upstairs we'll rush into the office, grab the makeup, get our asses out to the Annex and fix those people up...fast!"

Dinah approached the front door and greeted her visitor, "Good morning. You must be Mr. Devine."

"Yes, and this is my wife, Hillary," he said, gesturing toward the heavy set woman peeking into the Main Viewing Room. "We just wanted to come pay a little social visit. Hillary...Hillary?"

Hillary turned to look at Dinah. "Good morning. I...I...I'm...,"

Dinah recognized the reaction and said assuringly, "Good morning, Hillary. I'm so glad you came for a visit. I'm Dinah, the office manager at G&G's, and Gary's wife." Turning to Mr. Devine, she said, "Gary and Gilbert are just attending to a little detail. They'll be out shortly. In the meantime, I want to give you a little tour. Follow me, please."

Hillary was first to venture a few steps inside. Mr. Devine just stood in the doorway, longer than anyone Dinah had seen, his awe-struck steadily deteriorating into dumbstruck. Hillary motioned with her head, and he responded with a few short steps.

Dinah followed Mr. Devine's gaze to an interee who stood in Anton's former resting place. Capt. Harold Hillbury, besides being a police reservist, was a member of an amateur barbershop quartet. He stood wearing a red and white striped coat, one arm uplifted like a fencer, the other, outstretched, holding a straw hat. An imaginary final note seemed to reverberate from his open mouth. Dinah explained nervously, "The burial poses and costumes at G&G's are chosen by the interees themselves, or their families."

Mr. Devine blinked quickly a few times. "Yes. Yes, of course," he said, turning to Dinah, "I see. I agree. Very imaginative. I'm sure everyone is very happy with the results."

Dinah escorted Hillary and Mr. Devine through the Main Viewing Room to the Upper Level, into the Richelieu Room. Mrs. Stoner and Mr. Peterson sat against the far wall, by the window. Their poses and the tilt of their heads created the impression they were snubbing the praying gangster in the corner.

Dinah overcame her nervousness and said, "Seated by the window, we have Mr. Peterson. His son is writing a book based on Mr. Peterson's wartime London stories."

"Very good. Very good," Mr. Devine said, looking around the room in wonder.

Hillary said, "I must take a peek at your man in the bathtub." She took her reluctant husband by the elbow and led him down the hall to the bathroom.

Mr. Devine stood in the bathroom doorway, averting his eyes. Hillary turned to Dinah and bubbled, "I just love it. I love to see men bathe. They're just like little boys, playing with the soap suds and getting so squeaky clean without even knowing it. John, dear, isn't this so exciting?"

Mr. Devine opened his mouth, but no words came out. Finally he stammered, "I understand you've also opened a new room, the Perpetual Garden, and an Annex."

"That's right. The Perpetual Garden is on the Promenade Level."

Dinah took the Devines back downstairs, through the Main Viewing Room toward the office and the stairway beyond leading to the Perpetual Garden. She paused at the open office door. Gary had just sat down and grabbed clumsily at his pocket for a pen to hold. Gilbert slammed his bottom desk drawer and sat upright and alert. "Gary, Gilbert, look who dropped by for a visit. John and Hillary Devine."

Gilbert, oblivious to the smear of blush on his collar, rushed from behind his desk to shake Mr. Devine's hand. "Nice to see you again, Mr. Devine."

"John, please."

"John. And it's so nice to finally meet you too, Hillary."

"It's nice to finally meet you, Mr. Jackson."

"Gilbert, please. And this is Gary Colbert, my partner."

"Gary," Gary said, taking Hillary's hand. "Nice to meet you."

Dinah said, "I was just taking the Devines to see the Perpetual Garden, and the Annex. Perhaps you two would like to take them?"

Gary said, "Our pleasure. Let's see the Annex first. This way, please."

Gary noticed Mr. Devine looking past him into the office at Lester. "And this is Lester. He chose to be interred right here in our own office. And I might add, we're very happy he did. We've come to think of him as..." Gary scratched under his eye. "...a silent partner."

Dinah rolled her eyes, and slapped Gary's arm as he and Gilbert walked past her to lead the Devines to the Annex.

Outside, between the house and the Annex, Gary waited while Mr. Devine paused to breathe deeply the fresh air, and to stare for a moment through the tree tops into the endless expanse of sky. "It turned out to be a beautiful day, didn't it," Gary said, taking a step forward.

"Yes. Yes. Beautiful," Mr. Devine answered, following Gary's lead with a tentative step toward the Annex. "Tell me," he asked, looking around him, "have you made inquiries into buying adjacent property for expanded parking?"

Gilbert turned and said, "That would be a good idea. That's the one problem we have here at the first G&G's."

Mr. Devine took a few more short steps then turned toward the house. "Built in the mid Twenties, I would guess," he said. "How's the wiring? Do you have any trouble with the plumbing?"

"No problems with anything," Gilbert boasted. "The circuit breaker is of the latest design. The county put in a new storm sewer in this area just six years ago. And the streets are plowed by the city in the winter."

"It's all true," Gary said, walking ahead to hold the Annex door open. Mr. Devine stepped inside, pausing to examine the floor, walls and ceiling, saying, "Very nice. You would never know it used to be a garage. I'm very impressed."

Hillary brushed past him and stepped right up to the Cord. When she finished ogling the car's luxurious interior, she began studying the man behind the wheel. Gary worried about the makeup job he and Gilbert had performed. They weren't experts like Hillary. "Hillary, do you have any suggestions on how we can spruce up the decor in the Annex?" he asked. "That poster over there, for instance, do you think it fits?"

Hillary stepped back from the Cord and looked across to the far wall. "Well, now that you mention it, it does seem to be a distraction. Perhaps something in more muted tones. But I do love the floral arrangements."

While the Devines studied the poster and floral arrangements, Gary turned to Gilbert and made subtle pointing motions toward the door. Gilbert nodded, saying in a proud voice, "If you love the floral arrangements here, come, we'll show you the Perpetual Garden."

Not waiting for an answer, Gilbert turned and opened the Annex door, inviting the Devines back outside and onward to the fresher interees in the Perpetual Garden.

Speakers hidden behind the profusion of flora in the Perpetual Garden softly played lilting music from a looping CD system discreetly placed behind a mound of sand in the rock garden. A pair of Mr. Wiggins' brightly colored finches lit on the branch of a miniature eucalyptus tree. Not a single seam showed in the green Astroturf.

Hillary stared in revulsion at the couple on the car seat. "We did hear about that tragedy," she said. "Somehow it just doesn't seem right having them buried here on that...that car seat."

Mr. Devine reproved his wife, "Now, Hillary. We've had this discussion before. It's the credo of the funeral home operator to give everyone who can afford it a decent interment. We mustn't judge."

Gilbert added, "In this particular case, Hillary, we felt it especially important to provide a pleasant atmosphere for this couple's final resting place. It's not our business to understand why people sometimes do the things they do. We have to leave some things to God."

Hillary was humbled. "Of course, you're right. I didn't want to appear insensitive. Please forgive me."

Mr. Devine nodded absolution. Gilbert noted the

motion and followed suit.

Mr. Devine took a last, long glance around the Perpetual Garden and said, "Very impressive, sirs. You've done a fine job with your concept."

John and Hillary Devine followed Gilbert back upstairs. Before joining them, Gary looked around the Perpetual Garden one more time, then breathed a sigh of relief.

As the Devines walked past the office to the front door, Dinah emerged, smiling warmly. "I hope you've enjoyed your visit," she said.

"Oh, we've just loved it," Hillary answered.

Mr. Devine clasped his hands together and bowed. "Dinah, Gary, Gilbert," he said. "We'd like to thank you for your hospitality and for taking the time to show us your...establishment. Hillary and I would like to return your hospitality by extending an invitation to join us for cocktails and dinner Sunday evening in our home." He handed each of them calling cards with his home address and phone number. "Six o'clock?"

It was more than an invitation. It was a command appearance.

After the Devines left, Gary tried calling Mr. Wiggins again. No answer. "You don't suppose he's had a heart attack, do you?" he asked Gilbert.

Gilbert turned stone cold. "We're out of business if he did. We have to get him to teach us his process. There's too much at stake to have the whole show so dependent on one man. Maybe we can get him to train

Rick and Ron, too."

"They're not ready yet. And you and me don't have time to do Wiggins' job. And neither does Dinah."

Gilbert said, "I know, but we have to do something. You and Dinah take care of things here. I'll drive out to Wiggins' and make sure he's all right."

Dinah stepped into the office. "What's wrong with Mr. Wiggins?"

"We've been having trouble getting hold of him," Gary answered. "His line's busy all the time. We're afraid he had a heart attack and was trying to call an ambulance or something."

"I just talked to him a couple days ago. The day you two went to check out the Hall of Holograms. He said he would deliver Mrs. Spencer to the second this morning then he was going to take the weekend off and drive to the lake."

Gilbert picked up the phone and called Rick and Ron at the second.

"Good morning. G&G's Funeral Homes," Rick answered, sounding very professional.

"Rick, this is Gilbert. Did Wiggins come by this morning?"

"Yes, about an hour ago. He dropped off Mrs. Spencer and took off. Said he was going away for the weekend. We uncrated Mrs. Spencer. We're having trouble setting her up, though. She doesn't stand right. She's kind of lopsided. What do you want us to do?"

Gilbert had visited the hospital to make the arrangements with Mrs. Spencer. He was impressed by her spritely outlook and whimsical sense of humor, despite being connected to a dozen tubes and monitoring devices. She chose a curtsy as her burial pose. She told Gilbert it would served a double purpose, "I can say thanks to the world and bow out at the same time."

"Just sit tight, Rick. I'll be right over."

Gilbert said to Gary and Dinah, "Wiggins is OK. He delivered Mrs. Spencer this morning. There's a little problem with her, though. I'll go over and take care of it."

"When's the service?" Gary asked.

"This evening. I'll stay there and take care of things, Gary. You can man the first today."

"OK. Give me a call if you need any help."

Gilbert tuned his car radio to a classical music station and practiced Devine's nodding gesture while driving to the second. He hoped to use it when Rick apologized for not being able to set up Mrs. Spencer.

Two blocks from the second, he was dismayed to see a building being torn town. It made the neighborhood look bad. An allegro in Vivaldi's Flute Concerto in D on his radio seemed to sing, "Urban re-new-al isagoodthing. Urban re-new-al is agoodthing." Gilbert stopped the car, got out and took a loose brick from the pile of rubble, and continued on to the second.

He found Rick in the Sunrise Room propping up Mrs. Spencer with a broom handle. His tone was unusually gruff as he admonished, "What are you doing with that broom handle. She's not a witch."

Gilbert was disappointed when Rick explained, but did not apologize. "I'm just testing to see if we can use a table or a chair or something to lean her against."

"Never mind that. This will take care of it," he said, carrying the brick to Mrs. Spencer. He lifted her dress and placed the brick down the back of her panties. The counterweight worked like a charm.

That evening, all through the service, Gilbert hummed Vivaldi's Flute Concerto in D and nodded at the slightest provocation.

Sunday evening, Gary had to brake hard as he pulled into South Grand Maison Ct. A large sign declared it private property and a guard motioned him to stop. "Good evening, sir. May I help you?"

"We're visiting the Devines. Could you direct us to their house?"

"Your name please?"

"Gary Colbert. And this is my wife, Dinah. And this is Gilbert Jackson," he said, pointing to Gilbert in the back seat.

The guard made a tick mark on his clipboard. "Very good, Mr. Colbert. Straight ahead halfway down the block on the right. The red stone house with the marble lions in front."

Gary slowly eased away from the guard, down the narrow road and into Mr. Devine's circular cobble-stone drive. Looking up at the gargoyle rainspouts and the slate roof and the heavy copper gutters of Devine's house, he said, "This place would make a good G&G's."

"I bet they have some beautiful antiques," Dinah said eagerly. She tugged at Gary's arm, pulling him to the front door. Gary adjusted his jacket, and rang the doorbell. The deep, three-toned gong sounded at a becalming, stately pace.

There was a clicking and a fumbling and the heavy front door creaked open, its bulk dwarfing Mr. Devine. "Good evening. Come right in," he invited.

"They don't make doors like this anymore," he joked as Gary, Gilbert and Dinah entered. "You could shoot a cannon at this one and it wouldn't budge."

Gilbert said, "The whole house looks like it could take a direct hit from a Scud missile and be none the worse."

"I'm sure it could," Mr. Devine replied. "Still, Hillary and I aren't taking any chances. We have a fully-stocked, copper-lined, reinforced concrete bomb shelter in the basement."

Gary shook Mr. Devine's hand. "Beautiful house, John."

Inside, Mr. Devine let his guests pause in the spacious vestibule to admire the carved oak paneling, dazzling Tiffany lamps and gallery of oil paintings on the walls. He had often commented to Hillary that he had mixed feelings about the ostentatious decor, protesting that sometimes it was a distraction—a distraction from his own presence and purposes.

He had also commented to Hillary that he thought she should answer the door when guests arrived. But Hillary had grown up with servants answering doors and felt it just wouldn't do for the lady of the house to perform such a task. John tried for years to convince her that answering the door would allow her to give visitors a guided tour through the house; a job she was much better at than he. But she wouldn't budge. "The lady of the house never answers the door," she explained.

Mr. Devine endured the compliments Gary, Dinah and Gilbert gushed out. They were the same compliments he had heard a hundred times before. When they were over, and he always knew when they were over, Mr. Devine answered all the questions he knew would be asked. He tried hard to make his comments sound spontaneous. "The house was built in 1924 by Geoffrey Reginald Bates III, the famous industrialist who made his fortune in the automotive aftermarket. His good friend, Henry Scripps Booth, designed the structure, basing it on a medieval stone monastery he had seen during a childhood visit to Austria. The fireplace mantle, the mahogany banister leading upstairs, and several of the intricately carved wood moldings along the ceiling were taken from a house of similar design which had been damaged in World War I and was slated for demolition. Many of the furnishings and much of the artwork is from the collection of Hillary's father, the late Henry Nelson Gregor, financier, philanthropist, art historian."

Gilbert had been examining a coat of mail when he heard Mr. Devine mention the late Henry Nelson. Instinctively, he started to reach for the visor on the ornate helmet to see if the late Henry was still inside.

Mr. Devine continued, "I think Hillary is mixing us something special in the drawing room. Let's retire there," he said, leading his guests through the immense dining room with its heavy, claw-footed table and chairs.

Dinah noticed the huge table legs and imagined Mr. Wiggins using them to make burial prostheses for elephants. She was shocked at how easily Mr. Devine walked over the antique oriental rug. It was old, nearly threadbare in spots, but still beautiful. She cringed when he did an about-face, digging his heels into the rug, explaining casually, "This room is so stuffy and formal, we really don't use it much anymore."

They walked through the dining room, through an arched hallway, through another room, this one dedicated to artworks from the Impressionist school, through another hallway, which led to a set of stairs to the right, a water closet straight ahead, and the kitchen to the left. They turned left then right before reaching the kitchen, through another arched hallway, this one with a very low ceiling. The low ceiling made the contrasting high ceiling of the drawing room at the end of the hallway even more impressive.

A short step down led them into the drawing room. After they entered, Mr. Devine sealed off the hallway with a door that blended perfectly into the dark wood paneling. Another door led from the kitchen and Hillary emerged, carrying a hand-cut crystal decanter filled with an amber colored liquid. "Oh, I thought I heard voices. Has John been showing you our house?"

"Yes, Hillary. It's a beautiful house," Dinah said.

"Just beautiful," Gary answered.

"Really nice, Hillary," Gilbert said.

"Well, do come in and have a seat. I've taken the liberty of mixing up a little recipe that's been in my family for years. We call it Amber Gold. It's always a favorite."

Mr. Devine said, "It is an excellent drink. Of course, if you prefer something straight?"

"No. I can't wait to try it," Dinah said.

"Sounds exciting," Gary ventured.

"What's in it?" Gilbert asked.

"Oh, well, now...that's an old family secret," Hillary blushed. "I suppose I can tell you it's made with scotch and a steeped, strained mixture of spice and herbal flavorings. It's good for preventing a variety of ailments. And as you can see, John and I are very healthy."

Mr. Devine smiled broadly and puffed out his chest, tightening the slight paunch of his stomach. "It's the truth," he said, knocking on the dark wood paneling. "I haven't felt better in my life. Have a seat, please. Hillary, dear, I'll help you pour."

Gary, Gilbert and Dinah sat down and sampled Hillary's brew. It was delicious, and while Hillary offered a second round, Mr. Devine tried to find a common ground of interest between his guests and himself. He talked about the Tower of London and Big Ben, pointing to several enlarged framed pictures he had taken of the landmarks.

Gary mentioned Mr. Jackson's son. "He's writing a book on wartime London."

"Yes," Mr. Devine said, "Dinah told us about that. Very exciting."

Dinah said, "It's a blessing those old buildings survived the war."

Gilbert then went into an animated soliloquy on the operation of the M1 Garand. Mr. Devine showed off his collection of pistols, one dating back to the War of 1812. Gary told the story of his old ROTC small arms instructor, who could empty a clip from a .45 so rapidly it sounded like a machine gun. "Accuracy didn't matter with the old .45," he said.

On the third round of drinks, Hillary steered the conversation toward food, and they soon adjourned through the spacious kitchen with its smells and aromas to another room adjoining the kitchen. While Hillary remained in the kitchen putting the final garnishes on the dishes, Mr. Devine explained, "This room used to be the servants' dining area. We like it, though, because it's so cozy and convenient."

"It looks very comfortable," Dinah said.

"Of course," Mr. Devine continued, "the chandelier and wine rack were added years ago, after we no longer needed full-time servants."

Before eating, Mr. Devine said an ecumenical grace. When he finished, and before his guests had a chance to raise their bowed heads, he glanced around the table to see if his prayer had made a good impression. It had. He could sense it. He straightened in his chair, adopting a serious, pious look. He paused for effect. Aware that pious moods could ruin dinner conversation if sustained too long, at just the right millisecond, he raised his wine glass. "I think you'll find this wine just right for chicken cordon bleu," he said cheerfully. "Hillary and I bought one of the last consignments of '98." He held the glass to his nose and inhaled before taking a sip. The others did likewise.

"Delicious."

"Excellent."

"It seems made for cordon bleu."

Mr. Devine was a gracious host, full of wit and charm. He recounted his start in the funeral home business. "Those were exciting days. I was just an embalmer's assistant, mind you, filling in at St. Peter's Funeral Home. They gave me a sleeping room on the third floor and I really got to know the business. But I was getting ready to go back to school and continue working toward my degree in marketing. Then, one of the salesmen at St. Peter's took ill and the director asked me to take over his territory until they could find a permanent replacement. Well, the pre-need sales strategy was just beginning to take hold back then and I found that I made more on commissions in the last two weeks of the summer than I had in the previous eight weeks as an embalmer's assistant. So I changed my major to mortuary science and kept my sales relationship with St. Peter's for the rest of my school years.

"I loved the business," he continued. "That first autumn, I got in tight with one of the fraternities and we co-sponsored a Parent's Night/Halloween Party where...how shall I say it...the fermented cider flowed freely," Devine chuckled. "And in the spirit of things, so to speak, I got contractual commitments from fully one-third of the party goers. I must admit, and I think that you, being in the business, can understand, the money was a very attractive incentive for me. It's amazing how strongly people feel about having a nice funeral. And the nicer you can convince them it will be, the more you stand to gain."

Hillary added, "I remember John's first Halloween party. That's where we met. Remember, John?"

Mr. Devine nodded and gave his bride an embarrassed smile. "Yes, dear, I remember well."

Hillary continued, "John was so dashing. And so in control of the party. I was so impressed with how he joined right in with the revelers, then guided the party so smoothly into the sales, almost like it was an afterthought."

Mr. Devine flushed. "Enough about us. Gary, Gilbert, Dinah. Tell us, how did you decide to enter the business?"

Gilbert took a big bite of cordon bleu and gestured

for Gary to tell the story. Gary was sure Mr. Devine knew he had buried Aunt Winifred for them, and he suspected Mr. Devine was aware they weren't happy. But, not wanting to offend his gracious host, Gary coughed and rubbed his eye with his napkin. "That's an interesting story, John," he began. "You may recall that Gilbert and I used your services for our aunt, Winifred Gladstone. And although the service went fine, very beautifully in fact, except for that misunderstanding with the postage stamp, we hit upon the idea that an alternative to the conventional burial service could be offered to the public. To tell you the truth, John, it was the cemetery operator who really got us going. I happened to mention to him after the service at the cemetery that on an acre per acre basis, land in his cemetery would sell for about one-hundred times the most expensive property in the most exclusive neighborhood in our community. He just laughed in my face and said, 'Yeah. Ain't life sweet.' So, we came up with the idea of bypassing the cemetery altogether and providing an interment alternative for those squeamish about cremation."

Devine leaned back in his chair, lifting a toast, "Excellent. Excellent strategy. We try to discourage cremation, the profit margin being what it is. And you know, I think the time is right for a new push to discourage it. I'll take the matter up with the Association next month, and I'd like to mention to them that I think your perpetual display, even if it can't be fully sanctioned by the Association at this time, could be an excellent way to get this notion of cremation out of the public's mind.

"Yes, we're ready for a new push in this area," he continued, turning to Gilbert. "If cremation ever really catches on, and it seems the churches aren't going to be any help in this matter, we've got to find some way to put it in a bad light.

"All through the years," Mr. Devine complained, putting down his wine glass, softly pounding the table with his fist, "we've had to answer to the cremation-ists' challenges. Back when they sold it on the grounds that it would guarantee against accidental live burial, we were forced to open our embalming rooms to reporters and writers to show that accidental burial is equally impossible with modern embalming techniques.

"Then," he said, turning to Dinah, "when the cremationists started selling that silly romantic notion of spreading ashes to the four winds, we had to counter by pointing out that nobody wants to find human remains scattered across their front lawns when they go to pull up dandelions."

Mr. Devine sighed. "It's been an uphill battle and we've fought hard." Turning to Gary, he admitted, "And although we've done everything we can to increase the margin on cremation services, nothing can ever compare to the good old-fashioned custom of a big spread with lots of flowers and bells and whistles.

"And I'll tell you another thing, if you'll indulge me a bit longer, that ashes to ashes, dust to dust quote was something that really had us on the run for a while. Fortunately, it's just a figure of speech now. We always have to be on guard against the public taking certain Biblical sentiments too literally. It's our business.

"Yes," Mr. Devine finished, "I'm going to make sure the Association sees perpetual display for the opportunity it is—a sure-fire way to get people to stop and think about their earthly remains."

"But John," Dinah asked, "even with embalming, don't the earthly remains eventually decompose?"

Mr. Devine raised his eyebrow. "Why of course they do, Dinah," he said frankly. "After embalming, the body decays horribly. Slowly and horribly, with penicillin mold forming in little green spires, dragging out the natural decay process even longer." He paused a moment, then said, "Truthfully, I think a lot of people have some sort of worldly resurrection notion in the back of their minds. If so, they'd be better off not being embalmed. The sight of a resurrected embalmed body would be a vision straight out of the gates of hell!

"Luckily, no one sees that," he continued, with a sly smile. "And we don't think it's necessary to point it out to people after they have paid so much money for a beautiful memory picture of their loved ones lying peacefully, rosy cheeked in their caskets."

Mr. Devine looked to Gary, seeming to ask for a sign of assurance that he would keep Dinah in tow, that neither would rock the other's boat.

Hillary sensed tension in the air, and moved to

restore cordiality. "What you're doing at G&G's is so fresh and innovative," she said, smiling at her guests. "And so smart. I'm sure there's a great market demand to see dead people on display. Especially since the National Park Service started that policy. I can't tell you how disappointed John and I were when we revisited Mammoth Cave on our second honeymoon and couldn't view the wonderful skeletal remains of those Indians. Oh sure, one can go to a medical science classroom and see a skeleton, but they're all bleached and disinfected. It's just not the same."

Hillary rested her arms on the table and leaned forward with a sigh. She stared into the burning candles. Her face reflected the yellow glow, and shadows rippled over the loose skin under her widening eyes. Mr. Devine swallowed hard.

Lost in reverie, Hillary continued, "The happiest times of my life were as a child roaming through the Museum of Natural History and seeing all those big dinosaur bones. Bones. Bones. Everywhere bones. Or that too-brief scene in *Ben Hur* when the ships collide and one of the slaves exposes his arm bone. Such a work of art. People seem to want to deny they have bones, but I love them. Big, strong bones. Oh, if people only knew the joy."

"Yes dear," Mr. Devine interrupted, "It is a fascinating subject, but shouldn't you check on the crepes? I want our guests to have them at their peak of perfection so they'll understand why I'm carrying around a few extra pounds."

Hillary leapt from the table. "My crepes! Oh my!"

When Hillary served the crepes, she apologized, "Oh, they are just a little past their peak."

Gary cut into one of the still moist crepes with his fork. The texture was just slightly rubbery, but the taste was delicate and refined. He swallowed and smiled at Hillary, saying, "Delicious, Hillary. Very tasty."

Gilbert swallowed his second mouthful and added, "No bones about it!"

After the dessert, they all retired to the drawing room for a brandy. Mr. Devine offered cigars to Gary and Gilbert, and Hillary turned on the air cleaner and ventilation fan. Mr. Devine, Gary and Gilbert sank back in easy chairs, soft, worn leather enveloping them. Hillary and Dinah sat on a settee, away from the smoke.

Gilbert sat comfortably, satiated from a full meal, relaxed by a snifter of brandy. He took a puff on his cigar and blew the exhaust out his nostrils. "This is just what this country needs—a good $5 cigar."

Mr. Devine waited until the cigars were burning strong and his guests had finished their first brandy, before saying, "I want to congratulate you again on doing the pioneer work for perpetual display. It's a bold concept, and with the right promotion it could really catch on. My little attempt, the Hall of Holograms, was just my way of testing the waters. The Hall is going to make it, thanks to you, of course. But there are limits to what we can make from hologram sales and display. But with perpetual display, I firmly believe the sky's the limit."

Gary and Gilbert continued puffing and drinking, waiting to hear more, the smoke and alcohol beginning to make them dizzy. Dinah turned to Hillary, looking for a clue to what her husband was leading to. Hillary smiled nicely, but said nothing.

Mr. Devine had the floor. "Yes, the sky's the limit," he said. "I've been batting around a few ideas with my legal and financial advisers, and others, and we've come to the conclusion that, just like a good $5 cigar, this country needs widespread, full-scale application of the perpetual display concept. This country needs it and is practically screaming for it. I'm in tune to these things, you know. But, it's an awesome responsibility, bigger than G&G's, bigger even than John Devine. But it's a duty that must be performed. Some of the best ideas this nation has offered the world have started out just like perpetual display. The work and inspiration of just a small group of dedicated people who get the ball rolling before passing on the next stage of development to the right people. To the people who can make it happen."

Mr. Devine didn't pause for a second, lest his guests voice objections. Objections could come later, after his pitch was over. "You've done the tough field work on this," he went on. "And for that you can be proud. I sincerely hope you'll agree with me that the time has come for the flower that's blossomed from the seed you've germinated to be transplanted to a bigger pot, a more specialized pot, a pot with all the right fertilizers and wherewithal for that flower to live and grow to its full potential.

"This is a critical time for G&G's perpetual display. And I think you'll agree with me, it would be a crime against progress and human social evolution if this great new idea were nipped in the bud, so to speak, by a selfish clinging. Perpetual display belongs to the world, and to the people who can make it grow. Without growth, stagnation and decline set in.

"Gentlemen, and Dinah too, of course, what I propose is to buy G&G's Funeral Homes, complete with technical processes and inventory. In exchange, I'll retain the grand G&G's name, a name I'll put on the map, and possibly in the next edition of the *Encyclopedia Americana*. Naturally, I'll install my own management team, and give you a very fair price. Then, twenty years down the road, with you all living in comfortable retirement, you can sit back and tell everyone how it was you who got the ball rolling. You'll be very proud indeed."

Mr. Devine paused, trying to read the minds of his stunned guests. His heart quickened when the silence continued for two, three, four seconds. He smiled inwardly when Gary, Gilbert and Dinah looked to each other for direction, none offering to provide it. Devine took his cue, filling the vacuum. He pulled a large envelope from the book shelf behind him. "I've taken the liberty of drawing up my proposal in writing, along with a draft of a contract between us. Take it home and study it, discuss it among yourselves, make changes if you wish. But remember, the time is now. The iron is hot. The sun shines. Discuss my proposal and we'll talk again by week's end."

Gary rose. His face was pale. He could only think of the green problem with his 'inventory.'

Gilbert reached for the envelope with an unsteady hand. "We'll certainly look this over, John."

Mr. Devine and Hillary escorted Gary, Gilbert and Dinah through the house to the front door. Dinah thanked the Devine's for the delicious meal, adding, "Hillary, everything was so delicious. If you could just part with your family's recipe for Amber Gold..."

"Well, perhaps I could make an exception. For you. Give me a few days to write it down."

"That would be splendid, Hillary, thank you. Good night."

"We'll be talking soon, Dinah dear," Hillary said. "Good night."

"Good night all," Mr. Devine said with a smile, adding, "I'm so glad we had this chance to talk."

Gary said, "We'll certainly give your proposal some thought, John, but I don't think it's something we can seriously consider. G&G's has become such a large part of our lives."

"It can always be a part of your lives, every time you pass a perpetual display home, in any corner of the country. I understand how you feel about giving it up, but I'm sure that once you've had the opportunity to study my proposal at length, you'll see that it's the right thing to do."

Gilbert said, "Very interesting idea, John. Very surprising too. It's taken us by complete surprise. We'll certainly consider it, though. Good night."

"Good night, Gilbert. I'm sure you'll be very happy with what I'm prepared to offer."

Not a word was spoken by Gary, Gilbert or Dinah until they passed through the guardhouse gates. And even then, the only communication was an exchange of glances. While Gary drove, Gilbert opened the envelope and scanned for the bottom line. His hand shook nervously as he handed the proposal to Dinah. She found the bottom line and turned to Gilbert, shocked. Gilbert grinned widely. At a traffic light, Dinah held the proposal before Gary, pointing to the bottom line with her finger. Gary stared in disbelief until the car behind him gave a short toot on its horn.

Gilbert fidgeted and tapped his toes and fingered the door handle and lock in the back seat. When Gary finally pulled up Gilbert's drive, Gilbert yanked the door handle and jumped out, the knot in his stomach and lump in his throat about to burst from excitement. He slammed the door and waved good-night at Gary and Dinah through the front passenger window.

Gary fumbled for the power window switch before Gilbert could get away. "Gilbert," he said, "We'll read Devine's proposal tonight and drop it off at the first tomorrow morning. Dinah and I have to be at the second early. Give us a call there after you've read it."

Gilbert maintained an appearance of calm. "OK.

Good enough. Talk to you tomorrow. Good night. Good night, Dinah."

"Good night, Gilbert."

Gilbert walked steadily and deliberately up his driveway until he saw Gary's red taillights turn the corner. Then he ran to his door fumbling for his keys. He felt like a drunkard. The keyhole kept moving as he stabbed at it with random keys. Finally getting the door open, he ran down the stairs into the basement, held a pile of laundry to his face, and shouted a muffled cry of excitement. He did a lively Irish jig, then a clumsy ballet pirouette, during which, he hit his hand against the washing machine. The pain excited him more and he broke into a shadow boxing routine, which he sustained until he dropped from exhaustion into the pile of laundry. He lay on the basement floor and convulsed a couple of times like a cockroach drowning in pungent insecticide. Spent, he rested his head comfortably on the towels and t-shirts that lay scattered across the floor. He pulled a dirty sheet over himself and dreamed of money.

Dinah undressed to her slip, eying Gary's face as he lay on the bed reading Mr. Devine's proposal. Gary looked severe. Stone faced. Perplexed.

Dinah knew that before he came to any decision, she must seduce him. Then, as Gary slept on the decision, thoughts of Mr. Devine's proposal would meld with pleasant thoughts of her warm, willing body. The sweet dreams would influence his subconscious ciphering over the pros and cons of Mr. Devine's offer, making the pros proer, and the cons insignificant.

With sultry motions, Dinah stepped to the bed and positioned herself on top of Gary, her breasts resting heavily on his stomach. Gary set the proposal on the nightstand and closed his eyes. Dinah softly fondled his shoulders and said in a husky voice as she rubbed herself slowly yet forcefully against his kneecap, "That can wait until tomorrow."

Gary looked down at her vixen face, then at Mr. Devine's papers, then again at her vixen face. He reached for the lamp on the nightstand and shut it off.

CHAPTER 17

As Gary and Dinah worked in the Sunrise Room putting the finishing touches on the latest display at the second, Rick entered. "Gilbert's calling from the first."

"OK, Rick," Gary said, tossing Rick the displayee's Afghan shawl, "I'll get it. Help Dinah finish up in here."

Gary went to the office and closed the door behind him. "Hello, Gilbert? ... Yeah, I read it, did you? ... You seem pretty happy about something. ... I know it's a lot of money, but ...Yeah, but ... I know, that's right, but ... but ... Gilbert will you shut up a minute? What about the green problem? Devine wants our 'inventory' and exclusive rights to the process. He doesn't know his 'inventory' will turn green and the process doesn't work. We'd be guilty of fraud. Not only would he sue to get his money back, we'd have to pay lawyer's fees, probably end up in jail, and lose everything. And what about Wiggins? He's the one who holds the funeral home license. We'd have to convince him to sell, too. We can't make any agreements without him. No, Devine's offer is out of the question. ... No, I haven't talked to Wiggins, not for a couple weeks. He seems to wait till we're out before dropping off customers. ... No, I don't know what's going on. ... Uh huh, yeah, you might have something there. I don't know what to do about it. I'd sure like to talk this over with Wiggins. I'll try calling him today. ... OK, talk to you later."

Gary pressed the plunger with his finger, keeping the phone cradled between his shoulder and chin. It fell. He caught it, and by the time he repositioned it on his shoulder, it had a dial tone. He dialed Wiggins' number. No answer. He walked slowly, deep in thought, back to the Sunrise Room.

Dinah said, "I sent Rick to get your coat at the cleaners. What did Gilbert say?"

"He's a nut case. He's not thinking straight. I'll have to wait till he comes back to earth. I'm going to drive out to Wiggins' this afternoon. Can you handle things here?"

"You can't go this afternoon, you're supposed to officiate at the service. Don't you remember? Can't you go tomorrow?"

"No. I have to warn Wiggins about Devine wanting to buy G&G's."

Dinah manipulated the fibers of the displayee's shawl between her fingers. "Is the green problem really that important?" she asked. "We could tell Mr. Devine that our people need periodic maintenance, just like anything else. It's not that unusual."

"If Devine doesn't agree, he can withdraw the offer and spread word about our problem. We could all land in jail, or get lynched. No way! We're just going to give Devine a simple 'no,' without any elaboration."

"Well you'll have to drive out to Mr. Wiggins' this evening," Dinah said, giving the fibers a sharp twist. "While you're there, Gilbert and I will have a chance to go over the books. I'm afraid we've been neglecting them since we opened the second."

"OK. But I was hoping to bring Gilbert with me. Do you really need him to go over the books?"

"Yes. Sometimes I can't read his entries for the first. Can't you handle Mr. Wiggins' alone?" Dinah taunted.

"I just thought Gilbert might help me clear things up with Wiggins."

"Oh, you'll do just fine, dear."

That afternoon, while Gary was conducting the service, Dinah slipped into the office to call Gilbert. "Hello, Gilbert? Gary is driving out to Mr. Wiggins' tonight and I thought you and me could go over the books for last month. ... Yes, he wants to talk to him about the offer. ... No, he says he wants to warn Mr. Wiggins. Gary doesn't want to sell. He's worried about trouble because of the green problem. ..." Dinah laughed, "Well, we got our bags packed and our passports ready. But I don't know, he has a point. I don't want to become a fugitive. I told him maybe Mr. Devine wouldn't mind doing a little routine maintenance, but Gary thinks it would be dangerous to spill the beans about the problem to anyone. ...Yes, I'd like to, too. Talk to you tonight."

After the service was over and all the guests and gawkers left, Gary and Dinah dined on microwave pizza in the office at the second. As Gary got up to put his coat on to leave, Dinah said, "We should get together with Gilbert tomorrow night and discuss things."

"What's there to discuss?" Gary asked.

Dinah got up from her chair and silently gathered up the dirty plates. Gary grunted and left for Wiggins'.

A cold, light drizzle began falling halfway to Mr. Wiggins' house. The rain was just heavy enough to reconstitute the dried motor oil on the road. Gary slowed down, trying to remember how long it had been since he checked the tread on his tires.

It had been pouring heavily on the dirt road leading to Mr. Wiggins' farmhouse. The potholes were filled with water, making it impossible to gauge how deep they were. They reminded Gary of bomb craters in Vietnamese rice paddies. He thought of C38 to Mancelona and the Nazi commandoes he had routed. He remembered the musty cabin and his war prize. Then he thought of Dinah last night. 'She's been acting strangely. The things she did last night. And after a big meal, too! What did she mean, 'we'll discuss things tomorrow'?'

Pulling into Mr. Wiggins' drive, Gary imagined himself an OSS officer checking on reports of a mad Nazi scientist performing unthinkable experiments on walking dead concentration camp interees.

Gary's headlights scanned Mr. Wiggins' backyard. The house was dark, and the blue Step-Van was nowhere in sight. Gary got out and looked in the basement window. It was covered from the inside with aluminum foil, but a sliver of light shone through a gap in the caulking.

He knocked on the back door. No answer. He knocked again, then ran back to the window. The sliver of light was gone. Gary returned to the back door, thinking Mr. Wiggins had turned the light off before coming upstairs. Still no answer. He searched the yard for the Step-Van. The old tractor was still there. It would always be there. But the Step-Van was nowhere in sight.

Gary walked to the barn and peered through a dirty, cracked window. The storm had passed and a moonbeam shone through a hole in the roof. He couldn't make out the color, but there was a large van inside. Gary glanced back at the house and the back door, half expecting to see Mr. Wiggins waiting for him. No Mr. Wiggins. No lights.

It had been a long, unnecessary drive, Gary thought. He became irritated that Mr. Wiggins didn't stay in closer contact with his business partners. Determined not to leave without seeing Mr. Wiggins, he returned to the back door and knocked again, hard. Then he ran to the basement window and shouted, "Mr. Wiggins. It's Gary Colbert. I saw your light on. Do you need help? I can call an ambulance."

The sliver of light reappeared. Footsteps and shuffling noises sounded through the window. The kitchen light came on and Gary could see Mr. Wiggins approach the door.

"Hello there, Sonny. Caught me taking a cat nap.

Come on in. What brings you all the way out here on a night like this?"

"We've been worried about you, Mr. Wiggins. We haven't seen you for days, and we haven't been able to reach you by phone. Is everything all right?"

Mr. Wiggins offered Gary a chair at the kitchen table. The kitchen was different. The crusty stains from boiled-over pots had been scoured from the stove. The refrigerator had also been cleaned. The rust stains in the sink had been scrubbed and bleached, and the chips and black worn spots in the porcelain retouched. A box on the floor in the corner was filled with the menacing stuffed crows that used to hang from the walls and ceiling. Gary wondered if Mr. Wiggins had remarried.

"Oh, everything's fine," Mr. Wiggins assured Gary. "Been kind of busy lately, you know, working on the green problem and all. Was just downstairs working on it. Just turned out the light to take a nap when I heard you knock. Can I fix you a cup of coffee?"

"No thanks, Mr. Wiggins. I can't stay long. I just wanted to keep you posted on what's happening. I thought you should be aware that Mr. Devine has made an offer to buy G&G's Funeral Homes, lock, stock and barrel. And your process is part of the lock, stock and barrel."

"The barrel."

"Huh?"

"The barrel," Mr. Wiggins repeated. "My process

must be the barrel. I got barrels of pickling compounds downstairs. Just makin' a joke."

"Oh, yeah. Anyway, I'm worried that Mr. Devine's offer is really just a ploy to get information about the process. Have you been contacted recently by anyone suspicious?"

Mr. Wiggins fidgeted. He stepped over to the sink and filled the coffee pot with water. "Suspicious? Contacted? No. No, can't say I have. I wouldn't worry about anything, though. I'm sure it will all work out for the best. How much did you say he's offering?"

"Not enough. It's a lot, but it's not enough for our freedom. Do you know what people would do if they found out about the green problem? I'd sleep a lot easier if you could come up with a solution. How's it going?"

"I've tried everything. I never knew it would be such a tough nut to crack. They just seem to want to turn green no matter what I do. Kind of like they figure it's their birthright. But, it could be worse. At least I found out there's no breakdown of the cell walls. My process works like a charm that way. My people will still be intact a thousand years from now." Wiggins paused to frown. "But I got to tell you the truth, I'm about ready to give up. It's beginning to look like a job for a microbiochemist. You see, it's the epidermis. It undergoes some sort of change. It's an actual molecular change. A bit beyond my field. The change could have taken any form, we're lucky all it does is make people wrinkle a bit and turn green. Believe me, it could have been much worse."

Gary thought of Mr. Devine's spires of penicillin mold. He stared blankly at Mr. Wiggins, Mr. Devine's voice echoing through his mind. 'A vision straight out of the gates of hell. The gates of hell. The gates of hell. A vision. A vision. Straight out of hell.' Gary massaged his forehead with his hand. He looked at Mr. Wiggins again. The words came back. 'A vision straight out of the gates of hell.'

Mr. Wiggins chuckled as Gary got up to leave. "Don't worry, Sonny. I'm sure everything will work out. If you decide to sell, get every penny you can out of Devine. I'll leave all the negotiating to you."

Driving back home, the water had soaked into the ground and Gary could now see how deep the potholes were. He wondered why the seriousness of the situation wasn't sinking in to Dinah, Gilbert, and now Mr. Wiggins. "Am I missing something?" he asked himself.

It was late when Gary got home. Dinah was already in bed. Gary stood a moment in his pajamas, looking at the outline of curves beneath the blankets. He gently pulled back the covers and slipped in beside Dinah. He ran his fingers along her arm and traced the line of her cheek. Dinah snorted and slapped his hand away. She rolled over to the far side of the bed and continued sleeping.

Dinah awoke the next morning to the sound of Gary showering. She saw his pile of clothes on the floor at the foot of the bed, the way they always were. But she couldn't help wondering if Gary had just gotten home. She had gone to bed alone, and woke up alone. She snoozed until she heard Gary's electric razor, then joined her husband in the bathroom to take a shower, the way he sometimes did when she was first into the bathroom. "Where were you last night?"

"At Wiggins'. I was at Wiggins'. Can't you even remember things from one day to the next?"

Dinah turned on the water in the shower. It was lukewarm for a few seconds before turning ice cold. She turned the water off and walked out of the bathroom without a word. Gary shouted after her, "I'm going to get up early from now on. It's nice to have hot water."

Dinah went into the kitchen and put enough water in the coffee maker for one and a half cups of coffee. While it brewed, she brought in the morning paper. She skimmed through the first section, then opened a jar of raspberry jam, took a spoonful and splashed it across page three. She hesitated. It was too overt. She wiped the jam off, then unplugged the toaster and turned it upside down over the paper. The crumbs drifted down, sticking to the jam residue. After holding the paper over the trash basket and brushing away the loose crumbs, she was satisfied that page three looked enough like an honest accident to make Gary agonize over whether to retaliate. She folded the paper and poured herself a full cup of coffee.

Gary pulled into the parking lot at the second to let Dinah off, keeping the motor running. "I have to go to the first to tell Gilbert about Wiggins," he said coldly.

"Try to come to some reasonable decisions," Dinah said, opening the car door.

As she stepped out, Gary eased up on the brakes just enough to make getting out of the car a carnival ride for Dinah. Dinah slammed the door. Before she could storm out of earshot, Gary hit the power lock switch, its mechanism responding with a loud thunk. He wished the window had been rolled down so he could hit the power window switch, too.

Over coffee in the kitchen at the first, Gilbert told Gary, "Ron is going to wash all the windows. He wants Rick to help. If you won't be needing him at the second, do you mind sending him over this afternoon?"

"No, I guess not."

"What's the matter? You seem kind of down in the mouth this morning. Everything go OK at Wiggins' last night?"

"Yeah, everything went OK. It's Dinah. She's in some kind of snit about something. Treating me like I was a stranger. Pulling all kinds of little crap. Pissing me off."

"So what else is new? You can't let her push you around like that," Gilbert said, leaning back in his chair. "What does she want?"

"I think it has something to do with Devine's offer.

She wants to get her hands on all that dough, but she isn't thinking of the consequences."

Gilbert leaned forward. "You have to listen to your wife, Gary. After all, she is a partner in this. And she's intelligent and always has good ideas. Let's all three of us meet tonight and come up with a course of action about Devine."

"Yeah, I guess so."

"So, how did it go with Wiggins? Is he still alive?"

Gary was about to answer, but held his tongue. He leaned back in his chair and craned his neck, first looking out the back door window, then into the hallway, past the office and into the front vestibule. "Let's go into the office," he said.

Gary hadn't been in the office at the first for ages, it seemed. He noticed the changes. Lester now held an airline flight schedule in his hand, and a tourist brochure for Hawaii was sprawled across his desk where the *New York Times* used to be. A framed certificate from the American Funereal Institute hung above Gilbert's desk. Gary recognized Dinah's calligraphy. "Where's mine?" he asked.

"Oh, that? It was just something I got surplus at the printer's. It was just a sample. They gave it to me free. I only got one. If you want, I'll take it down."

Gary felt a tinge of jealousy. The least Gilbert could have done was run off a copy for him. And Dinah could have told him about it, instead of sneaking around behind his back, practicing her calligraphy for Gilbert. "No, that's all right," Gary said.

"It looks impressive. I've got to get one for the second."

"So, what happened at Wiggins'?" Gilbert asked.

Gary put Gilbert's certificate out of his mind and closed the door. It felt good to be back. He answered enthusiastically, eager to conspire. "You're not going to believe this, Gilbert, but Wiggins' has cleaned his kitchen. The birds are all in a box in the corner, one step away from the trash bin. He washed all the crap off his stove and refrigerator. I think he even got a haircut, too, I'm not sure. Something's changed. What makes a man clean his kitchen after twenty years?"

Gilbert shuddered. "What was inside his refrigerator?"

"I don't know. I didn't look. Why?"

"I dunno. So, anyway, what does Wiggins think of Devine's offer? Did you tell him?"

"Yeah, I told him. I warned him. I said I thought it was a ploy to get information on the process, and we're all going to land in jail if Devine finds out about the green problem."

"What did he say?"

"I guess I didn't get through to him. The old fart. He said, 'If you decide to sell, get every penny you can.' Do you think his mind is slipping?"

"I don't know," Gilbert answered quickly, "Let's figure it out this evening with Dinah."

"OK. Hey, do me a favor, Gil. Call her and tell her I want to look around here a little before I go, and I'll be there in a while."

After touring the first, checking that everything was being dusted and the cosmetics were holding, Gary left for the second, avoiding the freeway, taking the long route.

He walked through the front door just in time to help Dinah catch a six-foot fichus she was carrying to the Sunrise Room. Her left hand slipped, but her right hand held tightly on the lip of the plant's mammoth pot. As Gary grabbed the falling plant, Dinah tripped over his right foot, sending the tree, Gary and herself sprawling. Both Dinah and Gary instinctively closed their eyes for protection from flying dirt and fichus limbs. When they opened their eyes, they were lying on top of one another, their lips inches apart. Neither made an effort to move.

After sending Rick to the first to help Ron wash windows, Gary apologized for the carnival ride, and Dinah for the newspaper. They then locked the front door, and hurriedly disrobed. Giggling and self conscious at first, they were soon oblivious to the stares of their silent audience.

That evening at home, Dinah mixed an ersatz pitcher of Amber Gold. Gary dusted the furniture in the enclosed back porch. The day had been warm and it was the first time in months they were able to use the porch. Dinah brought in the pitcher and three glasses. "Did you remind Gilbert to bring his copy of Mr. Devine's papers?"

"No. Don't worry, he'll remember."

Dinah poured samples of Amber Gold, and they talked about the welcome warm weather, resodding the yard, hiring Rick and Ron to paint their garage. The doorbell rang, followed by three short knocks. It was Gilbert's way of announcing his arrival. While Dinah answered the door, Gary poured another drink. He savored the flavor, letting the liquid trickle through his teeth and over his tongue. From the other room he heard Gilbert's loud voice, sounding like a boy ready to start play after school. As Gary swallowed, he heard Mr. Wiggins' bellow a hearty greeting. Gary leaned forward to keep from choking.

"Look what the cat dragged in," Gilbert said, entering the porch.

"Mr. Wiggins! Good to see you in our neck of the woods."

"Well, you know, after all the trouble you took to come see me last night, I figured I ought to come down here and see you all. I guess I've been kind of scared...scarce lately."

Gary regarded the old man. What was he scared of? Where did he get the new clothes? Why did he get the new clothes? "Have a seat, Mr. Devine...Wiggins. I'm glad you're here. We have a lot to discuss."

Dinah invited, "Come in, sit down. Let me pour you a drink. It's as close as I could come to Hillary Devine's secret recipe. You'll remember it, Gilbert. Mr. Wiggins, I'm sure you'll like it. It's supposed to be very good for your health."

Mr. Wiggins accepted the drink and took a gulp. His nose twitched and his face screwed. "Yeech! What's in this?"

"I'm sorry, Hillary hasn't given me the real recipe yet," Dinah fretted. "Don't you like it?"

"No ma'am! But you know, it could be the answer to the green problem," Mr. Wiggins said, holding his glass up to the light.

Gilbert took a sip and mimicked Mr. Wiggins' reaction. "Yeech! If this stuff ever hit the market, we better be prepared to work overtime."

Dinah stood with pitcher in hand, silent and pale. Gilbert said, "I'm sorry, Dinah, I was just joking. It's really every bit as good as Hillary's. Mr. Wiggins, you've been drinking too much pickling compound. You don't know a good drink when you taste it."

"Huh? Oh yes. Yes, you're right," Mr. Wiggins blurted. "It is delicious. I had a bit of a cold last week and my taste buds aren't back to normal. Dinah, dear, I'm sorry. I didn't mean anything." Mr. Wiggins took a large gulp from his glass. Forcing a smile, he said, "Can I have another?"

After another round of drinks, they got down to business.

"Let's take the money and start a business with fewer headaches," Gilbert said.

Dinah said, "We won't have to start a new business. We can retire."

Mr. Wiggins said, "I wouldn't mind selling. Maybe we can hold out for even more."

Gary could see the consensus was against him. "OK, let's list the pros and cons," he said. "First the pros. Anyone?"

Gilbert enthusiastically championed the pros, saying, "We can get the hell out of this business. No more green problem, no more makeup, no more public relations...and lots of free money—Profit!"

Dinah added, "I agree with Gilbert. We may never get another chance like this. And we can take that vacation you've been promising me."

"I wouldn't mind a vacation, myself," Gilbert chimed.

Mr. Wiggins said, "My lumbago's been acting up and I wouldn't mind a change of pace."

Gary's face reddened in frustration, and he quickly spelled out the cons. "Well yeah, that's all great, but now the cons. Number one, Devine thinks he's buying a reputable outfit...an honest business...an...oh hell, you know what I mean—a perpetual display funeral home with an inventory that does what it's supposed to, and not turn green. If we sell before finding an answer to the green problem, not only will Devine sue the pants off us, and there goes all our 'free money,' we'll also be sued by all the relatives of the people we've interred. And there goes all the profits from anything we do for the rest of our lives. You guys are nuts. We're in this for the duration. We have no choice. So stop dreaming about making easy money selling to Devine. It won't happen!

"And Mr. Wiggins," Gary continued, "we'll hire a

microbiochemist or whatever it is you need. And another thing, what if your lumbago puts you in the hospital for a month? Who's going to put people through the process? You think we can just close up shop for a month, maybe longer? You're going to have to train one of us to take over when you can't."

Mr. Wiggins just smiled and said, "I'm sure everything will work out." He then quickly changed the subject, talking football with Gilbert, and gardening with Dinah, leaving an exasperated Gary to sputter and fume between gulps of Amber Gold.

After Gilbert and Mr. Wiggins left, Gary said to Dinah, "That was a waste. Why can't I get you people to realize, we can't sell to Devine, or anyone, for that matter. And that fart Wiggins, 'I'm sure everything will work out.' What kind of idiot is he? The bastard, I couldn't even get him drunk to find out what he's been up to."

"No," Dinah said, irritably, "instead you got yourself drunk. And Mr. Wiggins is a very nice man. You shouldn't call him names. And another thing, have you ever stopped to consider that it might be you who has the problem? The rest of us are perfectly willing to trust Mr. Devine. Sure, he has to be told, but we can certainly work something out with him. After all, he is a businessman. I wish you would stop being so obstinate. Three-quarters of the voting shareholders are in favor of selling. Sooner or later, you're going to have to face that."

"No way!" Gary shouted. "Don't pull that on me.

Even if we don't have it written out on paper, it's implied that any major decisions have to be made with unanimous approval. We're all in this together, equally. Whatever happens affects me just as much as you people."

"Just try once to be more flexible," Dinah said, adding in a sweet, venomous tone, "I'm sure everything will work out."

CHAPTER 18

The next morning Gilbert received a phone call at the first. "Good morning, G&G's Funeral Home. ... John? ... Very good, thanks. How's everything at Devine Funeral Home? ... Glad to hear it. ... We're still discussing it. Some of us are leaning toward, some against. I don't know what to tell you. ... Tonight? I don't know. Gary and Dinah are keeping the second open late for an evening service, and I agreed to stay late here at the first to accommodate some followers of Madam Kitty. They want to try some retrocognitive clairvoyance. ... Yes, got to keep the customers happy. ... Tomorrow? OK by me. I'll call Gary and Dinah right now and check with them. I'll get right back to you."

Gilbert hung up the phone, worried that Mr. Devine might withdraw his offer. He only had one day to change Gary's mind. He called the second. "Good morning Dinah, I'm glad it's you. I just got a call from Devine. He wanted to meet with us tonight, but I told him about Madam Kitty coming here. I hope Aura Lee comes, too. But anyway, I think Devine's getting impatient. I told him tomorrow, but I'd have to check with you guys. We have to act quickly or it could be all over."

Dinah answered, "I swear, if it is all over, it's all over for Gary. I've tried everything. He only has visions of doom and gloom. Sometimes that man can be so difficult. I'll be really mad if he lets this slip through our fingers."

"I've been thinking," Gilbert said. "Maybe he'll agree to sell if we make Devine sign a disclaimer absolving us of any wrongdoing if the inventory doesn't stay perpetual for whatever reason. Maybe we could add a phrase to the contract, something like 'whatever problems with G&G's become the problems of the new owner,' something like that."

"Tomorrow night is OK with me, Gilbert. Here's Gary. You talk to him. And good luck with Aura Lee."

"Hello, Gilbert?"

"Gary, Devine wants another meeting tomorrow night. Now what I have in mind is, we don't have to tell him anything specific, we'll just add a clause to the contract that says he can't sue us if something goes wrong with the inventory."

"No. It's too tricky playing around with contracts. You don't know anything about it. And neither do I. But I do know that even if we add your phrase, we're still in trouble because you say 'if anything goes wrong.' That doesn't cover our situation, because something is already wrong. Give it up, Gilbert. We just have to keep running G&G's ourselves, forever."

"Devine still wants to see us," Gilbert persisted. "He sounded very willing to make concessions. In fact, that's the word he used. He said 'If there's any problem that's holding up the decision, I'm sure concessions could be made.'"

"But for him to agree to concessions," Gary protested, "we'd have to tell him what he's conceding to. And if he doesn't like it, he would be well within his rights to call the whole thing off and squawk to the newspapers. It's a catch-22, so just forget it."

Desperate, Gilbert played his last card. "OK. I'll forget it once and for all and never mention it again if you just agree to meet with Devine and hear him out. We won't have to volunteer any information. We'll just hear what he has to say."

"And when we tell him we won't sell, that will be the end of it?" Gary asked. "You'll forget all about it and get your mind back on work?"

"Promise."

"Tell Devine he can come out to the second tomorrow night. Seven o'clock."

"It's a deal."

Gilbert called Mr. Devine. "... Well, frankly, it's Gary. He has certain reservations. But he did agree to meet with you one more time. Tomorrow night at seven at the second. ... Your office at eight? I don't know. ... Something to show us? Well, OK."

The next night Gilbert, Dinah and a reluctant Gary drove to Devine Funeral Home. On the way, Dinah excitedly asked Gilbert, "So, how did it go with Aura Lee last night?"

Gilbert looked out the backseat window. "I don't know. She didn't come. I called her this morning, and she just said something's bothering her and she doesn't want to start seeing anyone just now. We talked for a while, though."

"Well, that's good," Dinah said. "Don't give up on

her," she added hopefully.

"Never mind about Aura Lee, Gilbert," Gary said angrily. "I still wish you would have stuck to your guns and insisted on Devine coming out to the second. Those were the conditions I set."

"But Devine seemed quite excited," Gilbert said defensively. "He said he had something very important to the deal to show us."

"And you didn't even think to ask what was so important that he couldn't bring it with him to the second? Geeze, Gilbert. Sometimes I wonder about you. Let's go in, see whatever it is he has to show us, and leave. This will be the end of it. That's the only reason I'm here. And I'm going to hold you to your promise, count on it."

The angel met them at the door and ushered them into Mr. Devine's office. Mr. Devine silently motioned for them to sit on the sofa. It was more comfortable than the stiff-back chairs Gary and Gilbert sat in when they made arrangements for Aunt Winifred, but Gary couldn't shake the feeling that Mr. Devine wanted them to be comfortable for making arrangements for G&G's.

Mr. Devine came right to the point. "I think I know what's troubling you. The green problem."

Gary, Gilbert and Dinah turned white.

Mr. Devine paused, like a grade school principal milking all the trauma he could squeeze out of naughty students caught red-handed in their mischief. He then slowly, wordlessly took a few steps and sat on the edge of his desk, warming to the students slightly, but maintaining a hint of reproach in his face. He took a deep breath. "Gentlemen, and Dinah," he said, "I've known about the green problem for quite some time." He reached behind and pushed a button on the intercom. "Mr. Crisler."

A tall figure with expensive clothes and steely eyes entered from the adjoining office. Mr. Devine introduced, "Mr. Crisler. My attorney." Mr. Devine paused for effect, then continued, "You see, I've known about the green problem for quite some time. I didn't want to tell you that, but you've forced my hand." He reached for the intercom again. "Gentlemen."

The door to the adjoining office slowly opened again and two solemn figures emerged. Mr. Devine said, "I think you all know Mr. Westlaw and Mr. Wiggins."

Mr. Westlaw and Mr. Wiggins entered sheepishly, hands clasped in front of them like manacled prisoners being paraded before a jeering throng. They stood to the side of Mr. Devine's desk, behind Mr. Crisler, heads bowed, not daring to brave the stares directed at them.

Mr. Devine relished the heavy silence. He waited and waited, until he perceived Gary's jaw loosen. Before Gary could speak, he said, "I'm still willing to buy G&G's. In fact, I insist upon it. You see, I'm a man of vision, and I have plans. Misters Westlaw and Wiggins will be heading G&G's now. My interest will be strictly financial. G&G's will live up to its potential as a money maker, and I'll reap the benefits while keeping the whole thing a respectable distance from my...my more conventional operations."

Gary looked over at Mr. Wiggins. "Mr. Wiggins, how could you?" Gary turned to Mr. Westlaw and said, "You, I can believe. You're just a slime and a rogue. But Mr. Wiggins, we're partners. How could you do this?"

Mr. Wiggins cleared his throat, mumbled something, cleared his throat again, and said, "Mr. Devine has offered me the chance to run my own home again. I want to get back full into the business of funeral homin'. This isn't a business for nice folk like you. After hearing Jeremy's ideas, I knew you weren't the ones to run G&G's properly. You'll understand. And I did insist you be paid a premium price for your work in setting up the G&G's perpetual display concept. Please, give me credit for that."

Mr. Westlaw stepped from behind Mr. Crisler. "I've been thinking about G&G's since it started," he said. "I knew you guys were on to something. You just aren't letting it live up to its potential. I have the ideas to really make it fly, and Mr. Devine is going to give me complete freedom to do just that. I'm sick of being a hack journalist. Do you know what it's like? No respect, editors treating you like dirt, impossible deadlines, eating on the run, indigestion, alcohol, hassles, money problems."

Mr. Devine interjected, "Misters Westlaw and

Wiggins have some very exciting ideas. And I'm willing to sit back and let them do their thing." He gave Mr. Crisler a nod. "My offer stands," he continued. "I don't want any ill will between us. We'll settle this once and for all right here, right now, so we can all part amicably."

Mr. Crisler handed Gary a document, saying, "All of you, sign at the bottom where indicated." He pulled out his notary stamp, and G&G's was sold.

CHAPTER 19

"So you see, Kevin," Gilbert said with a laugh, looking out the car window at the thickening Fijian jungle growth, "what else could we do? Devine had us by the balls. Well, he had me and Gary by the balls; he had Dinah by the...by the..."

"Yes, Gilbert?" Dinah asked. "By the what?"

Gilbert turned around to look at Dinah in the backseat, who repeated, "By the what?"

Gilbert's eyes darted about, stopping briefly at Dinah's breasts. No. They darted lower. No!

Dinah crossed her legs and folded her arms. She tilted her head slightly, directing her ear toward Gilbert, letting him know she expected an answer and wasn't going to let him off the hook.

"By the dimples," Gilbert finally said as Dinah's smile involuntarily broke through. "By those mean little dimples," he repeated, reaching into the backseat to pinch Dinah's cheek.

Dinah recoiled, bumping Gary's knee with her foot. Gary opened his eyes with a start, looking this way and that. Dinah and Gilbert stared at him, no recognition of who they were registered in his eyes.

"Gary?" Dinah said, shaking his arm. "What's the matter? Have a bad dream?"

Gilbert said, "I was just telling Kevin about how Devine had us by the balls."

"Huh? Oh, yeah," Gary answered, rubbing the sleep from his eyes.

"It's quite a story, Gary," Kevin said, bringing the car to a stop at a traffic light on the edge of Suva, where he lived and worked. "If I were you, though, I would have sold out to Devine immediately. Take the money and run like hell, that's my motto."

Gary looked over at his wife, who sat smiling, eager to see the new sights, content to be in strange surroundings. Gilbert, too, in the front seat, was eager and content, looking confident and on top of the world. Gary took a deep breath and looked out the car window, forcing himself to become absorbed in the Fijian scenery.

Kevin drove through the old section of Suva. The British architecture of the buildings seemed out of place in the tropics, yet somehow fascinating. They stood like strong and stalwart memorials to the confidence of the old British Empire. Kevin pointed out the newspaper where he worked as they passed, driving onward to the wharf, where they snacked on an assortment of seafood at one of the dozens of small eateries. Afterward, they strolled lazily about the wharf. Gary, Gilbert and Dinah gathered around a thin, wrinkled, Indian vendor. Kevin stood off to the side, admiring the vendor's pitch, not wishing to interfere with his livelihood.

"And this is the famous Fiji cannibal fork," said the Indian. "Everyone who comes to Fiji must buy a cannibal fork. It was used to pluck the meat from prisoners...only the select prisoners from the highest social standing. You see how it works?" he asked, demonstrating on his forearm.

Gary winced. Dinah took a half step back in disgust, thinking of the funeral home, glad the old Indian was thousands of miles from her former wards. She thought of the wrinkled, preserved Anton, unable to keep herself from imagining he would taste like beef jerky. She took another half step back, bumping into Gary.

Gary looked at her plump forearms. He picked up one of the cannibal forks. "Is this how you do it?" he asked, applying the fork to Dinah's flesh, bringing it to his mouth, pretending to chew.

Dinah's eyes widened and she pulled her arm away from Gary, slapping his hand. "Stop that, you cannibal."

Kevin laughed.

Gilbert asked the vendor, "Do you still have cannibals here?"

"Oh, no no no. There are no more cannibals in Fiji. It is against the law. But you can still get cannibal forks; they are a great remembrance of the former Fiji." The vendor turned and motioned a native Fijian working in the noodle stall next to his display of souvenirs. The Fijian, with thick, heavy limbs, dark brown skin and wide, friendly smile approached. The Indian said, "Here, you buy your cannibal fork from a real cannibal. Mistah, my friend, is descended from a tribe in the outer islands who specialized in raiding the other islands in search of the best prisoners available."

Mistah nodded and reached to shake Gilbert's

hand, saying with a deep voice, "I'm from the number one tribe of cannibals in Fiji. Happy to meet you." He picked up one of the forks. "With a fork such as this," he boasted, "I could easily strip the cooked flesh down to the bone in one pull. I cannot admit doing so, but I can say my ancestors did so many times. They lived to be very old and had many babies. I have five sons and three daughters."

Gilbert picked up a cannibal fork and fondled it. He liked its rugged, rough-hewn texture. He bought six, telling Gary and Dinah, "These will make great salad tongs. Or wedding presents."

After strolling about some more, they drove to Kevin's house to settle in for the night. "Tomorrow, I'll help you plan an itinerary," Kevin said. "There's a lot you can do here. But I recommend you retire to one of our outer islands. I've contacted an old friend on one of them and he and his family would love to take care of you."

They awoke the next morning to a light rain. Something in the dank air, however, promised the clouds would burn off, bringing clear skies and bright sunshine for the afternoon.

"No jet lag problems?" Kevin asked, doling out portions of boiled rice and pickled cabbage.

"We're too excited for that," Dinah said cheerfully, adding, "It'll catch up to us later, no doubt."

"And when it does, we'll just outrun it," Gilbert added.

Gary dipped his spoon into the bowl of boiled rice Kevin set before him. He stared at it a moment, and when Kevin turned his back, tipped the spoon to let the flavorless mush drip and plop back into the bowl, all the while, making strange faces for Dinah and Gilbert.

Dinah put a spoonful into her mouth. "Yum! Kevin, this is delicious!" She smiled at Gary.

Gilbert caught on to the joke. He ate a spoonful and said, "Yeah! This is what breakfast was meant to be. I could eat this stuff three times a day. How 'bout you, Gary?"

"Sure beats cannibalism."

Kevin pulled out a chair and the moment he sat down, the phone rang. He jumped to his feet as if propelled by a large spring in the seat cushion. "Damn! That happens every time," he cursed. "Hello. ... They are? ... Oh shit. ... OK."

"That was the paper. Something big is brewing in Parliament. One of our Indian members is going to resign in protest of the Indian land rights issue." He chugged his coffee. "I got to get going. Feel free to wander around the neighborhood and look around. I'll be back around noon."

As soon as Kevin left, Gary said, "You heard him. Let's wander around the neighborhood, maybe we'll find a diner."

After finding Gary a solid breakfast of heavy, doughy donuts and chocolate milk and coffee, they came back to Kevin's and waited. Noon came and went. And they waited. Then they took a siesta outside in the shade of the back porch, which overlooked a small yard with two palms and a mango tree spaced naturally, almost poetically, between tall grass and orchids. They didn't stir to life again until late afternoon.

Gilbert lay on the floor of the porch, his head resting on a rolled-up blanket. Suddenly, at the sound of squawking, he sat up, looking intently among the branches of the mango tree for the source of the racket.

Gary lay shirtless on the other side of the porch. He opened his eyes at the sound of Gilbert's movements. "Man, I'm tired," he yawned.

Gilbert looked over and said, "You've come to the right place to rest. Even in the middle of the city, it's peaceful...except for that crazy bird. Look, there it is."

Dinah sleepily shifted and stretched in the chaise longue at the sound of Gary and Gilbert's voices. "What day is it?" she asked lazily.

Gary thought a moment. "Hmm...You know, I'm not really sure." He turned toward Gilbert.

Gilbert, still concentrating on the bird in the mango tree, looked toward Gary and Dinah, puzzled. "You know, I really don't know either." He looked out again at the tree, then past to some wispy clouds floating high in the bright blue sky. "One thing I'm fairly certain of is that it's right now, and we're somewhere on Earth."

Gary and Dinah looked out at the backyard, then

at the blue backdrop and lacy clouds far in the distance. Gary said in a slow, groggy voice, "I can't say for certain, Gil, but I think you're right. This probably is somewhere on Earth. It has to be."

"Does it?" Dinah teased.

Gary and Gilbert looked across the porch at each other. The bird in the mango tree let loose its cry, "Aww-roc Aww-roc Aww-roc oc oc oc oc," then took flight, disappearing in a blaze of bright green and orange.

"Maybe not," said Gary.

The front door opened and Kevin entered, all apologies. "I'm sorry you guys. It took a bit longer than I expected. I tried calling, but I guess you were out. What did you see?"

"Oh, we walked around a bit then napped all afternoon out on the back porch," Dinah said.

"I'm sorry."

"No, it was very restful. We needed it."

"Just the same, I'm not going to be a very good host. Hell's-a-poppin' and I'm going to be busy for a while. You guys should get going and see the real Fiji. I told the editor I'm doing an island tour tomorrow to get local reaction to the resignation. He bought it! There's daily plane service to the Yasawas. I'll take you up there and introduce you to my friends, the Saeagas. They're a wonderful family. It'll be good to see them again."

The puddlejumper landed amid coconut palms and pandanas. Gary, Gilbert, Dinah and Kevin rose and stretched after the cramped, harrowing ride. "Come on. This way," Kevin said, pointing out the window to a band of taxi drivers. "We'll get a ride to the dock and catch a shrimp boat to the Saeagas' island."

"They own the island?" Gilbert asked.

"No. I don't know who owns the island," Kevin answered. "Maybe Marlon Brando owned it once."

"I'm glad I brought my camera," Dinah said.

Gary, Gilbert, Dinah and Kevin, landlubbers all, survived the three-hour boat tour of the Yasawas Islands. After several stops to meet dugout canoes trading copra and straw mats, they arrived at the Saeagas' island, the late afternoon sun just beginning to hint at the spectacular sunset it had planned.

Kevin made some inquiries at the little wharf while Gary, Gilbert and Dinah unloaded their things from the shrimp boat. A group of boys watched, giggling and pointing. Kevin walked over and talked to one, who immediately got on his bicycle and rode off, a big grin on his face. Returning, Kevin said, "He's going to tell the Saeagas we're here. They don't get many foreigners out this far, so it's a big deal to them. They like to show off their island and beaches and seafood. Be prepared for a feast of sorts."

"Ready whenever you are," Gilbert said, "I could eat a horse, or a whale, I suppose."

They walked down a road that turned into a trail

that turned into a jungle path and back into a trail and a road. Sitiveni, Minali, Mikal, and Captain Bligh met them at the outskirts of the village.

Kevin walked ahead and greeted Sitiveni and his wife, Minali. Their teenage son, Mikal, stood off a few feet, anxiously eying Kevin's backpack for the telltale bulge of books Kevin always brought him. Captain Bligh sniffed Kevin's pant legs, barked at the smell of shrimp and romped over to extend the same greeting on Gary, Gilbert and Dinah.

Kevin placed a small bundle of dried kava root in front of Minali, and after greetings and introductions, they all settled in front of a fire. While Minali mixed the kava roots with water to prepare the murky, tranquilizing brew, Kevin distributed books and newspapers and, to fulfill his official purpose being there, halfheartedly asked the Saeagas' opinion of the Parliamentary resignation, reading two columns worth of story into their silent shrugs of dismissal.

"We're very glad you're here," Sitiveni said to Gary, Gilbert and Dinah, raising his cup of kava with both hands, chugging it in one gulp, showing the newcomers how it's done.

Gary looked at the dirty-dishwater colored brew and slowly raised his cup with both hands, looking toward Gilbert for assurance. Gilbert sniffed his cup and raised it, saying, "We're very glad to be here." He put the cup to his lips and swallowed stoically. When the cup was drained, he smiled at the tingling sensation in his mouth and nodded in appreciation.

Gary followed suit, then Dinah, Kevin, Minali and Mikal.

Satisfied his guests were happy, Sitiveni filled the cups again and said, "Tomorrow we build a new two-room hut in your honor and you stay in our village as long as you want and tell us what is happening in the world and help Mikal study his lessons so he can be a chief speaker in Parliament when he is of age."

Dinah regarded Mikal. With his strong arms and limbs and chiseled features, he had the magnetism to be a great leader. She determined to tutor him in oratory and debate, subjects she studied long ago and always admired in people who successfully mastered them. She was already in love with the Fijis and wanted to do her part in their advancement.

A rustling in the brush beyond the Saeagas' thatched hut caught Captain Bligh's attention and he took off like a sleek catamaran, kicking up sand as he went. Minali, Sitiveni, and Mikal laughed and called the neighbors to watch the show. The neighbors stopped and pointed. Little children ran after the dog, stopping when they reached the edge of the brush. Everyone followed the Captain's progress through the rustle of thick undergrowth. A great commotion followed, then silence and deathly still.

Captain Bligh emerged from the undergrowth prancing, his head held high, a limp bandicoot in his mouth. The children jumped and screamed with delight, chasing the Captain, who kept one step ahead of them, holding his kill tightly, occasionally growling, sending the children scampering. The dog threw the dead rat-like creature in the air and pounced on it, re-enacting the great hunt, standing erect and proud.

Minali said, "That's the Captain. Every day the bandicoots come and he watches them. Only when visitors arrive and he has an audience does he give chase."

While toasting the Captain with a round of kava, Gary examined the strange rat-like animal he had caught and thought of mailing it to Mr. Wiggins for his collection. He checked himself, angry he had let the memory of the traitor pollute the beautiful beach at the Saeagas' village.

Kevin left the next morning. He told Gary how to deliver mail to the visiting shrimp boats and that he would return to see how they were doing whenever he could. Gary, Gilbert and Dinah spent the rest of the day helping the villagers build the hut that would be their home.

Minali led them and a throng of neighbors in collecting the great pandanas leaves that would be thatched together to become the walls and roof. In late morning Sitiveni, Mikal and several other men from the village came carrying a strong, straight tree trunk on their shoulders. They sang songs all the way, announcing their approach. They let out a perfectly synchronized war whoop as they heaved the trunk from their shoulders onto the ground. Mikal took special interest in the digging of the hole for the main post; the hut would later be his home with his betrothed from Nanuya Levu, where the women were reputed to have the strange power of being able to summon giant sea turtles from the depths with their song.

When the hole was dug, in the pause before the post was laid, Minali explained traditional Fijian hut building techniques to the visitors, lest they taint the house with white magic untempered by native influence. "Before the missionaries came," she said, "and Fiji was made up of many islands led by many warring chiefs, it was customary in building a hut for the chief to let a man stand in the hole and hold the post erect while the others filled in the dirt around him. In this way the man's spirit would always be protecting the hut."

"Hey, that's a great idea," Gilbert said. "I'll go down there and hold the post for you. I have a friend who's into that kind of stuff." Turning to Gary and Dinah, he added, "Maybe Aura Lee will go out with me if I tell her about this."

Gary and Dinah looked at each other, thinking they had misunderstood Minali's lecture. Mikal looked at Gilbert with a raised eyebrow. He said something in Fijian to the other men, who looked at Gilbert, unable to contain their laughter. One said, "Yes, yes. You go down in the hole. We will be very careful not to shovel sand in your eyes when we bury you."

"Hey! Wait a minute! You mean you didn't let the guy out of the hole? Hey, no way! I'm not going down there. Send Gary, he's much stronger than I am. I wouldn't be able to hold the post steady, and you'd have a crooked house."

Gary laughed, "Thanks a lot, Gilbert. But you already volunteered."

Mikal said, "I would be honored to have you hold the post for me, Gilbert. I would be famous throughout Fiji. No one has participated in this ceremony for many decades."

Dinah offered, "Hey, here's what we can do, a kind of modified tradition for the modern Fiji. Gilbert, you go down the hole and we'll lift you out each time as the sand gets up to your knees. Then before we fill in the hole completely, we'll cut off some of your hair and leave it in the hole. Sound good?"

Mikal and the others smiled broadly and nodded enthusiastically. Gilbert shrugged his shoulders and agreed, "But you better lift me out or there'll be hell to pay."

Under that threat the village men lowered Gilbert into the hole and set the post in with him. They sang a song as they shoveled sand into the hole. When the sand reached Gilbert's knees, Dinah gave a signal and the men hoisted Gilbert up a notch to a loud round of cheers, dancing and whooping. They continued the process, clipping a tuft of hair from Gilbert's head, tossing it into the hole before finally hoisting Gilbert up and out, then filling the hole completely.

At the celebration that night, Gilbert was the guest of honor. He was seated in the best spot in front of the fire, surrounded by tall torches that shimmered and reflected their golden glow across all present. Small children reverently touched the bare spot on his head. He was inducted into the tribe as an honorary member, and given a key to the village made of filed mother-of-pearl. The drink flowed, the abalone sizzled, and the singing and dancing were performed with such spontaneity and mirth as had not been seen on the island for as long as even the oldest villager could remember.

Gary, Gilbert and Dinah watched the sun set ten, twenty, thirty times, until they lost interest in counting the days. The coral seas, excursions into the tropical forest, visits to neighboring villages, trips by dugout to other islands, periodic visits from Kevin, the good cheer and warmth of their hosts, feeling useful helping the people bone up on their English, and apprising them of the latest geopolitical gives and takes...it was idyllic and tranquil, a much needed rest.

Then Kevin appeared one chilly, overcast day. He was drinking kava with Minali and Mikal around the family cooking pit when Gary, Gilbert and Dinah returned from a mid-morning stroll down the beach collecting driftwood from the other islands of the Yasawas. "Bula," Gary said, proud to display the Fijian word he had learned.

"Bula to you, too," Kevin answered. "Sorry I haven't been able to visit in a while, but this thing with the Parliament fired up again and kind of snowballed.

Kept us newshounds hopping."

Gary thought of Westlaw. If Kevin was a news-hound, Westlaw was a news mangy dog. Kevin was reassuring and trustworthy, if a bit secretive and evasive. Westlaw was scurrilous and suspicious. Gary imagined scraping Westlaw's bones with a cannibal fork, chewing his gizzard and spitting it out for the bandicoots. Still, if it weren't for the dog, Westlaw, and the traitor, Wiggins, he would never have been rid of G&G's green problem, never would have lazed in Fijian sun with Minali, Sitiveni, Mikal and the rest of the villagers.

Dinah asked, only half caring, "What's the news from the outside world, Kevin?"

"Well," Kevin stalled, "it's a bit weird. I don't know how you're going to take this."

"Take what?" Gilbert asked.

"Well, I've been getting letters from your brother, Ken."

"Yes?"

"It seems he's a bit upset that Rick and Ron agreed to stay on at G&G's. He didn't give any details, but there was something about a 'sick concept' the new owners had. He's pretty mad at you guys. Here, he sent this," Kevin said, digging into his pocket.

Gilbert took the letter. He read aloud:

Kevin:
Pls. relay following to Gilbert, etc. It's my unfortunate duty to inform you that G&G's is now sham. Sick concept.

Rick and Ron brainwashed. Thanks a lot. Rot in hell!
–Ken

"'Thanks a lot. Rot in hell!'" Gilbert shouted. "What's he mean by that?"

"'Sick concept'? What's he mean by that?" Gary asked.

"And 'Rick and Ron brainwashed'? I thought he liked his sons working there," Dinah added.

Gary speculated, "Something must have happened. Ken did like Rick and Ron working there. I wonder what...," he had to search his memory for the name, "...I wonder what Devine meant when he said his management team had some new ideas. What have they done? What could be done? But why blame us? 'Rot in hell!' That bastard! Do you think he means me and Dinah, too?"

Dinah set aside her driftwood. "That management team could do anything," she spat. "Maybe it's time we thought about getting back and seeing what's been happening."

"Yeah, you're right," Gary said reluctantly. "Much as I'd like to, we can't stay here forever. Maybe it's time we did start for home. What do you think, Gilbert?"

"I think you're right. I hate to say it, but I think you're right."

"And remember, guys," Dinah pleaded, "Ken was probably upset when he wrote that. Let's find out why before we start calling him names."

CHAPTER 20

Air pockets and wind shears jostled the big 747 during most of the final leg home. Babies cried, small children ran off their energy up and down the aisles, mothers shouted and scolded, the air conditioning broke. "Gary, why did I let you talk us into taking the long route home?" Dinah complained. "We could have landed in L.A. two days ago."

"Well, we're going to land in New York soon. We went halfway around the world to visit Fiji; it would have been a shame if we hadn't continued on and done a circumnavigation of the globe. How many people do you know have circumnavigated the planet they live on?"

"Sometimes I wonder what planet you live on."

"Yuk, yuk, yuk. You'll thank me later."

Gilbert put on his Groucho Marx sunglasses and tried to cheer Dinah. "Hey Dinah, we're all from the same planet, Xorton Regula. Have you forgotten already? If you think this trip was bad, wait till we circumnavigate the galaxy to get home, to the one true home—Xorton Regula, pearl of the Milky Way."

The pilot broke in on the intercom. "Good morning fellow travelers. We're beginning our approach and ask that you check to make sure your seatbelts are still fastened."

"Thank God," Dinah said aloud.

"We'll be running into some heavier than normal turbulence," the pilot continued, "but it's nothing to worry about. Just effects of Hurricane Dinah, which petered out yesterday afternoon, bringing clear skies and sunny weather behind to the greater New York area."

Gary and Gilbert looked at each other, then at Dinah. They smiled, but didn't dare say anything. A pocket of turbulence hit the plane. Outside the window the wing flexed visibly. A stewardess lost her balance and her soft rump brushed against Gary, sitting in the aisle seat. He smiled broadly. Seeing Dinah glower at him out of the corner of his eye, he said hastily, "I was just thinking of checking into a hotel at the airport for the day. It's been a long trip for all of us and we could get cleaned up, take a long rest, and see where we can rent a Winnebago and drive the rest of the way home. What do you say?"

"Sounds great," Dinah said sarcastically. "But do you really want to rent a Winnebago? They don't have stewardesses."

"No, but this one will have you, dearest."

"Please, Gary, you're making me airsick."

Gilbert said, "Yeah, let's take a couple of days and drive the rest of the way. That's a great idea, Gary. I'm not ready to face Ken and see what's become of Rick and Ron, or G&G's for that matter."

"Dinah? Sound good?" Gary asked. "It will be a nice rest. Maybe we can swing down to Mammoth Cave and take a second honeymoon."

"If we're going to swing anywhere for a second honeymoon, it'll be to Niagara Falls."

"OK. A Winnebago to Niagara Falls. But first we'll rest up at the airport. OK?"

"OK."

He asked Gilbert, "OK?"

"OK."

Gilbert took off his sunglasses and held them in front of him. "OK?" Nodding the glasses up and down, he squeaked from the side of his mouth, "OK."

Dinah rested her face in her hands. "Xorton Regula," she sighed.

"That's everything," the man behind the counter said. "Here are the keys. Have a good trip."

"Thanks. I'm sure we will."

Gary joined Gilbert and Dinah outside, inspecting the giant vehicle. Dinah said, "Gary, this was a marvelous idea. This thing has everything: beds, stove, toilet, shower. And I really feel refreshed after a good night's rest in a real bed. That was a good idea, too. I'm sorry I got cranky on the plane."

"That's OK. I'm used to it."

Gilbert climbed into the driver's seat. "Let's roll, good buddy. Who's gonna be my navigator?"

Dinah slid open the side door and stepped into the great RV, taking her shoes off, settling into a recliner behind Gilbert. Gary took the lounge chair beside Gilbert and opened a manila envelope containing maps. "Course plotted and laid in, sir."

"Ignition system, check," Gilbert said, turning the key. "Full ahead, impulse power." He shifted into gear and eased off the brake.

"Let's open a hailing frequency," Gary said, searching for a CB, settling for AM.

Gilbert tested the horn. "Ahh. B flat. Perfect."

Gary turned to Dinah. "And awaaay we go."

Gilbert was unsure how much acceleration the big RV could muster. He waited at the edge of the rental parking lot, looking for a hole in traffic to wheel the Winnebago onto the busy street. Finally, he took a lesson from the truckers, and nosed into the traffic, leaving it to the onslaught of cars to accommodate him. A wide left turn put him in the middle of the avenue, in the center lane for left turns. He nosed in again and edged to the right lane, then drove a mile and a quarter to a traffic light, which he intentionally hit at the red to check the braking power of the rig. Finally onto the highway west, bearing toward the interior of the strange country.

He relaxed at the wheel after getting on the highway. "This place is nothing like Fiji," he noted. "How can all these people afford cars? Where do they have to go in such a hurry?"

"To get home to take a pee," Gary answered.

"If they would all get Winnebagos they wouldn't have to be in a hurry to get home to take a pee; they could just put their cars on autopilot and step back to their own mobile piss pot."

"Yep, this place is nothing like Fiji," Gary agreed, looking out the window. "Look at all these maniacs in their cars, stupid bumper stickers..." Out of the corner of his eye, Gary saw a seated figure on a billboard. He turned to look, but it was too late. "I swear that billboard had a guy on it who looked just like Anton."

Dinah rubbed her bare feet into the thick carpet. "Anton?" she laughed. "On a billboard? You need a couple more night's sleep on a good bed, Gary."

"Yeah, Gary," Gilbert added, "you can forget about Anton. That's all lightyears behind us. Nothing but smooth sailing now. We'll put some distance between us and that airport and grill some steaks at the campground tonight."

"Maybe a couple martinis or a jug of wine," Dinah suggested.

"Now you're talking," Gary said. "I'm going to take a swim before dinner and watch the sun set. I really got into sunsets."

"They were beautiful," Dinah sighed. "I'm going to write Minali and Sitiveni a letter tonight. Do you think they'll really send Mikal here for college?"

"Why not? We'll help foot the bill. It's a great investment. In ten, maybe twenty years we'll be personal friends with the prime minister of Fiji."

"Now don't push him, Gary. He'll do what he feels is best. He doesn't have to become prime minister."

"No, of course not. But, you know, I kind of think..."

Gary stopped, squinting his eyes. "Look! Look up ahead, on the right. Slow down, Gilbert."

"What?

"Slow down. Look at that billboard on the right. Dinah, look!"

Gilbert slowed the Winnebago. "NO! It can't be!" he shouted. "Tell me I'm seeing things."

"You're seeing things, all right, as well as I am."

"Oh my God!" Dinah said. "It's got to be a mistake. What have they done?"

A happy smile beamed down at them from the green, twisted, wrinkled face of Anton, his peg leg in full view, his arm held high in greeting. The billboard read:

> *GRUESOME GARY*
> proudly announces
> another GG's Funeral Home
> coming soon
> to a neighborhood near you!

They drove in silence for several minutes. Gilbert finally ventured, "It has to be a joke. It can't be for real. Westlaw and Wiggins must have found out we were coming back to save Rick and Ron, and they put up that billboard to shake us."

"Gruesome Gary?" Gary wondered aloud. "Who is Gruesome Gary?" Gary suddenly went cold, his face losing its color. "I hope there's nothing to connect me with this. I don't want people calling me Gruesome Gary." He paused, "It does have a certain ring to it, though. Kind of catchy. But why 'Gary'? Why didn't

they come up with a name for Anton? Astonishing
Anton. Asymmetric Anton..."

"Those sound like names of professional wrestlers," Dinah said.

"So does Gruesome Gary."

Gilbert remembered, "Devine said he'd put the
G&G name in the encyclopedia. Maybe he wanted to
keep his word, like if he didn't, we could sue for
breach of contract."

"I don't know, Gilbert," Gary argued, "G&G stood
for Gary and Gilbert."

"Gilbert and Gary," Gilbert corrected.

"Well, whatever. They dropped the ampersand
and the Gilbert and Gary."

"They didn't drop the Gary," Gilbert answered, a
tinge of hurt and envy in his voice.

"Yeah, aren't I lucky."

"Never mind whose name they dropped," Dinah
said. "As far as I'm concerned, they dropped both your
names. Gruesome Gary is not what we had in mind
when we named our funeral home. Gruesome Gary's
Funeral Home. What kind of name is that? It's...it's
gruesome."

Gary said, "It has to be Westlaw's doing. He was
the one with the big ideas. I wonder what else he had
in mind."

"Wake up, Dinah," Gary prodded. "We're getting
near Niagara. We have to make a decision. Do you
want to stay on the American side or drive over to

Canada?"

Dinah adjusted the recliner and looked out the window. The billboards advertising Niagara Falls honeymoon hotels were springing up like wildweeds. She was groggy and felt like drinking a cup of coffee before making a decision. She yawned and stretched, finally deciding there was no decision to make. She secretly liked the tacky commercialism of the Canadian side, with its boat rides and little museums, and motels featuring heart-shaped beds. "Oh, I don't know, Gary. We might as well go...we might as well..." She squinted. "On the right. Next to that gas station. Look!"

Another Gruesome Gary billboard beckoned, the same seated Anton waving down tourists, promoting the American side:

See Gruesome Gary's Funeral Home.
Better than a wax museum!

A mile down the road another billboard featured the seated, waving Anton, this time with a double ring of golden halos above his head. Underneath, the legend read:

OVER 7200 SERVED!

Dinah leaned forward, head between her knees, nausea churning her stomach. "This is too much, Gary. I don't feel like a second honeymoon anymore."

"Should we stop and see the funeral home, at

least?"

"Hell yes!" Gilbert said.

"Hell no!" Dinah said sternly. "We have to get home and talk to those people."

Gilbert objected, "We should scout out what they're doing, first."

"I agree with Gilbert, Dinah. We should see just how far they've gone."

"If it's better than a wax museum, I don't want to see. Keep driving," she ordered.

A few miles further, another billboard read:

Visit LOVE CANAL
A Planned GG's Interment Community

"No!" Dinah shrieked, pulling at her hair, shaking her head. "No!"

"Dinah, we have to stop and see this one. We have to find out what's going on," Gary implored.

"We have to stop, Dinah," Gilbert pleaded. "I think it is important we start checking out these Gruesome Gary's Funeral Homes. Anyway, I've had enough driving for one day. You can wait in the car if you like."

"OK, you guys. All right. We can stop, but I'm going in with you. I have to see for myself that it's not as bad as I imagine."

Gilbert followed the signs to the Love Canal Interment Community and wheeled the Winnebago into the parking lot, and into a section reserved for

RVs. He read off the license plates from across the country. "New York. Pennsylvania. North Carolina. Virginia. New York. Tennessee. Look, here's one from Arizona."

Gilbert pulled into a spot next to the RV from Arizona, and they climbed down from the posh vehicle and boarded a shuttle ferrying visitors to a neon-lit entrance. There, a large poster of Anton hung above the ticket windows. A sign on one window advised, 'Group Tours.' Another, 'All-day Family Passes.'

After buying all-day family passes, they were given little plastic booties and told, without explanation, to put them on. At the exit, thirty feet down a barb-wire chain-link fence, they noticed people removing the booties and tucking them into slots in sealed waste receptacles.

The streets of Love Canal were clean. Antiseptic. The lawns had all been removed to a depth of eight inches and replaced with crushed stones spray painted green. People strolled about popping into shops and houses. "There's a diner," Gary said, "let's get a cup of coffee and see if we can get any information from the waitress."

"Coffee sounds good," Gilbert said.

"Information sounds even better," Dinah said.

A lone customer sat at the counter, staring into a cup of coffee. The waitress was busy at the grill and made no acknowledgment she had noticed them enter. Even tucked in a bun under a hat, her black hair was shiny and beautiful. Both waitress and customer were cordoned off by a velvet rope that ran the length of the diner, separating the counter from the table area. Gilbert picked a table and pulled a chair to sit down.

The chair didn't budge. Gary tried a chair on the opposite side. It didn't budge either. Dinah lifted the tablecloth and looked underneath the table. "Hey! The chairs are bolted to the floor. What's going on here? Hey, Gary, why is that section roped off?"

"I don't know." He hailed the waitress, "Excuse me, Miss. Are you open? Miss?"

The waitress turned, a cup of coffee and a piece of pie wedged in her stiff fingers, a tinge of green developing around her full lips. Gary jumped back. Dinah covered her mouth to muffle a cry. Gilbert stared transfixed by her beauty, shocked, knowing what she would become. Gary said, more to himself than to Gilbert or Dinah, "She's on perpetual display."

Dinah's voice cracked, "What...what about the customer?"

Gary leaned over the rope and examined the customer's face. His tinge was developing, even more noticeably than the waitress'. As if saying, "Now you know our little secret," the waitress turned back to the grill, the coffee and pie still fixed in her grip.

"I don't understand. Who?...How?" Dinah said.

Gilbert offered, "He must be an old trucker who liked hanging out in diners, and she was a waitress who loved her job. I'd love to see how they get her to move." He glanced over his shoulder toward the door and carefully stepped over the rope to peak behind the counter. The waitress was standing on a circular wooden disk fixed to a motor and timer mechanism. Gilbert wanted to see it cycle, but a family with two children entered, catching him by surprise. Gilbert froze.

The children ran into the diner, jumping back warily when Gary and Dinah turned toward them. "It's all right," Dinah said, "we're real." Turning to the parents, who followed, she said, "Quite a place, isn't it?"

The parents smiled. "Our kids wanted to see it."

The little girl pointed at Gilbert, the waitress, and the customer. "Hey dad, who are they?"

"Oh, I don't know. They must have all died of food poisoning at the same restaurant."

"Oh."

The waitress went into cycle. The children laughed and clapped their hands. A bead of sweat formed on Gilbert's forehead. Gary spoke to the father, telling the children, "Did you see the clowns across the street? That's really something to see."

The children ran to their parents, taking them by the hands, dragging them out the door. "Let's go see the clowns. Hurry up, we want to see the clowns."

"It's OK, Gilbert, they're gone."

"Whew! I was getting tired. Thanks, Gary. Hey this is a great idea. We should have thought of it."

"Let's go," Dinah said. "We still have lots to see."

They left the diner, and walked down the main road, stepping inside houses to see people on display wallpapering their kitchen, watching TV, rocking in chairs powered by hidden mechanisms. Further down the road, a crowd was gathered in front of a little chapel. A sign above the door read:

Wee Chapel of Love
Rev. Cecil P. Williams (deceased), Pastor

Gary, Gilbert and Dinah got in line. A muffled voice from inside spoke for about a minute, then clicked and whirred. Each time it clicked and whirred, a couple exited carrying a piece of paper, and another couple entered. A sign in the foyer explained:

> Enter the Wee Chapel of Love and exchange wedding vows directed by Cecil P. Williams, the "marryin' pastor" of Love Canal, U.S.A. Please fill out your authentic   Wee Chapel   spurious marriage certificate and place it in the Reverend's left hand. Deposit $2 in slot on podium. Pull crank. Exit to the left.

The certificates were stacked neatly on a table by the door. Gary turned around to see a happy, eager throng waiting to get inside. He leaned toward Dinah and whispered, "We'll have to go through with it now. There's no way out."

The couple in front of them wrote their names on a certificate and handed their camera to Gilbert. "Would you take our picture, please?"

"Sure. I'd be happy to." Gilbert readied the camera as Reverend Cecil started the ceremony. He waited for just the right moment and snapped a picture. The Reverend clicked and whirred. "Perfect shot," Gilbert said. "Hey, my friends forgot their camera. Can I take a picture of them and give you their addy?" he asked.

The newlyweds hugged and smiled. The groom said, "Sure, glad to."

Gary placed the certificate in the Reverend's left hand, deposited two dollar bills in the slot and pulled the crank. A microphone inside the Reverend's slightly open mouth spoke, "Dearly beloved, we are gathered here in the Wee Chapel of Love in Gruesome Gary's Love Canal Interment Community to join this couple in matrimony. If anyone knows any reason why these two should not be wed, let them speak now or forever hold their peace." After a short pause, the voice continued, "I now pronounce you husband and wife. You may kiss the bride." Click, whirr.

Outside the chapel, Gary folded the certificate and stuck it in his shirt pocket. Dinah spoke in a severe tone. "You really enjoyed that, Gilbert, didn't you? Did you get a good picture?"

Gilbert was taken aback. "No Dinah, it was horrible. You don't understand. If we're going to carry on a successful reconnoiter operation, we have to blend in with the crowd. I didn't enjoy it at all. Despicable business."

"OK, Gilbert. You're the expert spy. But don't you

think we've seen enough?"

Gilbert scanned the main road down to the next intersection, where an exuberant crowd was gathered. Whatever it was, it was a bigger draw than even the Wee Chapel of Love. Dinah said, "I don't want to see it, but you boys can go if you like. I'll start walking back to the RV and meet you there. Give me the keys, Gilbert."

Gilbert eagerly dug into his pocket and handed the keys to Dinah. "This could be important, Dinah. We'll just be a few minutes."

While Dinah strolled back toward the parking lot, Gary and Gilbert turned and headed for the next intersection. They talked freely. "This place is really something," Gary said.

"Devine wasn't kidding when he said Westlaw had some big promotional ideas."

"And look at the public acceptance. It's amazing. I wonder how he pulled it off? This is the most tacky concept in the history of mankind. And yet, here it is."

"Beats the hell out of me," Gilbert said.

At the intersection an old department store had been refitted with an elegant facade built up two stories. Long white columns stood on either side of double bronze-colored doors. Eager people entered with wide eyes; those exiting wore focused eyes and thoughtful expressions. Gary and Gilbert stopped in their tracks, speechless. Gary finally said, "I thought he wanted to keep his name out of it."

Gold letters, two feet high, emblazoned across the

full frontage of the building spelled out:

DEVINE'S FUNEREAL MUSEUM

They stood in silence for a moment, then with weak-kneed, shaky steps, they approached, joining a crowd of about twenty waiting at the museum's entrance. Automatic sliding doors, glass tinted black, checked their progress. Stenciled in gold lettering, a sign on the doors read:

Please wait.
Next tour begins in just a few minutes.

When the doors slid open, they entered with the throng into a darkened room. A voice from a speaker in the foyer announced, "This tour group is at full capacity. Please stand clear of the sliding doors. The next tour of Devine's Funereal Museum begins in just a few minutes."

The doors slid shut. Soft lights illuminated the inside of the museum, to the accompaniment of muffled tribal drums. A dim spotlight brightened and zeroed in on a white-haired gentleman in a dark blue three-piece suit. Gary gasped and nudged Gilbert in the ribs. Gilbert covered his mouth and stared, speechless, straight into the face of Mr. Devine.

The slightly distorted, mechanical-sounding voice coming from the microphone in Mr. Devine's mouth was Mr. Westlaw's. "Welcome to my museum of funereal practices through the ages. My name is John Devine, and I used to take part in some of the curiosities you'll see later in the tour."

Mr. Devine's right arm rested stiffly at his side, his left was raised, palm up, in a perpetual gesture telling all comers to enter, relax, reflect, follow. A beam of bright light sliced through the air, illuminating a painted scene of cavemen, ape-like missing links, carrying a limp saber-toothed tiger to their encampment, leaving behind the bloody remains of one of their fellows. Mr. Devine spun to the left, gesturing toward the scene. The music volume inched up. Mr. Devine said, slightly louder to compensate for the music, "In the savage days of man's distant past, fallen comrades received no regard. The dead were left to the jackals, no concept of a human soul, no provisions, no considerations."

Mr. Devine turned on his wooden disk back toward the group, his left arm still held stiffly in gesture. The disk propelled him on its track further along into the tour. With unmoving footsteps, he came to rest at the next scene. The music picked up tempo, Egyptian strains playing to a spotlit mural depicting a pharaoh lying in state, gold mask on his face, jars of grain and oil stacked in front of walls covered with wedge-shaped cuneiform writings.

Mr. Devine continued, "Only when a sense of the eternal human soul developed, did civilization begin. The dawn of the new age of mankind ushered in by a belief in an afterlife, elaborate and touching burial provisions left as evidence."

The wooden disk slipped a gear and Mr. Devine rocked slightly before gliding along, arm gesturing to the next spotlit scene. The group followed, some pausing to reflect on the pharaoh until his spotlight dimmed to pitch.

Harpsichord music at the next scene was courtesy of Handel. Mr. Devine's disk made a half turn, pointing his gesturing arm in the direction of an open casket occupied by a fat, unattractive, wax resemblance of a man. A few weeping relatives stood off to the side. "Until recently, this is how the final send off of man's eternal soul was interpreted. Notice the sadness and sense of remorse on the faces of the observers. Notice the desire to make the deceased comfortable in a human sort of way, almost as if those who laid his head on the satin pillow were making a conscious effort to prevent him from taking the last step in his great journey. Is this dignity?"

Two notes from a kettle drum signaled the spot-light to quickly fade. The room fell to total darkness, except for a single, sharply focused spotlight on Mr. Devine's face. "Follow me. Bear witness to the next great evolution in funereal customs."

Strips of pink neon flickered and took along the baseboards, providing a path for the tour. Mr. Devine moved ahead of the group quickly, more quickly than before, like he was being catapulted from the deck of an aircraft carrier, the speed causing him to wobble slightly from side to side. He finally came to an abrupt halt, his gesture pointing toward a darkened area which immediately became awash in a blaze of light that stunned the group's eyes. The light revealed a mural of the green and wrinkled Anton, seated with arm held high in greeting, smiling to the strains of synthesized bagpipes with a rock beat. In a loud voice, Mr. Devine proclaimed, "Gruesome Gary ushers in the new age! Perpetual display! The epitome of funereal evolution is here, now. Gruesome Gary's patented process displays you in the best light. Our special space age polymer sealants preserve, while allowing nature's lovely patina to shine through. Come one, come all. Be forever with us, in Gruesome Gary's gallery!"

A Sousa march replaced the bagpipes, and another set of blacked-out sliding glass doors opened. The group exited wearing thoughtful expressions, nodding in affirmation. Gary watched them, scratching his head. "It's a good thing Dinah didn't come. I don't think she could have taken this."

"I don't think I can take this. What are we seeing here, Gary? Tell me, what is going on?"

Gary shook his head. "I don't know. And I don't mind telling you, I'm afraid to find out. I'd like to get back on the plane and return to Fiji."

"If it weren't for an outside chance with Aura Lee, I'd like to join you. I wonder what she must think of me now. I hope she doesn't blame me for all this. I hope she doesn't go along with all this; she is a bit spacey."

"Let's go back and tell Dinah. Then we'll broil a couple steaks and belt back a few beers and camp for the night. If we get an early start, we can be home tomorrow evening."

Dinah removed the meat from the broiler in the Winnebago and sliced into one of the pieces. Blood-red juice ran from the pink meat inside. She put it back under the broiler and joined Gary and Gilbert, who sat outside on lawn chairs sipping beer, exhausted. She took a can from the cooler at Gilbert's feet and cracked it open. "The meat's almost done, guys. Are you sure it was the real Mr. Devine and not a dummy or a wax figure?"

"It was the real thing, all right," Gary answered.

"I wonder how he died?" Gilbert asked. "He seemed OK when we left."

"He must have died of shock at Mr. Westlaw's ideas," Dinah commented, taking a deep sip of beer.

"Maybe he got in the way and Westlaw bumped him off," Gary suggested. "He wasn't such a bad guy, really. Devine, I mean."

"What about Hillary?" Dinah asked. "I wonder how she's doing."

"Maybe Hillary poisoned him," Gilbert suggested. "Maybe she put too much bleu in his cordon bleu."

"Or gold in his Amber Gold."

CHAPTER 21

Next morning Gilbert took the first shift driving. The countryside passed unnoticed, no longer scenery to be enjoyed, just miles to traverse. It was all highway, and no urban streets. The camper handled smoothly and he was soon going the speed limit.

By evening, Gary had the wheel for the final stretch. The road had turned into a taxing blend of potholes, turbulence from semis, lane-hopping econoboxes, thinking what to say to Ken. And Rick and Ron. And Mr. Westlaw. And Mr. Wiggins. The Winnebago fit in Gary's driveway, with just inches to spare. Gary shut the engine off and took a deep breath.

Dinah unfolded herself from the small sofa and opened the door, nudging a sleeping Gilbert on her way out. The house was the same as when they left, and the time they were away seemed like just a long weekend.

Gary sat at the driver's seat, feeling slightly depressed as he looked out at the side of his house. After seeing something new every day, the familiar sight seemed confining. It provided nothing to wonder at.

He fished receipts out of his pocket for the two quarts of oil he had added along the way, tucking the slips under the visor. "We'll return this thing tomorrow morning, Gilbert. You can sleep in it tonight if you want to."

Gilbert yawned. "Huh? Yeah. OK."

"It's good to be home," Gary said, trying to shake

the sense of depression. "Let's make a pot of instant and call Ken...if he's still speaking to us. Maybe he can give us some background on what's been happening."

Gilbert sniffed deeply, like he was coming down with a cold. "OK, you call. I'm still asleep."

The house smelled musty, and felt like a time capsule. Dinah put a pot of water on the stove while Gary opened windows. Gilbert sat at the kitchen table, in a semi-sleep state.

"Gilbert, wake up," Dinah said, setting out three coffee cups, pouring hot water in each. She measured in the coffee and stirred.

Gilbert looked at the steaming cups and grimaced. "I guess we'll have to drink it black," he said.

Gary entered the kitchen and stared at the muddy potions, dissatisfied. He thought for a moment and opened the refrigerator. It was empty except for some jam, a few cans of beer, a jar of salad dressing sealed around the rim with a black growth, and a damp, caked box of baking soda. He tried the freezer. Ice cubes, margarine containers filled with stew and leftover vegetables, little aluminum foil packets, and a half-eaten microwave dinner.

The corner of a blue and white wrapper peeked from behind the microwave dinner. "Hmm, what's this?" he asked. "A Three Musketeers bar?" He pulled at the blue and white wrapper, but it didn't budge, stuck to the bottom of the freezer by frozen condensation. He tugged harder and the wrapper tore, revealing a capital 'T.' "It is a Three Musketeers." He tore away the microwave dinner. The candy bar lay exposed amid a wasteland of encrusted ice. He took a frozen margarine container and hammered at the icebound candy bar. It yielded at the third blow.

Gary cut the bar into three segments with a serrated bread knife. Dinah and Gilbert sat at the table, sipping their coffee, watching. Gary plopped one segment into his coffee and offered a segment each to Dinah and Gilbert. Gilbert put a hand over his cup. "Will that work?" he asked.

"No," Gary answered. "But it's better than nothing."

Dinah shrugged and pushed her coffee cup toward Gary. Gilbert took his hand from his cup and Gary distributed the remaining segments. The segments floated while the chocolate melted, forming an oil-blue coating on the coffee's surface. Gary stirred each cup, determined to prove his effort worthwhile. The spongy center of the candy bar started to dissolve, black coffee turning a creamy shade of brown. With great satisfaction, Gary raised his cup and proclaimed triumphantly, "Now we can call Ken."

"One for all and all for one," Gilbert toasted.

Gary took out his phone and sat down at the table with Gilbert and Dinah. "Hello? Hello? Ken? It's Gary. ... Gary Colbert. We're back. ... At home. ... Great trip. Great. ... Yes, well, that's OK. We didn't know what you were talking about till we got back and started driving cross country. He's got billboards on the highways. ... I know that's not all. We stopped at Love

Canal. We're all in shock. We had no idea it would turn out like this. ... Yes. I know. I don't blame you. Have you talked to Rick and Ron? ... OK. Yes, Ken. ... I understand. ... OK. ... Oh, I'm sorry. ... We'll. ... OK. We'll go see Rick tomorrow. ... OK. ... OK. ... I'll let you know. And tell Jan not to worry. ... OK, he will. ...Talk to you later."

Gary let his hand drop to his side, as if the phone were too heavy to bear. "Rick and Ron don't live at home anymore. They've moved into the first. I guess Rick is running it and Ron is doing a lot of traveling. They haven't talked to Ken or Jan in weeks. Last time Ken saw them, they wheeled up his drive in a brand new Camaro. He's worried they're in over their heads."

"What'll we do?" Dinah asked.

"I told Ken we'd go talk to Rick tomorrow. That's all we can do. It's really out of our hands if they want to stay with the new operation. They're both eighteen. We'll just go say hi and see what happens and hope Ken isn't too mad at us if they don't want to quit."

"A new Camaro?" Gilbert asked. "I wouldn't blame them if they don't want to quit. The little shits."

"I know," Gary said.

Dinah stayed home to clean the house while Gary and Gilbert cleaned the Winnebago and returned it to the local rental outlet, Gary following in his car. From there, they drove to the first to talk to Rick.

Outside the first a crowd of teenagers, friends of

Rick, milled about, listening to boomboxes, dancing, acting as touts for passing motorists. Gary parked on the street. The teenagers shouted, "Hey man, it's this way. Go on inside."

As Gary and Gilbert walked up the front walk, they heard a teenager shout from the crowd, "Yeah, go in. And don't forget to leave a donation." The crowd giggled, pleased at their friend's cheek and bravado.

"Assholes," Gilbert said to Gary.

Inside, visitors strolled from display to display, loudly critiquing each interee's choice of burial pose. An interee near the door held a plate of souvenir glow-in-the-dark keychains molded in the shape of the seated Anton. In the other hand he held a covered pot with a slit in the top. A hand-painted arrow pointed from the word 'Donations,' directing patrons where to put their money.

Gary and Gilbert approached the kitchen, past the closed office door, looking for Rick. Several teenagers sat at the kitchen table drinking beer and talking loudly. Gary and Gilbert entered. One of the kids greeted them. "Hey man, no one's allowed back here. You get lost or something?"

The group stopped talking to outdo each other in chuckles and laughter. Another said, "Hey man, deliveries in the rear."

Gilbert said, "Hey man, deliveries in your rear."

Gary scanned the group. "Where's Rick?"

One of the boys put on a pretense of surprise and indignation. "The Man? You want to see The Man?" he said. "Nobody sees The Man without an appointment. Sorry dude, you're shit out of luck. Come back tomorrow."

Gary and Gilbert turned and walked away. The group in the kitchen laughed and congratulated each other. A girl's voice yelled after them, "Don't forget to leave a donation."

Gary and Gilbert paused outside the office door and knocked once, twice. A voice from within yelled, "Get lost. I'm busy."

Gilbert nudged Gary aside. Without a word, he leaned back and kicked down the door. It gave with a loud crash and tumbled into the office. The kitchen crowd fell silent. The girl's voice asked, "Are you guys going to let them get away with that?"

The boys sprang into action, rushing Gary and Gilbert. Gary and Gilbert stepped inside the darkened office, where Rick was sprawled in cutoffs, sitting beside a girl in cutoffs and a cropped neon-colored T-shirt. Another couple were entwined on a large bean bag chair. A pornographic movie played on a big screen television in the corner and the smell of marijuana filled the air.

Rick rose. "What the fuck. What the fuck do you think you're doing?"

The kitchen gang grabbed Gary and Gilbert by their arms. "Sorry boss," said one of the boys, "we told them they needed an appointment, but I guess the assholes don't understand English."

Gilbert broke free and made a fist. "Here, try some

body English," he said, throwing a punch that sent the boy tripping over the fallen door into the wall opposite the office. The boy holding Gary took a step toward Gilbert. Gary grabbed his neck, squeezing the mass of nerves under the boy's left ear. He kicked the back of the boy's knee, pulled him off balance, and threw him into the hall, where he landed in a heap on top of his comrade.

Recognizing Gary and Gilbert, Rick said groggily, "Hey, it's all right. I know these guys." He stumbled and took a step and shook Gary's hand. "Uncle Gary. I didn't expect to see you here. I thought you guys moved to the Bahamas or something."

"Fiji. We went to Fiji. And we would still be there right now if your father hadn't asked us to come straighten you out. What the hell have you done to my business?"

Rick took a step back. "Hey, wait a minute, it's just free enterprise. We're just out to make a buck like everyone else."

Gary turned and looked at Gilbert, shaking his head at the hopelessness of helping Ken.

Gilbert looked around the room at the movie and the overflowing ashtrays, and at a sheet-covered mound in the corner. His heart sank and he stormed over and pulled the sheet off, revealing Lester, green skinned and shriveling, the inscrutable expression now twisted and grotesque. Gilbert stared at Lester's face a moment. He swallowed hard and turned toward Rick, pointing a finger in his face. "Don't ever cover Lester with a sheet again. I don't know who the hell you think you are…" Gilbert turned abruptly and stormed out of the office, the youngsters stepping back in surprise to let him through.

Gary shook his head again and followed Gilbert. As they walked down the hallway toward the front door, the teenagers shouted after them, "Assholes."

They walked out the front door, visitors looking upon them with disapproval. Gary was still shaking his head, but he was glad to be out of the first, glad he had seen Rick and fulfilled his obligation to Ken. In the car, he said to Gilbert, "Let's go back to my place and get some lunch and cool down. Then I want to see Westlaw and Wiggins."

Gilbert winced as Dinah pulled the last sheet from her living room furniture. Dinah folded the sheet and said defensively, "I know you think it's silly to cover my furniture, Gilbert, but I don't say anything about your housekeeping habits. So how did it go with Rick?"

Gary answered, "Not good at all. That silly little pecker has turned the first into a teenage hangout. Beer drinking, marijuana…Rick was wearing cutoffs in the office, for God's sake!"

"We had some trouble with the crowd hanging out there," Gilbert added. "Had to kick in the office door to see Rick. He's in there with some friends smoking pot and watching porno tapes. What really pissed me off is they stuck Lester in the corner and covered him with a sheet."

Dinah glanced down at the sheet in her hands and tossed it aside. "Oh, I'm sorry," she said. "I know how you and Gary felt about Lester. Isn't there anything we can do?"

"We'll pay Westlaw and Wiggins a visit at the second and tell them what's going on," Gilbert said. "Maybe they'll put the screws on Rick. Want to come?"

"Yes. I would like to find out what's going on...but I don't especially want to talk to Mr. Westlaw."

"OK," Gary said. "Gilbert, want to call Ken and tell him we tried talking to Rick?"

Gilbert bit his lip. "Not yet," he said. "What'll we tell him? That Rick is running a den of iniquity? Let's see what we can get Westlaw to do about it first."

"All right."

"Anyway, I have to go make a call. Be right back," Gilbert said, exiting toward the kitchen.

Dinah looked after him. "What's that all about? Who's he going to call?"

"Aura Lee."

"Oh?"

Gilbert came back into the living room with spring in his step and a smile on his face. "Aura Lee is going to meet us at the second. Then we'll all go have a bite to eat. My treat."

"Great. I'm hungry."

"Oh Gilbert, that's wonderful."

After the scene at the first, the crowd at the second seemed to possess unusual decorum. There were no boomboxes or dancers on the front lawn and visitors conversed in hushed tones.

They were met at the front door by Aura Lee, who was waiting, wearing a serious expression. Gilbert hesitated, staring intently to be sure it really was Aura Lee. She wasn't wearing her purple poncho, and her hair was done in a tasteful permanent. Single, diminutive zircons dangled from her ear lobes, replacing the huge quartz crystals. Gilbert looked into her worried face and smiled. Aura Lee's face lost its concern and relaxed, breaking into a coy smile for Gilbert.

He took her by the elbow. "Aura Lee? Is it really you? You're more beautiful than ever."

Aura Lee lowered her eyes and blushed. "Thank you, Gilbert. I'm glad you called me. I felt I really had to talk with you. Things have...I..." She didn't finish, noticing Gary and Dinah. "Hi Dinah, Gary."

Gary answered, "Hi, Aura Lee."

Dinah gave Aura Lee a sisterly smile.

Gary asked, "What do you think of what has happened while we were away?"

Aura Lee raised her eyebrows and tilted her head slightly. An errant curl broke rank and brushed across her forehead. She paused in thought for a moment then took a deep breath. "It's all gotten to be a bit much for me."

She turned back to Gilbert, looking him deep in

the eyes. "Kitty...I don't know...Kitty has become really strange. I never did like her. Now she's moved Jain here and is working with Jeremy." She paused as if embarrassed at using his first name. "Westlaw. Westlaw came up with this idea to present Gruesome Gary as the founder and patriarch of GG's. Westlaw supposedly gets spiritual and financial advice from him through Kitty...they've set up a subscription-based website. The advice is one of their selling points. And if that weren't bad enough, Kitty held a ghost marriage for Gruesome Gary and Jain. She said that the energy released from their spiritual copulations would filter down to all of us. She's really gotten carried away.

"But what worries me most," Aura Lee continued in a quiet voice, "is that she's got a lot of people attending her seances and believing everything she says. I think she's even starting to believe it herself. I feel really horrible about it all."

Aura Lee lowered her head again and leaned toward Gilbert. Gilbert put his arm around her shoulder and gave her a hug. Her forehead brushed against his lips and he kissed her.

Before Gilbert's passion turned entirely toward Aura Lee, Gary said, "We'll all talk over dinner. Right now, Gilbert and I are going to have a little talk with Westlaw and Wiggins."

They turned and walked through the front door, Gilbert leading Aura Lee by the arm. Dinah circled around back of Gilbert and took Aura Lee's other arm.

"Let's look around and you can tell me all about what's been going on," she said. "I don't want to see Mr. Westlaw."

Dinah and Aura Lee turned right and headed slowly toward the Sunrise Room. Gary and Gilbert headed for the office, in search of Mr. Westlaw and Mr. Wiggins. A young receptionist smiled as they approached. "May I help you?"

"Yes. I'm Gary Colbert and this is Gilbert Jackson. We'd like to see Misters Westlaw and Wiggins."

"Well, I can tell you now, Mr. Wiggins isn't in. I'll see if Mr. Westlaw is free."

Gary said, "Just tell Mr. Westlaw it's Gary Colbert and Gilbert Jackson. I think he'll make himself free." Gary was shocked at how rudely he had spoken to the receptionist. He added warmly, "We're old friends."

The receptionist buzzed the intercom. "Mr. Westlaw, there's a Gary Colbert and Gilbert Jackson to see you. Shall I send them in?"

After a long pause, the answer crackled back, "Yes, yes, by all means, send them right in."

Mr. Westlaw opened the office door. He stood in the doorway beaming, offering handshakes and slapping Gary and Gilbert on the back. "Well, look who it is. Come on in. I'll bet you never expected to see your little funeral empire grow so big so quick."

Gary and Gilbert stepped into the office. Mr. Westlaw closed the door and stood for a moment, blocking it. "I trust you're pleased with what we've made of G&G's?" he asked.

"It's really amazing," was all Gary could think to say.

Gilbert looked around the office at the certificates on the walls, the action-figure dolls clothed and bent to show various pose choices, the polished maple menagerie that used to be in Mr. Wiggins' basement, Mr. Wiggins' empty desk. "Where's Wiggins?" he finally asked.

Mr. Westlaw smiled broadly and gestured expansively. "Have a seat, gentlemen. Please." He sat down behind his desk. "Wiggins maintains an office here, but he spends most of his time at our Training, Process Equipment, and Supplies Distribution Center. He trains all our franchise owners and puts together the equipment and mixes up and packages the solutions they'll need. He's really found his niche. I got to tell you, that man is happy as a lark."

Gary thought of the stuffed crows that used to litter Mr. Wiggins' kitchen, doubting his old farmhouse was big enough for a Training and Distribution Center. "Where is this Training and Distribution Center?" he asked.

Mr. Westlaw leaned back in his chair. "Devine's old operation. After he died, we took it over. His son is helping Wiggins run it. First-class kid, Devine's son. Knows a good opportunity when he sees one."

Gary looked at Mr. Westlaw, unable to keep from smiling. He couldn't help admire Mr. Westlaw's moxie. He had obviously been working hard, putting a lot together. Gary wondered just how far Mr. Westlaw would go to succeed. Voice cracking a little, Gary hesitantly asked, "What happened to Devine?"

Mr. Westlaw leaned farther back, putting his hands behind his head. "Sudden heart attack, poor fellow. Luckily, all the legal papers were signed and I was able to work with his lawyer to, uh..." Mr. Westlaw searched for the right words, "To see to it that things worked out to everyone's advantage."

Gilbert asked, "But we saw Devine on display at Love Canal."

Mr. Westlaw chuckled. "That was our greatest coup, Wiggins' and mine. 'What a great boost for the business,' we thought, 'to have a former funeral director pushing our product.'" Mr. Westlaw stifled another chuckle with a cough. "Well, I'll tell you, it didn't take much to convince that scatterbrained wife of his to go along with it. So, Wiggins put him through the freeze dryer and we shipped him off to our Theme Park at Love Canal. I understand he's a top draw," Mr. Westlaw added triumphantly.

Gary shifted uncomfortably in his seat and cleared his throat. He looked over at Gilbert, who looked back, mouth agape. "About your 'Theme Park,' Mr. Westlaw," Gary asked, "don't you think that's going a bit too far? And all those billboards with Anton...?"

Mr. Westlaw leaned forward, pulling his chair closer to the desk, folding his hands, laying them in front of him. "Not at all," he said, matter-of-factly. "You've been away for a long time...what seems a long time, anyway. Things can change fast back here, not at all what I'm sure it's like in those little backward islands in the middle of nowhere. This is America, man! Anything's possible." Mr. Westlaw stared briefly into space, then added, "And if it's not possible, we'll make it possible." He chuckled again, delighted at himself.

Gary was annoyed. "I've been wondering about the name of your establishment..."

Mr. Westlaw smiled sheepishly. "Oh, that. Well you see, right from the start, we decided to make Gruesome Gary...Anton...part of the act. We have him traveling around the country with Ron appearing at all the grand openings. And I'm putting together a campaign to get Gruesome Gary named *Time* magazine's Man of the Year, maybe for 'putting the fun in funerals,' or something silly like that. Sorry about the 'Gary' part, though, but the name really sings. Nothing personal, I assure you."

Gary stared blankly at Mr. Westlaw, admiration for his moxie turning to disgust at his chutzpah.

"Mr. Westlaw," Gilbert said, "I'd like to ask you about Rick and Ron. We visited the first earlier today and didn't like what we saw. I don't know what you've done to Rick, but he's acting like some kind of mafia lieutenant. Kids drinking beer and smoking dope, calling him 'The Man,' treating visitors with contempt...you better do something about it, fast."

Mr. Westlaw leaned back, a paternal smile of understanding covering his face. "Oh yes, Rick. Rick and Ron. Well, what can I say?" he said, raising his hands in surrender. "In their own way, they're as important to GG's as me or Wiggins. They're the younger generation, you see. And I believe in giving them guidance in the right direction and letting them have a...oh, how shall I say it...a bit of latitude to do their own thing. That Ron, now he's going to be the sharp one. Already he's on the road being our eyes and ears. Doing a fine job, too. Why, just last week he reported from Arizona that the patina takes too long to develop out there, what with the dry climate and all. That's the kind of information we need. Wiggins went right to work on it, altering his chemicals to compensate. Now we can boast of our climate-specific formulas.

"And Rick," Mr. Westlaw continued, "...well, Rick might need a little more time. We put him in charge of the first, mainly because it's already filled and not taking on any more customers. He can't do any real harm there. And he's fixed up the attic for a place for him and Ron to live. Gets them out from under their mother's apron strings. I'm not the least bit worried about them."

Gary took a deep breath, happy that Gilbert had inquired about Rick and Ron. He looked at Gilbert, gesturing with his hands that he had heard enough and was ready to leave. Gilbert gave Mr. Westlaw a stiff nod, stood and extended his hand across Mr. Westlaw's desk. "Mr. Westlaw. It's been a long, strange trip...best of luck to you," he said with more dismissiveness than sincerity.

Mr. Westlaw rose and shook hands. "I'm certainly glad you stopped by. I'll tell Wiggins you said hello. Oh, and if you ever want to visit our Theme Park again…we're adding new exhibits all the time…just let me know. I'll give you some free all-day passes."

Gary and Gilbert exited the office, smiled politely at the receptionist and went to look for Dinah and Aura Lee. They found them standing in front of Jain, who was seated at a round table, gazing into a crystal ball set in the center. Dinah saw them approach and asked, "How did it go? What did they say?"

Gary answered, "Wiggins wasn't there. They've taken over Devine's old place and Wiggins is using it as his laboratory and a training center for people who buy into the franchise. Westlaw…Westlaw is about what you'd expect him to be."

Gilbert added, "He isn't going to be any help talking to Rick, even though we told him what was going on at the first."

"Oh, yes, I've seen the first," Aura Lee said. "I'm so sorry you had to come home and see what they've done to it. Kitty didn't like it either. I think that's why she had Jain moved here, that and I think she wanted to be closer to Jeremy…to Westlaw."

Gilbert put his arm around Aura Lee. "I'm sorry everything worked out like it did."

"I'm not. At least now I'm free of that silly witch, Kitty."

"And we're free of all this nonsense," Dinah said.

They left through the front door, passing the offer of souvenir keychains, walking slowly down the front walk. As a body, they turned to look at the funeral home one last time. The early evening sun was disappearing behind its roof, turning the front of the building gray, like a giant tombstone. They took a step back, standing just outside the building's shadow.

Aura Lee said in her quiet voice, "I think what bothers me most about all this...this and the old G&G's, and all funeral homes actually...is that not only does it mock what should be a very personal, satisfying celebration of metamorphosis, it's also the final insult a person can do to the ecosystem. Preventing their bodies from being used to feed new life after they're dead. I really believe that's what this means," she said, pulling a scrap of paper from her purse. She read, "Then shall the dust return to the earth as it was: and the spirit shall return unto God who gave it."

Gilbert leaned over and kissed Aura Lee on the temple. She looked up at him and smiled, a tear in her eye. Gary put his arm around Dinah, and they all turned, happy to leave the funeral home behind.

Thank you for reading this…interesting?...tale. It's worth noting that funeral customs vary widely from culture to culture and from century to century, and at least in the U.S. are rapidly evolving due to such pressures as expense, land use, general ecology, and a growing demand for and acceptance of more personal relevance and expression in all things. More information on real-world funeral and burial alternatives, including facilities that are likely now in your own city or town, can easily be found by doing an Internet search. Best wishes to you in all you do.

You are warmly invited now to return to the site where you purchased this book and leave a few words in the comments section, be they good, bad or ugly. The author and everyone involved in the production of this book appreciate your interest in helping keep reading alive here in the digital age.

About the Author:

Gary Freeman, twin brother to the classic '57 Chevy, was born in Detroit in the months leading up to the dawning of the Space Age. Though he developed a dislike for reading at an early age from having been forced to read *Hardy Boys* books, which he found kinda stoopid, he grew up to write for newspapers and magazines, finally falling into a fairly steady gig at one of the big car companies as a copy editor/proofreader (which is rather astonishing if you read the teacher comments on his third grade report card, "We hope Gary will try to improve his penmanship and spelling. He makes careless errors and does not check his work. Many words are misspelled and his writing is so messy that it is impossible to read." Miss P. was actually his favorite teacher of all time, and reportedly very sexy too, even to a third grader!)

So when the car company stalled and the good gig gagged, he went into show biz, acting in several low-budget indie films (you might actually be able to get a copy of such films as *After the Blood Rush* by searching real hard). Buoyed by the success of *ATBR*, he collaborated with famed underground cartoonist Matt Feazell on the screenplay for *The Amazing Cynicalman*, though Matt provided most of the storyline because he's really funny and it's his character. *TAC* is actually a pretty good film and DVDs are available at modest cost at www.cynicalman.com.

Gary did indeed write *Gruesome Gary's* following an uncomfortable and expensive experience helping arrange a funeral years ago, and that is him on the cover, though weirded up a bit. He is currently writing a new work, which he only describes as a horror/comedy PSA on a timely topic.

Made in the USA
Charleston, SC
27 September 2014